About the author

Raised by wolves, Stephen Walker was born in that Pennine Shangri-la, Sheffield. Like all the town's inhabitants, he is immortal.

Over the years, he's unearthed numerous people stupid enough to employ him as a graphic artist and mural designer. But his first love is unemployment, to which he one day hopes to return.

The power of invisibility is his to use as he sees fit. Semi-retired, he spends his days entertaining visitors by playing piano in the style of Mrs Mills while pondering the mysteries of this and other worlds.

KT-162-112

BY STEPHEN WALKER

Danny Yates Must Die
Mr Landen Has No Brain
(Coming in Summer 2000)

Voyager

danny yates must die

Stephen Walker

HarperCollins*Publishers*

Voyager
An Imprint of HarperCollins*Publishers*
77–85 Fulham Palace Road,
Hammersmith, London W6 8JB

www.voyager-books.com

A Paperback Original 1999

1 3 5 7 9 10 8 6 4 2

Copyright © Stephen Walker, 1999

The Author asserts the moral right to
be identified as the author of this work

A catalogue record for this book
is available from the British Library

ISBN 0 00 648380 1

Typeset in Meridien by
Palimpsest Book Production Limited,
Polmont, Stirlingshire

Printed and bound in Great Britain by
Caledonian International Book Manufacturing Ltd, Glasgow

For nice people everywhere

Acknowledgements

The author would like to express his appreciation of the following: Harry Walker; Nellie Walker; Ma'amselle Tufty; Steve Morgan; Anne Micklethwaite; Mary Burgess; Jean Collins; Ian Parkes; Tony Simonen; Audrey Bradley; Zena, The Warrior Princess; Paula Turton; Mr C. Monkeys; and finally my editors, Jane Johnson & Jim Rickards for not calling me up more than ten times in one day.

one

'Just look at that; Superman's breaking twenty-eight laws of physics. And it's not even noon yet.'

'Doesn't bother me. I'll be dead within fifteen minutes.'

Teena Rama raised a Dan Dare eyebrow. She stood in a doorway, looking across a tiny shop at a boy up a ladder. His back to her, T-shirt half hanging out, he stapled comic books to a wall, finding an assassinal rhythm any supervillain would envy.

Kerchung. There went Superman.

Kerchung. There went Spiderman.

Kerchung. There went Batman.

A Doc Marten back-heeling the door shut, she clomped down three wooden steps then browsed among tight aisles of comics, model kits and 'cult collectables'. 'So,' she asked, 'how do you reckon you'll be dead within fifteen minutes?'

Kerchung. 'This is an industrial stapler,' he said, 'used for fastening tank parts together. It's unbelievably dangerous in the wrong hands.'

1

'And are yours the wrong hands?' '

'Completely. By the time I've finished stapling the most expensive stock to the walls, there'll be so many holes around the entire place'll collapse.'

'So hadn't you better stop?'

'I don't want to. That's what three years working here does to a man.'

'It doesn't seem that bad,' she said.

'Do you have nightmares?' he said.

'Never.' She took a battered paperback from a rack by the window: Herbolt Myson, Victorian Sleuth. While speed reading it, she told the boy, 'I have a recurring dream about an angel dispensing knowledge to the peoples of the world, who are all like children not understanding the simplest of concepts. I try to see her face, knowing she must be the most beautiful thing in Creation, but can't get her to look at me. Then, just as I'm waking, she turns my way.'

'And?'

'And she's me.' She returned Herbolt Myson to his rack, after three chapters, deducing the Pennine Hell Hound to be Sir Charnwick Hoyle in a five-shilling dogsuit bought from Mlle Beauvoir's theatrical costumiers. When she abandoned the tale, Myson was still pondering the odd nature of the hound's woofing; quite unlike any Hell Hound he'd ever encountered.

She glanced across at the boy. He still had his back to her. She said, 'You do know you're allowed to look at me?'

'I won't be looking at you at any point in this conversation.'

'Because?'

'No offence, but you're bound to be gruesome.'

She inspected one of her dreadlocks. It needed re-dyeing. 'I suppose I could have made more effort with my appearance today.' Then she flicked it aside. 'But it never occurred to me that any man I'd meet in a comic shop could afford to be choosy.'

'I have a nightmare,' said the boy. 'It's about shelves. I'm here, stock taking, and the racks come to life – oh quietly at first, so I don't notice. And as I work, they creep up on me, nudging each other with wooden elbows, sniggering stupidly among themselves. Then one taps me on the shoulder. I turn. And they're encircling me, like Pink Elephants on Parade. They close in on me, crushing me, smothering me, falling on me, killing me. And I wake, screaming, to discover I was awake all along. Well; today I'm killing that dream.'

'Even if it means killing yourself?'

Kerchung.

'Have you considered a holiday?' she asked.

'They come along with me.'

'Who do?'

'Shelves – on holiday.'

'But not really?'

'Yes, really. I sit on the coach, looking forward to a good time, then I look around. And they're filling all the other seats, reading newspapers, smoking pipes, one leg flung over the other. Little baby shelves kick the back of the seats in front and get told off by their mother shelves.'

'I see.' Choosing to lighten the subject matter, she pulled a comic from a low rack. 'How much is this *Fish Man. He Swims*?'

'One pound seventy-five.'

'And this *Hormonal Fifty*?'

'One pound seventy-five.'

'And *The Human Leech*?'

'One seventy-five.'

She placed them back on the rack, none containing the information she needed. On tiptoes she scanned the rack's upper reaches. 'None of your stock seems to have a price tag.'

'Osmo's orders. He says, "Daniel, my dear boy, we are tigers in the jungles of commerce. Customers are our prey. Keep them confused, disorientated. Show a dapple of movement through the trees here, a dapple there. Keep them guessing. When they are suitably frightened, pounce."'

'Osmo?'

'The Great Osmosis, my boss and landlord. He models himself on El Dritch, Menacing Master of Mirage from *Man Fish. He Breathes*.'

'Don't you mean *Fish Man. He Swims*?' She referred to the comic she'd just studied, being a stranger to such things.

'No; *Man Fish. He Breathes*. Fish Man was half man, half fish. Man Fish is half fish, half man. You can't confuse the two, it's in the swim bladders. Osmo won't stock *Man Fish* because Man Fish always beats El Dritch.'

'Sounds a well-balanced individual,' she said.

'Osmo wears a bucket over his head, with smoke pouring from the eye holes. He appears from nowhere, checks for dust, delivers lofty, muffled orders then disappears in a cloud of smog. God knows why he takes so much interest in a dump like this when he has his fingers in every pie in town.'

'I believe I've had dealings with him.'

'Then you know what a pillock he is.'

Now she was by his step ladder. Knuckles on hips, lower lip jutted, she gazed up at him.

Kerchung.

How old was he? Nineteen? No age at all to die, but still a year older than her, and she'd packed a lifetime into her eighteen years. 'He seemed a little smarmy,' she said of the Great Osmosis, 'but otherwise okay.'

'That's because you've never had to endure a lunch hour with him.'

4

A comic fell from the ladder, hitting the floor. She scooped it up.

Strolling through the aisles, she flicked through pages that looked as though someone had wiped his trainers on them. Like extinguishing birthday cake candles, she blew dusty marks from paper. 'How much is this one?'

'What is it?'

'*Mr Meekly*.'

'Never heard of it,' he said.

She read out the front page blurb. It informed them that Mr Meekly, 45, a man in a brown suit, was responsible for handing out tax refunds. Alone among his colleagues, he delighted in redistributing money to the populace. And he was famous for it. Upon spotting his approach, women would lean out through their bedroom windows, asking, 'Why, Mr Meekly, are you coming to *my* house?'

And he'd say, 'Yes, Madam, I am,' even if he wasn't, because the more money he handed out, the better he felt. And, excited, they'd rush to the door, still in their nightwear, inviting him in for a cup of tea. And, though tea was all he ever received, he was content with that.

One day, a call arrived.

He was sent to Future City's new Atomic Underground.

The underground was vital for the city to compete with Tomorrowville's nuclear taxis, it was claimed. Some saw a more sinister purpose. They said there was no such thing as a nuclear taxi, although they could never prove it in televised debate.

The underground was still under construction when Meekly arrived. At the entrance, the foreman warned him it might be unsafe to enter the building site.

'Nonsense,' said the taxman. 'A man in there deserves his money, and his money he shall get.'

So the foreman handed him a yellow helmet, two sizes too large, patted it on 'tight' and sent him through a gauntlet of environmental protesters. Thrown house bricks bounced off that helmet. It was a good helmet, a life saver.

Meekly climbed the barriers then descended into the bowels of the Earth. Briefcase in hand, he made his way down dusty tunnels, giving the occasional polite cough.

Emerging onto the dimly lit platform, he spotted the man he wanted. Mike Mionman, 26, knelt – his back turned to Meekly – riveting square things to a wall.

Meekly stood still. He removed his shoes, one at a time, placing them neatly to one side, then tiptoed up behind the man, smiling, anticipating the look Mionman's face would adopt upon seeing the cash laden case.

But then . . .

. . . Disaster.

A child was loose on the platform.

Panicking, oversized helmet falling over his eyes, Meekly staggered around, arms outstretched before him, and toppled onto the track, as the Atom Bomb powered train approached on its final test run.

He took the full force.

Against all odds, Mr Meekly survived the collision; Future City did not.

And the radiation did things to his blood.

'Now,' read Teena, 'when exposed to travel delays, rude staff or ill-considered town planning, Mr Meekly becomes the Human Tube Line, powerful as an Atom Bomb, obdurate as a ticket collector, stupid as the fascist government's love of private roads when we should be travelling by bicycles or Out Of Body Experience as taught us by the Inuit.' She closed the comic, pulling a face she felt to be appropriate.

'Eco crap,' said the boy. 'In the early '90s, someone decided ecology'd be the next big thing in comics – that and talking turtles. Now do you see why I hate working here? All eco titles are a hundred and thirty-five pounds, sixty-eight pence.'

It stopped her in her tracks. 'A hundred and thirty-five . . . ?'

'Osmo's orders; "Daniel, the only people who care about the environment are those who can afford to avoid it. Charge them extra. If they don't complain, add VAT."'

'I see,' she said, not seeing. 'Well, I'll take it anyway. In fact, I'd like to order every back-issue of *Mr Meekly*, and any other comic in which he's ever appeared.'

'You do know that might be hundreds of issues, each at a hundred and thirty-five pounds?'

'Believe me they'll be more than worth it. Can you have them delivered?'

'No.'

'Why not?'

'I'll be dead. Osmo could deliver them. Just write your details in the counter's order book. I'm sure he'll find it in the rubble. It'll be the first thing he looks for.'

The implication of that comment was not lost on her. Rolling the comic up, she strode across the shop, and stopped at the foot of his ladder. Fists on hips, she looked up. And she said strongly, 'Excuse me.'

Kerchung.

'I said excuse me.' And she gave a forceful tug at one leg of his tatty jeans.

Danny Yates broke off from stapling, sighing loudly, eyes cast heavenward. Without turning to face this interloper, he knew what to expect.

They'd enter the shop, drab little things in black, usually dragged along, passive as wet rags, by equally dull boy-friends. But girls who came alone were the worst, unable to see the horror of the shelves. 'Gosh. How lucky you must feel,' they'd say, 'to be surrounded by this escapism all day long.' And they'd leave without knowing the scars that one sentence had left on him.

Again the girl tugged as though trying to pull his jeans off.

So Danny Yates looked down from his ladder . . .

. . . and almost fell off with shock.

'Hello.' She sparkled. 'My name's Teena; Teena Rama.' Cleopatra-painted eyes lowered to his lower portions, drilled into them with medical efficiency then returned to his eyes. A perfectly proportioned hand extended for him to shake, the girl saying, 'And judging by the rapidly swelling lump in your trousers, you've just found a reason to live.'

two

Then the building collapsed.

three

Lucy said hi.

Danny woke, to find his flatmate sat doing piranha impressions by his bedside. The twenty-one-year-old wore a second-hand Bay City Rollers T-shirt. Beneath each Roller's nose she'd marker penned a Hitler moustache. Fresh Faced Roller had two. Bad Hair Day Roller had three; one for his nose, one in place of each eyebrow. Roller Who's Name No one Remembers had no moustache; Lucy's pen had run out by then.

Explaining to Danny who the Rollers were, she'd once named them as, Uncle Bulgaria, Orinoco, 'A couple of others,' and Madam Choulet. They wandered around Wimbledon Fortnight tidying things up when no one had asked them to, and were therefore like your mother. Danny'd always felt she'd got it wrong somewhere.

She flicked a peanut in the air, mouth catching it, head stationary, her tongue clicking on contact. Cold, forward gazing eyes – and lower jaw jutting to catch each nut – gave the killer fish effect. But it was how he'd always seen her.

'Fancy a peanut?' she asked, not tipping her giant-size bag his way.

'I'm allergic to peanuts,' he said, still weak.

'Oh, yeah.' She chewed. 'So you are. You'd've thought I'd have considered that before buying them you.' She sounded as though she had.

'Where am I?' he asked.

'Looks like a chip shop to me.' Flick. Click.

Groggy, he looked around at jade coloured walls, at doctors, nurses, trolleys, opened screens, closed screens and beds. A machine by his side blipped. A clear plastic tube fed purple liquid into his arm. 'This isn't the hospital they usually take me to.'

'Nah,' she said. 'This was your first calamity in the north west of town, so they brought you here. Congratulations, you've now had life or death surgery in each of Wheatley's four big hospitals. How does it feel?'

'Wheatley General?' Again he looked around, this time seeing danger everywhere; behind those screens, in those beds, in that adjacent corridor which had no door to separate it from this recklessly open ward.

'Yup.' Lucy confirmed the location.

'But this is Boggy Bill territory.'

'Yeah,' she snorted, the ring through her pointy nose glinting. 'The laughs I've had over that video on those Sad but True shows.'

'But what if he knows I'm here?' Heart thumping, he sat up, throwing back the sheets. He looked at the floor for his shoes. His clothes, where had they put his clothes? 'I've got to get out of here before . . .'

'Lie down.' She pushed him back down onto the bed then held him there, 'You're going nowhere till the doctor's seen you.'

'But . . .' Again he tried to rise.

And again she stopped him, either not understanding

11

or not caring about the situation's urgency. Hard grey eyes stared into his. She gave her, 'Don't argue with me, Daniel,' look.

He stopped resisting, and she reclaimed her seat, pulling it closer to his bed. It scraped over tiles, making a noise like a braking lorry. The ward's other occupants looked at her then returned to their own concerns. She ignored them, retrieving the peanut bag from the floor, where she'd dropped it. And she asked, 'Why would he come for you? I'm sorry to break the news to you but I'm sure there's better people in this place to bump off.'

'Like who?'

'Like the Financial Director. If I was Boggy Bill, he'd be the first to go. Jesus, I'm not even Boggy Bill and I want to punch that bloke's lights out. And is the Financial Director dead? No. He's in the car park, walking his Dougal dog.'

'But you'd like to punch everyone,' said Danny. 'Boggy Bill picks his targets with surgical precision, planning for months ahead, biding his time, awaiting the right moment to burst from the trees and grab you.'

She frowned. 'Boggy Bill does?'

'All the time.'

'The Wheatley Bigfoot?'

'The Wheatley Bigfoot.'

'A creature with only one word in its vocabulary?'

'Yes,' he tried to make dwindling conviction sound like growing conviction.

'And that word is . . . ?'

'We don't need to go into that.'

'Yes we do, Daniel.'

He shuffled slightly in his bed, turning red, finally saying the words, 'Tamba-lulu.'

'Tamba-lulu. And what does that mean, Daniel?'

'No one knows.'

'Do you think Boggy Bill knows?' she asked cynically.

12

'No one knows.'

'And that's a cunning planner of revenges, is it?'

'Don't mistake a lack of formal education for stupidity.'

'Are we talking him or you?' Shaking the bag, she emptied a handful of nuts into her palm then swallowed them. 'Do you reckon Boggy Bill's cross-eyed? He sounds the type of monster who would be.'

'He's no laughing matter for some of us, Lucy.'

'So why would he choose you as his prime target?'

'Because of my brother.'

'And how would he know who your brother is?'

'He'd know.' He glanced round meaningfully, as though the thing was about to leap out from behind a closed screen or appear in the doorway, cunningly disguised as a nurse come to administer his bed bath. His blood froze solid at the realization that he'd been lying there for God knew how long, and at any time, Bill could have walked right in and torn his head off, giving its blood curdling cry of, 'Tamba-lulu?' which *could* be frightening, if uttered while your head was being bashed against a wall.

'Danny, you've been here all this time. If he was coming for you, he'd have done it by now. I refuse to believe he's blessed with patience, even if he did exist, which he doesn't.'

'He exists alright. Brian assured me.'

'And if your brother said the world was hollow and inhabited by a secret sect of Aztec rabbits?'

'He did.'

'He did?'

'Yeah.'

'When?'

'In a letter yester . . . I mean the day before my "accident". He felt someone should know the truth, in case the rabbits came for him with their obsidian blades.'

'And you believed him?'

13

'Not necessarily,' he conceded grudgingly. 'Brian may have a tendency to fantasize. But I like to keep an open mind. And let's face it, if anyone'd know the world was hollow, he would. Brian's been everywhere.'

'Everywhere except the planet Earth.' Flick. Click.

Danny scanned the walls for a calendar. There wasn't one. A clock on the far wall told him it was 2:30 in the afternoon but not which afternoon. 'How long have I been here? I was in the –'

'Six months.' She consumed half the peanuts in one go.

'Six months?' he said in disbelief.

'Pretty cool, huh?' Munch munch munch. 'I never knew anyone who'd been in a coma before – least, not for six months.' Swallow. 'Course, my flatmate before you – Keith – he was dead. But who could tell? But you, Danny, you've gone for it big time. Me, I'm proud of you. I may not look it but I am.'

'Six months?'

'Everyone at Poly wants to meet you, especially Annette Helstrang from Occult Pathology. She wants to dissect you; after you die, of course. Remember Annette Helstrang?'

He didn't; and didn't want to.

'You met her once. She frightened you. She dissected Keith, put him in this hu-u-u-u-u-u-u-u--u-uge pickling jar.' Lucy did a full stretch One That Got Away gesture. 'Then she put him on display in her living room. She did a great job. You should see him, Dan. He never looked better.'

'And for six months you've sat here, waiting for me to recover? Lucy, I don't know what to say.' Visions of Blackfriars Bob frisked, waggy tailed, in his head. And it had taken something like this for Lucy's true feelings to show through? Her lies and insults, the practical jokes that only she found funny, her over pushiness, her casual

14

fraud and theft, they didn't mean a thing, not really, not when it mattered. And maybe the two of them could have a future as flatmates, one that didn't involve her always trying to trample all over him whenever she was in a bad mood.

He took her non-peanut-flicking hand, squeezing it tight. 'Thanks, Luce. I won't forget this.'

She snatched her hand away. 'Yeah; like I've nothing better to do than sit around waiting for you. I told you when you first moved in with me; don't expect me to run round after you just coz I'm a woman; no washing for you, no ironing, no cooking. Coma watching was out too. Don't believe me? Check the contract.'

'But, then . . . ?'

'I only just found out you were missing. The hospital got in touch. You'd been plain "Anonymous" till two hours ago. I suppose that's nothing new for you. You started muttering my name and address. They figured you probably weren't, "That cow Lucy Smith," so they called me. Anyhow, I thought I'd better come round and see you.' She flicked another nut.

He frowned at her. 'You didn't notice I was missing for six months?'

She shrugged. 'Osmo said something about it a few times but, I dunno, I suppose I wasn't listening. Maybe there was something more interesting on TV; *Home and Away* or something.'

Danny was beginning to recall something. 'There was a girl at the shop . . .'

'With spotty hair?'

'Tangerine,' he corrected.

'Huh?'

'Tangerine; tangerine dreadlocks, big thick ones with lemon polka dots.'

'Whatever.' Flick. Click. 'She's dead.'

15

'What!?!'

'You killed her, Danny. The building fell right on her, squashed her like a polka dot lemon. It was only coz she'd thrown herself over you that you survived.'

Danny stared, numb, at the ceiling. In his mind's eye it gave way; just a crack at first, a tiny thing spreading, like black lightning, from one wall to the other. Then it was a torrent of falling masonry, chunk by heartless chunk beating the life from the most beautiful girl he'd ever seen – as though hurled by a mad god lacking the sense to know who should live and who should die.

This couldn't be right. He thought she'd have time to get out before the building collapsed, leaving him to face the fate he now knew he deserved. Deserved because she was lovely and brave and witty and clever – and innumerable other things he'd never know about her – while he was nothing.

What was he supposed to do now, with a life that had been spared for no reason? He didn't know. He just knew he felt empty and stupid and useless. Most of all he felt nothing because he didn't know what to feel. And that was what he hated himself for most.

Croaky voiced he asked, 'How did she . . . ?'

'How did she get home? She walked.'

'What?'

'She walked. You know, used her legs. Maybe she got the bus later. I dunno.'

'How could she walk if she was dead?' he asked, completely lost.

'She's not dead.'

'You just said she was.'

'I lied.'

'Why?'

'Teach you a lesson.'

'What lesson?'

'Not to go demolishing buildings on young ladies. In case your mother never told you, it's bad manners.'

@!%%$*@@&$*!!! 'So, what the hell happened to her?'

'According to the emergency services, when they reached the scene, she was with you. She'd dragged you from the rubble, given you mouth to mouth, performed emergency surgery with her credit card and boot laces, then kept you going with heart massage till they arrived. Seems she's some sort of hotshot doctor.'

Lucy retrieved a Gladstone bag from by her feet, placing it on her lap. Click, she opened it, pulling out a sheet of paper. 'On my way in I grilled the ambulance crew in question. They had a little trouble – her having been fully clothed when they met her – but, using hypno-regression, I got 'em to construct this photofit of her chest. It's a bit vague but I think it captures the essence.'

She studied it further. 'They're pretty good, though way too small for my purposes.'

And she held the picture for him to see. Indistinct, it reminded him of the flying saucer photos which sometimes appeared in *The Wheatley Advertiser*, only the exhibitor seeing in them what they purported to depict.

Lucy pointed out assumed areas of interest. 'As you can see, they're equally perky, which is unusual. Normally one's perkier than the other. Why do you reckon that is?'

He shrugged blankly.

'Of course no photofit's entirely reliable. I'll need to get some proper pictures.' She made a note, paper on lap. Lank, green hair hanging over one eye, she murmured along as her biro wrote; 'One ... must be ... as perky as ... the other.' The pen stabbed a full stop. She slotted the photofit back into the Gladstone, clicking it shut, placing it by her feet.

Danny contemplated the girl's use of mouth to mouth resuscitation. 'She kissed me?'

17

Lucy stuck the pen behind her left ear. 'Only coz she had to. I'm sure she must've pulled a face while doing it. Anyway, how are you? You okay?'

'I think so.' He mentally checked; toes, feet, legs, fingers, arms, neck, head. There was no discomfort nor disconcerting numbnesses. The small of his back itched. He scratched it. It wouldn't go away but that was all right, itching rarely happened to dead people. 'I feel a bit weak,' he said, finally finding something to complain about.

The tube in his arm slurped. He looked at it, concerned. 'Lucy?'

'Yup?'

'What's that liquid?'

She pointed at it. 'This?'

'Yeah.'

Leaning forward she scrutinized the tube. She unhooked it from his arm, stuck one end in her mouth and took a long hard suck on it that gurgled like a straw drawing on the bottom of a near empty glass. She reaffixed it to the tap on his arm.

He stared at the tap. He stared at his flatmate, horrified by what she'd just done.

'Ribena,' she shrugged and, bag in hand, left – swiping someone's grapes on her way.

Danny frowned at the tube.

Ribena?

Boggy Bill had been replacing his blood with Ribena?

18

four

The Great Osmosis appeared from thin air, late afternoon, accompanied by billowing smoke and the opening chord of the Beatles' *Her Majesty*. His stage magician's cape swirled melodramatically. Thunderous black fumes belched from his bucket's eye slits.

When Danny stopped coughing, following the smoke's dispersal to all quarters of the hospital, the esoteric entrepreneur slammed a grocery box down onto the boy's chest and boomed, 'Oh, perfidious betrayal!'

Another cloud swallowed the man. And, with a final flourish, he was gone.

Coughing one last cough, Danny tipped the box toward him for a better look. Its contents rattled.

This was trouble.

Big trouble.

The Dr Doom Detection Pen was a cheap, see-through biro

available at any stationer's. It didn't even write properly, failing on every other word. And the snot-green mug with the not-quite-on-right handle and full length crack? In what way could it ever be connected with the Green Hornet? The Deluxe Spiderman Webbing (snare any villain in seconds) was sellotape. But not good sellotape.

Danny dropped the biro back into the grocery box, with the rest of the junk. It was his property – Osmosis had always insisted – freebies from a sales rep who'd arrive once a month, dispense rubbish then depart without selling a single comic.

And there were the rats, two. He'd rescued them from the broom of the girl who ran the takeaway next door. She'd screamed hysterically when told he'd be keeping them because he'd felt all shops should have a pet. Each rat had had a five-pound note in its mouth, as though they'd entered the takeaway planning to buy a meal.

Osmosis had pooh-poohed the idea. 'Daniel, my boy, rats rarely appreciate the value of money.'

Regardless, Danny had put the notes in a piggy bank on the counter, doing it in front of them so they'd know where it was should they need it.

Now he checked the grocery box. Inevitably Osmosis hadn't returned the money with the rats. In the box, their noses twitched up at him. And he knew they deserved better than being squashed by broom heads, or having their money stolen by over-theatrical shop owners, or being unacceptable in hospitals when cuter animals would be welcomed as therapeutic.

Right!

That was it.

He looked around. No one was watching.

Sitting up, he placed the rats on his lap. Tearing four thin strips from the box, he bit required lengths from the 'Spiderman Webbing', and taped cardboard to rodent ears.

20

He pressed their new, longer ears on securely, to resist high winds.

There.

That was better.

Now they were rabbits.

Blam! Danny jumped.

Blam! Danny jumped.

Blam! Danny jumped.

Blam! Someone was firing a shotgun in the nearby woods. Another fired, then another, and another, till it became a chorus of hastily discharged pellets, each blast nearer than the one before.

And Danny knew all too well what it meant.

No time to waste, he placed his rattits back in their box, giving them one final stroke. Then he looked around to see if anyone official looking was watching. They weren't.

Since he'd awoken, not one member of staff had paid the slightest attention to him. Initially they'd all been gathered around the bed by the door, watching its occupant perform his card tricks. Their presence had deterred Danny from trying to leave.

But, fifteen minutes after the card trick man's death, they'd finally realized there'd be no more tricks from him and all the prodding in the world wasn't going to change that. So, bored, they'd gravitated to the bed furthest from the door.

That was his chance.

Now the man in the bed furthest from the door was showing them his magic tricks. Constantly smiling he produced doves from nowhere and threw them into the air. In mid flutter they transformed into much needed medical supplies which clattered to the floor around him, whereupon he donated them to the hospital.

The act elicited gasps and applause from the entranced nurses, doctors, surgeons and accountants. The man didn't even have the decency to look as unhealthy as Danny looked when healthy. But Danny'd figured it out; in this hospital, attention given related directly to entertainment value. Good; because Danny Yates had no entertainment value.

He leaned to one side and placed the rattits' box on the floor. Now the man produced bunches of flowers from behind a doctor's ear, handing them out to delighted nurses who sniffed at them and blushed coyly – even the male nurses. Now he handed flowers to the surgeons. And they blushed more than anyone.

Danny turned off the tap attached to his arm. He unplugged it then carefully slid it free of his vein, relieved to see the limb didn't become an opened sluice discharging liquid by the gallon. He licked the one drop of purple liquid that formed on his arm where the tube had been. It *was* Ribena.

Throwing back the sheets, he climbed from the bed as more applause erupted behind him.

A small cabinet stood by his bed head. Inside, he found his clothes folded into a neat pile, trainers on top.

Casting furtive glances over his shoulder, grocery box and clothing in his arms, the unnoticeable Danny Yates made his escape, as the world's most entertaining patient sawed himself in half.

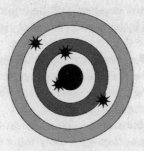

five

The Great Osmosis sat in the dressing room of a closed down Working Men's Club. Where once he'd heard the babble of club members awaiting the next act, he now heard silence.

And it didn't matter. He no longer needed the applause of fools. Holding his bucket steady on his head, he sat before the huge wall mirror. With the softest of cloths he polished his precious pail. When that pail gleamed with all the vigour of Lancelot's armour, he put aside the cloth. He placed the lid on the polish. He twisted tight its tiny latch. And he leaned forward, eyes narrowing to better admire the bucket.

In that mirror's cracked reflections he glimpsed the past . . .

. . . March 28th, 1984. In that club, a novice magician donned his white gloves and marked his debut by making his pretty young wife disappear.

He'd been trying to saw her in half.

Confused, but hiding his desperation, he looked beneath the cabinet. He looked above it. He checked either side of it. He checked inside it. He checked beneath the curtains. He checked above the curtains. Still he found no sign of her.

Accompanied by boos, jeers and beer glasses hurled from the audience, he fled the stage, in tears.

When he got backstage and sobbed against the wall, what did he see by the fire extinguisher? Nothing less than his new bride kissing the club secretary. She spotted him. She threw back her head and laughed.

Days later, jobless and wifeless, he sat by the ring road and cried into a bucket – the only thing that could never betray him. And he knew what he must do.

He stood up, donned that faithful bucket so he wouldn't see the onrushing traffic, and said goodbye to the world.

He stepped forward.

But, as he was about to step into the road, a miracle happened. A comic book blew onto his bucket. It was *Man Fish*, the last ever issue, where the soon-to-retire artist had finally granted El Dritch his deserved victory. Oh the writer had tried to hide Man Fish's defeat, with captions that claimed being torn in half, and squashed by a mountain, was part of Man Fish's master plan. Osmosis knew better.

His new career began with the founding of a small comic shop on that very site. He kept it spotless. Herbolt Myson was added to the stock, then model kits, then posters; all things that in childhood had given Osmosis hope of escape.

And a new dream was born . . .

. . . But now a boy threatened that dream. He'd destroyed the shop, the very foundation of Osmosis' empire. What if he should strike at other parts of that kingdom; the tenements, the skyscraper, the munitions works? An empire cannot stand without foundations.

And, as he gazed into that mirror, Osmosis again knew what must be done.

Danny Yates must die.

'Danny? What're *you* doing here?' Lucy stood at the far end of the hallway, in boxer shorts and a vest, holding a TV set. Hair dangling over one eye, she gave a shapeless grin.

Danny stood just inside the flat's opened front door. 'This is my home too – in case you hadn't noticed.'

Carrying the TV into his bedroom, she called through to him. 'Used to be your home. The Great Osmo materialized ten minutes ago. As of the moment you left hospital, you no longer lived here. Of course, technically, you've not lived here for the last six months, but your lease was still valid, so he's been debiting rent from your bank regardless. Did he mention that during his visit?'

Teeth grinding, Danny dug his fingernails, talon-like, into the sides of the grocery box he held pressed against his chest.

Lucy explained: 'At first he did it coz he thought it'd be what you'd have wanted had you lived, sort of a memorial. Then, when he discovered you *had* lived, he just plain emptied your account and went on holiday with it. I've never seen him so angry.' Her head popped round the door; 'If I were you, Daniel, I would *not* go round to complain,' then popped back again.

Her voice receded deeper into his bedroom. 'Anyway, he's given me your room. Is this your wardrobe? Or did it come with the flat? If it's not yours, bags it's mi

'Lucy, how could you do this to me? I tho

were friends. Well, no, I never thought we were friends but . . .'

'Don't get me wrong,' she said against the swish of coat hangers being test driven along wardrobe rails. 'There's nothing personal in this but you know I've always wanted this room. I'm a growing girl, Danny, or intend to be. Once I've had my breast implants, I won't even be able to get through my old room's door.'

'You're not really going through with that?'

'Too right I am. Soon as I've graduated, and earned some real money, my chest will be a whole new barrel of fish. Besides, it's not fair that whenever some new kid moves in they always get this room, when I've been here the longest.' Spring spring. Creak creak. Boing boing creak. 'This bed's great.' Boing. 'Did it come with the flat?'

He closed the front door, taking a final look around the dingy hallway. Today was the third anniversary of his moving in. On that first day, he'd inadvertently set himself alight. On the second, Lucy had electrocuted him; accidentally, she'd claimed, though laughing too readily whenever retelling the tale to friends. On the third day had been the blender incident. Subsequent events had taken a turn for the worse.

There'd been a third flatmate, Josephine. She sang; like Aretha Franklin, in her sleep – like Bill Franklyn, while awake. And she danced; like Baryshnikov, while asleep – like Barry Sheene, while awake. She acted; like Olivier, while asleep – like Olive Oyl, while awake.

Josephine Daly sold eighty million albums, won three Grammies, two Larries (and an Emmy for her X-Files guest spot as 'Snoring Alien on the Left') but had slept through the whole thing. She'd believed she only worked at Mr Kake's Bakery – her day job – never accepting Danny's attempts to tell her otherwise.

When two workmen arrived, one midnight, to put the

26

Sleeping Diva in a packing crate and mail her to Hollywood, Osmo'd immediately replaced her with Maria, the flatmate no one had ever seen. Clearly Danny would never get to see her now.

What to do next?

The rattits squeaked in their box, oblivious to all worry. Should he give them names? George and Ira? Arnold and Sylvester? For that matter, what sex were they? No way would he be checking, his Aunt Fi having always warned that only people you don't want to meet go round checking animal genitalia without veterinary need. And she should have known, having been married to Uncle Fred.

Danny's index finger stroked a rodentine back. Whatever sex they were, those two lumps of scraggy fur were all he had left in the world.

Lucy reappeared from her new bedroom, for the first time noticed his grocery box and, after a pause, asked, 'Did those rats come with the flat?'

When he left, Danny left ratless.

six

'Erm, hello?' Danny stepped forward, tentatively.

The young nun stopped writing, put the lid on her pen then placed it to one side. She slammed shut her hefty ledger and put it to one side. Chin on knuckles, elbows on desk, smooth faced, she gazed down from behind a counter so high it couldn't fail to make you feel inadequate.

And she gazed.

And she gazed.

She blinked once.

And she gazed.

Danny found her unreadableness disconcerting, but he found anyone in uniform disconcerting, having always lived in fear of the reintroduction of National Service.

'Hello,' said a soft, Dublin lilt. 'Would you be Gary?'

'No. My name's Danny; Danny Yates.'

'Well, good afternoon, Mr Danny Yates. Can I be of assistance?'

'You put homeless people up?'

'We offer refuge to locals who've fallen on hard times

after a lifetime devoted to this town's maritime industries, yes. Are you a sailor?'

'Not really.' His heart sank like a holed tug.

'A cabin boy?'

'Not really.'

'A ship's mascot?'

'Not really.'

'Have you ever been on a ship?'

He shook his head.

'A hovercraft, catamaran, or dinghy?'

He shook his head.

'A raft, crossing the mighty Atlantic?'

He shook his head.

'A bathtub crossing Windermere for charity?'

He shook his head.

'Have you ever been on any vessel on any water?' she asked.

'I celebrated my fourteenth birthday with a pedalo ride in what's now Osmosis Park,' he said. 'You had to be fourteen to go on one.'

'Well, I suppose that's somethin –'

'I drowned.'

Her expression told him to continue.

'A freak tidal surge overturned my boat, smashing it to smithereens. Washed ashore, face down in mud, I was only saved by an unfeasibly large mallard repeatedly jumping up and down on my back, thinking I was attacking its nest. The action emptied my lungs of water and got me breathing again. When I started coughing, the duck jumped down, quacked one last angry quack at me and waddled off. The park keeper'd said he'd never seen anything like it. If not for that incident, I might have been a sailor.'

'Heavens,' she said. 'But did the park keeper not try to save you?'

'He'd thought about it but really couldn't be bothered.

I have that effect on people. Since then, I've pretty much avoided open water. But then, I avoid most things because of . . . incidents.'

Eyes still gazing into his, she shrugged. 'Well, we can't have that, can we, Mr Yates? A non-sailor staying at a seaman's mission?'

He shook his head, having known all along that this would happen. Now he'd probably have to endure a lecture.

'Why,' she lectured. 'Such a thing would be an abomination against reason. What would Barnables, the patron saint of shipwreck survivors, have to say about that?' Her eyes looked toward a huge painting Danny took to be Saint Barnables. Like all Godly men, he possessed the face of a man whose sole pastime was strangling donkeys.

And, head down, Danny trudged toward the door, a futureless, homeless, penniless void opening up before him.

'Mr Yates?' she said.

He stopped.

'You've left something behind.'

He turned, puzzled, not aware of having brought anything in with him.

She took an item from beneath the counter, tossing it to him, then resumed her chin on palm pose.

He unfolded the thrown object. It turned out to be a sailor's hat. Baffled, he looked at her.

'Try it on,' she said.

He did. It didn't fit. But smiling, she winked. 'You look a mighty fine sailor to me.'

'This is where you'll be staying, the sleeping quarters; or "cabin", as we call it to make sea dogs feel at home.'

'It's empty.' Danny stood at the room's centre. Crunchingly narrow, its decor loosely echoed a galleon's lower quarters. Ship's wheels alternated with port holes along the walls. Lanterns hung from the low ceiling.

The nun stayed by the door. 'Completely empty.' She opened a steel locker beside the door, hauled out a rolled up web of knotted ropes and carried it across to the wall nearest him. She tied one end around a hook projecting from the wall and yanked it tight.

'You have to remember, Mr Yates, Wheatley is over sixty miles from the sea, in all directions. In its history, the town has produced just one, nominal, sailing man; Peghead Flannaghann, scourge of the leisure boat industry. Of course, back then there were no leisure boats, nor indeed a canal, nor any large stretch of water in Wheatley, nor any boat makers, nor sail manufacturers. Rigging was hard to come by, and expensive. All in all, Peghead Flannaghann's adventures are a bit of a let down to the thrill seeker.'

'Shouldn't that be pegleg?' asked Danny, watching her.

'In 1694, Declan Flannaghann, self-declared buccaneer of the pavements – though pavement quality was much poorer then than now – came down with a headache following an all night drinking session. To relieve his pain, his friends, for he had many among the underclasses, sawed off his head and replaced it, in grand pirate tradition, with a peg.'

His jaw dropped. 'They sawed off his head?'

'Sadly, none of his friends were medically trained. Nor were they reivers. Nor were they a full shilling. They may have misunderstood the term "cut throat pirate".'

'But they sawed off his head?' Danny was horrified. It was the sort of act he'd thought only Lucy capable of.

The sister continued. 'Undeterred by his lack of mobility, his shipmates' descendants kept him mummified in a public house where regulars would amuse themselves by spinning plates on his peg head, until the canal was built. Whereupon he was placed on a small barge and left to drift, causing aimless terror and consternation among passing traders, in conjunction with Sqwark the peg head parrot.'

Danny frowned. 'Are you making this up?'

'It's in the reference books. Flannaghann and Sqwark were accompanied by Bark the peg head dog, and Mark the peg head cabin boy. Atop the mast was Krark the peg head albatross. Once his friends had got into the groove, they just couldn't stop themselves. It must all have been quite a sight emerging from the mist, peg-heading toward you.'

And she crossed to the opposite wall. 'No one knows what happened to him after the 1880s. Some say his ghost still stalks the canal though boats no longer sail it. Some claim a daring soul has replaced his peg with a wonderful mechanical limb possessing a mind of its own; which is just as well, considering he himself lacks any sort of mind.'

She tied the webbing's other end to the wall. Its narrow span bisected the room at waist height. 'Some may say Peghead Flannaghann wasn't much of a hero for Wheatley to have but I like to think he was rather noble in his battle against the odds. And by all accounts . . .' she became flushed, '. . . quite rough.'

She yanked tight the rope, tied a final knot then stood back, admiring her handiwork. 'There.' Quietly satisfied hands clapped themselves free of dust.

Danny looked at her, across the newly completed hammock. 'So why does Wheatley have a seaman's mission?'

'Sister Remunerable.'

'Who?'

'My partner in this venture, and best friend in all the world. She was my bunkmate at the convent; taught me to drink gin, which was naughty of her but fun. The Mission was her idea. "Sister Theresa," she said. "Every town should have a seaman's mission, regardless of need." She was most insistent. She'll be delighted we have our second ever guest.'

'You have another?'

'We had. He packed his bags and set off to make his way in this world, not forty-five minutes ago. In many aspects he was not unlike you, a man who'd given up all hope until he found us. But I've blathered on enough. You want to get settled in. I'll leave you to unpack.'

'I don't have anything to unpack.'

She headed for the door, not looking back, said, 'Regardless,' and left.

Her footsteps receded, leaving Danny to test the hammock. He didn't bother. He'd seen enough sit-coms to predict the outcome. Setting the hammock creaking back and forth he considered the floor, deciding it'd be better to sleep on than the street. And he had this whole room to himself. And, unlike Lucy, a nun wouldn't help herself to his property, claiming Finders Keepers as English Law's one inviolable principle – when the item had been 'found' in a locked drawer, using a crowbar.

The sister's footsteps returned.

Her head popped round the door, her fingers wrapping around its frame. 'Do you play a musical instrument, Mr Yates?'

'No. Why?'

She just smiled then left.

Danny was lying on the floor when Sister Theresa returned. Smiling mischievously, she was hiding something behind her back. 'Hello again, Mr Yates. Lying on the floor are we?'

He said nothing.

She lay beside him. The hidden thing droned like a trod on octopus. Produced from behind her back, one end strapped to one hand, the once hidden thing distended and sprawled like an sick caterpillar across her chest. The thing dribbled to the floor and expired.

It was a squeezebox.

He squinted at it, suspicious.

The sister made herself more comfortable. 'I thought we could have a sing along. Do you know any sea shanties, Mr Yates?'

'None.' He hoped to discourage her.

'Fortunately, I know one. It's called The Rhyme of Long Gone Hats and is so authentic it practically reeks of salt. A sailor taught it me in a Liverpool bar.'

He glanced at her.

Gazing at the ceiling, she answered his implied question. 'Sister Remunerable took me there. "Tessie," she said, a Rothmans flapping in her mouth, "in order to understand sailors, we must first mix with them. We must ape their ways, however coarse." Sister Remunerable spends near all her time getting to know sailors. That's where she is today, seeking them out in the pubs of Newcastle on Tyne, before moving on to its many all-night clubs.'

Danny chose to say nothing.

'Mr Dimitri Stassanopolou, my sailor was called. Sister Remunerable introduced us. He had some very strange ideas about what nuns get up to.'

Her free hand entered the other strap and, fingering a bewildering array of buttons, she held the small accordion ready. 'Right. Here goes.' And she squeezed.

THE RHYME OF LONG GONE HATS:
Oh my hat lies in the Eastern Caucasus.

It was thrown there by naughty porpoises.
Sea horsie.
Sea horsie.
Sea horsie.
Sea horsie.
Sea horsie.
Sea horsie.
Sea horsie.
Sea horsie.
Sea horsie.
Sea horsie.
Sea horsie.
Sea horsie.
Sea horsie.
Sea horsie.
Sea horsie.
Sea horsie.
Sea horsie.
Sea horsie.
Sea horsie.
Sea horsie.
Sea horsie.
Sea horsie.
Sea horsie.
Sea horsie.
Sea horsie.
Sea horsie.
Sea horsie.
Sea horsie.
Sea horsie.
Sea horsie.
Sea horsie.
Sea horsie.

Sea horsie.
Sea horsie.
Sea horsie.
Sea horsie.
Sea horsie.
Sea horsie.
Sea horsie.
Sea horsie.
Sea horsie.
Sea horsie.
Sea horsie.
Sea horsie.
Sea horsie.
Sea horsie.
Sea horsie.
Sea horsie.
Sea horsie.
Sea horsie.
Sea horsie.
Sea horsie.
Sea horsie.
Sea horsie.
Sea horsie.
Sea horsie.
Sea horsie.
Sea horsie.
Sea horsie.
Sea horsie.
Sea horsie.
Sea horsie.
Sea horsie.
Sea horsie.
Sea horsie.
Sea horsie.
Sea horsie.
Sea horsie.
Sea horsie.

Sea horsie.
Sea horsie.
Sea horsie.
Sea horsie.
Sea horsie.
Sea horsie.
Sea horsie.
Sea horsie.
Sea horsie.
Sea horsie.
Sea horsie.
Sea horsie.
Sea horsie.
Sea horsie.
Sea horsie.
Sea horsie.
Sea horsie.
Sea horsie.
Sea horsie.
Sea horsie.
Sea horsie.
Sea horsie.
Sea horsie.
Sea horsie.
Sea horsie.
Sea horsie.
Sea horsie.
Sea horsie.
Sea horsie.
Sea horsie.
Sea horsie.
Sea horsie.
Sea horsie.
Sea horsie.

Sea horsie.
Sea horsie.
Sea horsie.
Sea horsie.
Sea horsie.
Sea horsie.
Sea horsie.
Sea horsie.
Sea horsie.
Sea horsie.
Sea horsie.
Sea horsie.
Sea horsie.
Sea horsie.
Sea horsie.
Sea horsie.
Sea horsie.
Sea horsie.
Sea horsie.
Sea horsie.
Sea horsie.
Sea horsie.
Sea horsie.
Sea horsie.
Sea horsie.
Sea horsie.
Sea horsie.
Sea horsie.
Sea horsie.
Sea horsie.
Sea horsie.
Sea horsie.
Sea horsie.
Sea horsie.

Sea horsie.

Sea . . .

'Can you stop singing now, please?'

. . . horsie.

Sea horsie.

Sea horsie.

Sea horsie.

10 PM.

Sea horsie.

Sea horsie.

Sea horsie.

Sea horsie.

'Can you stop singing now, please?'

11 PM.

Sea horsie.

Sea horsie.

Sea horsie.

Sea horsie.

'Can you stop singing now, please?'

Midnight.

Sea horsie.

Sea horsie.

Sea horsie.

Sea horsie.

Danny set about making a string of desperate phone
calls.

seven

First thing next morning.

Annette Helstrang awoke, threw back the sheets, sat up, stretched out in a great big, foot-stomping, yawn. Then she watched the floor, puzzled.

Between her bare feet, a pair of legs were protruding from beneath her bed.

'Lucy?' Early morning, Danny answered a knock at the Mission door, surprised to find her stood on the doorstep.

She grabbed his arm, almost yanked it from its socket, and dragged him to her psychedelic taxi.

'How did you find me?' he asked.

Fingers tapping steering wheel, in time to REM, she said, 'I asked myself where would the saddest of sad losers end

40

up in this town, chose the Seaman's Mission and rang the bell. You answered.'

Lucy drove along a tree-shaded road out of town, Danny seated beside her in the pink and purple cab she ran to supplement her student loan. Wedged above the rear view mirror was a rolled up copy of the comic book *Daisy the Cow*. Daisy would spend each issue's thirty-seven pages sampling different types of grass to see which tasted best. In the end, she always settled on New Zealand Rye; the message being that the familiar is always the best. *Daisy the Cow* was the number one comic strip among students. It was an irony thing.

'So, what's this about?' asked Danny

'I have a King Kong of a surprise for you.'

'You've found something of mine you've not stolen?'

'Don't get bitter on me, Danny.'

'Well what do you expect? You take my room, my rats, my grocery box, on top of all the other rotten things you've done to me over the years.'

'You don't want to know what I have to say?'

He folded his arms and looked out through the side window. 'Get on with it.'

'I, Lucy Jane Smith, who everyone said was neither use nor ornament, have found you a home.'

'Is it crap?'

'Daniel, this is not crap. This is with Annette Helstrang. You remember her from Hallowe'en?'

'The horror movie?'

'The party. She was at my Walpurgis do. Annette remembers you; remembers you big time. She was the nice one.'

'There was no nice one at your Hallowe'en do.'

'Course there was. She frightened you.'

'They all frightened me,' he complained. 'They all frighten me at all your do's. I don't know where you unearth your friends but, frankly, I'd rather you didn't.'

41

'You're one to talk,' she retorted. 'With the state of your friends.'

'What's wrong with my friends?'

'Chuff, Biffer and Bloaty Elvis? Need I say more?'

'Chuff was a good enough name for you when you went out with him.'

'For three hours, Daniel, for three hours. And believe me, it's the last time I blind date anyone on your recommendation. So where is your "mate" Chuff during your time of crisis? Practising that hilarious trick of his with the U-bend?'

'Everyone thinks it's funny except you.'

'Danny, they laugh out of pity.'

He told her, 'I spent the early hours on the Mission's pay phone, trying to call my old friends. Do you know, every single one of them moved house while I was comatose?'

'Yeah, that's what they tell you.'

'No, really. Each number was answered by someone I didn't know. And none had a forwarding address. What do you think the odds are against that?'

'With you, pretty long; you were never that lucky before. Anyway, the party. Annette was the one in the cyberman suit.'

He looked at her. 'That was a girl?'

'A girl? You know what was inside that baco-foil? Winona Ryder, or as good as. And you turned down a chance to snog that?'

He thought about this. 'Which Winona Ryder?'

She frowned, intent on the road ahead. 'Which Winona Ryder? Which d'you think? The one works down the chip shop, says she's Elvis.'

'But she's not the same in every movie is she? She's a human chameleon. In some movies she's nice. In some she's nasty.'

'She's Winona Ryder in *Beetlejuice*. Happy?'

'She'd do, I suppose.'

'You suppose.'

'I preferred *Edward Scissorhands* Winona.'

'Oh, I'm sorry; you see, I forgot that a classy bloke like you has to be careful which Winona Ryder he's seen in public with.'

'Just as long as she's not *The Crucible* Winona.'

Lucy chuckled malevolently. 'Oh yeah. I remember you running out the living room in a panic, half way through that one.'

He shuffled in his seat, turning red, and gazed out through the side window. 'I was not in a panic. I was just . . .'

'You were just what?'

'I was checking things.'

'What things?'

'Things that needed checking.'

She smirked and accelerated. 'Anyway, Annette's sweet. Everyone says so. And frankly, cybermen are not scary. She's a little eccentric but you like that in a woman. And, Danny, God strike me down if I'm lying but, although she wears one, Annette does not need a bra.'

'Here we go,' he groaned.

'"Here we go," what?'

'Have you ever considered therapy for this fixation?'

'What fixation?' she asked.

'Your breast fixation.'

'I have no fixation.'

'They're your sole topic of conversation.'

'No they're not.'

'Yes, Lucy, they are.'

'No, Daniel, they are not. I have a full and varied range of conversational subjects.'

'Such as?'

'Such as Annette Helstrang, who I was in the process of describing when you so rudely interrupted.'

'Okay, so tell me about her.'

'Danny, this girl has rock hard nipples. Every morning, climb from bed, go downstairs, collect two eggs from the fridge, close the fridge door, get a frying pan, go back upstairs, walk into her bedroom. Tap once, tap twice, crack those eggs, one on each breast. Sizzle sizzle sizzle. Sunny side up, you've got breakfast. That's how firm we're talking. I know how important spigotal hardness is to a man in a home-sharing scenario.'

'Lucy, nipples are not a factor.'

'Mine were.'

'No. They weren't.'

'Don't lie.'

'They were never important.'

'What you saying? You saying they're rubbish? You saying they're too close together? Too far apart? Too identical? Too unalike? Too high? Too low? Too inbetween? Too two? Do they lack character, charm and mischief? Do they lack thrust? Do they thrust too much?'

'Yes.'

'"Yes," what?'

'"Yes," all that stuff you just said.'

'You've not even seen them, for Godssake; apart from surreptitious glances when I've been wearing something clingy. And don't tell me you didn't look. Coz I know you did.'

'No, Lucy, I didn't.'

'Yeah, right,' she sneered, and crunched gears.

'No, seriously, I didn't.'

'Yeah. Right.'

'No. Really.'

'Really?'

'Breasts are too passive,' he said. 'All they do is hang there.'

'What do you want them to do? Attack you?'

'I'd just like them to do something. Nothing dramatic. Nothing clever. Just something. Anything.'

'Well that's where you're wrong,' she said. 'Because breasts are the best things ever and don't need to do anything in order to be entertaining. Just sitting here my own chest's a veritable fun fair. And no one can have too much of them.'

'I suppose you want me to look at them now,' he sighed.

'You'd be the last person I'd show them to. Wait till I get my new ones. Try ignoring them, Mr I'm So Squeaky Clean I Don't Even Look When They're Shoved In My Face. Not that I'll let you see them. I'll probably wear a double thick overcoat every time I see you. And you'll just have to dream about what you're missing. Probably keep you awake at nights, craving.'

'What about this Annette woman?'

'They're too small. She'll never make an impact at parties; not with her, "Hey, boys, I'm a non-underwire-dependent cyberman," malarkey. Size, that's what gets you noticed. And you can tell her that from me.'

'I meant, tell me about this home offer.'

'She called me an hour ago, saying you could move in with her.'

'But I don't even know her.'

'Who can figure it? Must be desperate. I don't think she gets many callers, what with being flat chested.'

'So, what's the catch?'

She drove on, gaze fixed on the road ahead.

'Lucy?'

She drove on.

'Lucy?'

'No catch.'

'What's the bond?'

A lump slid down her throat before she answered, still looking straight ahead. 'No bond.'

'References?'

'No references.'

'Rent?'

'No rent.'

'Terms? Conditions?'

'No terms. No conditions. Simply be there. But, Danny, under no circumstances mention her embarrassingly small breasts. Between you and me, she attaches far too much importance to such things. I tried to avoid mentioning them on the phone when she called but somehow it slipped out.'

'Is there anything about this place you're not telling me?' he asked. 'It's not in an earthquake zone or something?'

'Believe me, this is *the* house to be. And, Danny?'

'What?'

'Imagine cracking those eggs.'

'So where is it?'

'666, Hellzapoppin Cul-de-sac, Nightmareville.'

'What?'

'Ha ha, only joking. It's on Plescent Street, Wheatley 48, a really nice area, all manual lawnmowers and salad sandwiches. I've done loads of pickups there and never once got a tip – a sure sign of affluence. Do you know they have a residents' committee? People round there talk to their neighbours, Dan. Can you believe that?'

'And you're sure about this?'

'Positive. You've landed on your feet better than a cotton-wool cat with eighteen legs and cast iron paws. Annette has a cat, by the way. It's called Ribbons. Be nice to it, it bites.'

'Lucy?'

'Yup?'

'Why are you helping me?'

'I'm not helping you.'

'You're going out of your way to take me to a new home.'

'I'm not helping you.'

'Yes you are.'

With a screech of tyres the cab swerved to a halt, half climbing the kerb, Lucy scrunching on the handbrake.

Danny's momentum flung him forward. His seat belt stopped him from melding with the windscreen.

She reached across and unlocked his door, letting it swing open. Upright again, one forearm on the wheel, the other on the back of her seat, she stared him in the eyes. 'You want to get out?'

'No.'

'Then don't say I'm helping you.'

'But . . .'

'You want to get out?'

He sighed, gazing at the ceiling, then reluctantly pulled the door shut. 'You're not helping me.'

'Damn right I'm not.' And she steered the cab away from the kerb.

'Eyes up, shipmates. Plescent Street ahoy.' Lucy turned her cab up a sloping avenue on Wheatley's outmost outskirt.

He watched passing rows of neat trimmed housing. Whitewashed picket fencing contained hedges topiaried into trains, snowmen, castellations, airborne kites, friendly dinosaurs, friendly dinosaurs flying kites, kites on castles and snowmen on trains. Each bordered a perfectly square garden.

He'd once seen a documentary: in America, an identical street had built a Berlin Wall at each end then issued residents with 'passports' to keep the riff-raff out.

Danny was riff-raff; or he'd have known there were such

places in Wheatley. 'You're sure this is the right place?' he asked. 'There's not another part of town with the same name?'

'Course I'm sure. What kind of cabbie do you take me for? I know this city like the back of my hand. Aargh! What's that on the end of my wrist?'

'Your hand,' he said, as unamused as on the first three million occasions she'd cracked that joke.

'Only joking.'

'This is the place.' Lucy scrunched on the handbrake, engine noise dying away.

He gazed out through the windscreen, puzzled, seeing only cherry blossom trees to either side and the crown of the road ahead. Straight backed, head raised to peer over the crown, he saw the green fields of open country beyond. His gaze flicked across that landscape. 'Where?'

'There.'

'Where?'

'There.'

He watched her, suspecting a practical joke. 'Where?'

'Straight ahead.'

Again he looked, still seeing nothing.

Then he grew excited. 'You're saying, all that country-side, as far as the eye can see, is my new home? The woman owns the countryside? Lucy, this is fantastic.'

eight

Danny climbed from the cab, letting its door swing to behind him. It clunked as Lucy pulled it shut.

He stepped forward, eyes fixed on distant fields and a white cottage gleaming in the sun. An imaginary choir sang as he imagined summer days spent running through that long long grass, lazing by that cool cool lake, climbing that distant ridge against a sunset that couldn't fail to be glorious in such a setting. And he knew at last he'd found happiness.

He heard Lucy approaching behind him. He wanted to hug her, to take her in his arms, spin her round and round and round in slow motion, laughing and giggling stupidly. He decided not to, fearing violence.

'Danny, the girl's a student. How could she afford the countryside? She owns just these houses.'

'Which houses?'

'Either side.'

'There are no houses either side.' His gaze remained on the fields, still dreaming of the days ahead. And this woman? Annette? Beneath the cyberman suit she was *Beetlejuice* Winona, or as good as? And she liked him? It was as though all the rotten luck he'd ever had was now being cancelled out by the law of averages.

Lucy's grip forced his head leftward. She said, 'Look twenty feet, straight ahead.'

'What about it?'

'Concentrate really hard.'

He did – convinced she was wasting his time when he could be running around that valley, like the Railway Children as the final credits rolled and they knew everything would be perfect from now on. Ahead he saw nothing but full-bloom cherry blossom stretching down to a stream that seemed made for stickleback jam jar fishing.

Then he frowned.

The harder he looked, the darker those trees became and the fewer of them there were. They twisted, thickened, threatened. Branches became arms. Twigs were fingers reaching out to scratch the eyes of unwary passers by. Bark became the faces of souls who must have done terrible things in life to be so anguished in death. The daisies punctuating the cherry blossom turned into coarse grass to grab the ankles of those foolish enough to encroach, and to tug them to the ground before consuming them.

He frowned deeper. Something was materializing.

It was a black smudge, floating, spreading, as though being sketched in charcoal by some mad artist. It became huge, brooding, a gaunt silhouette. It had chimneys, twelve, one on each outcrop. Screaming-faced gargoyles appeared beneath the eaves. Things stuck out for no purpose. Things stuck in for no purpose. Things stuck.

Windows were eyes. A door was a mouth. A crazy, yellow brick path connected street to door; an invitation to enter at your peril.

And it was a house, a great, complacent toad of a house waiting to unroll its tongue and reel in the careless.

'Jesus.' Danny gasped and stepped back. The cab blocked his uncoordinated retreat.

'Now look right.' Lucy's grip redirected his head.

On the street's other side, a second house appeared, faster now he'd learned the trick. It exactly mirrored the first.

How many houses like this were there? Was the town full of them and he'd never noticed?

'See them now?' she asked.

'See them? They'll be in my nightmares for the rest of my life.' He glanced behind him but the rest of Plescent Street was still square-gardened suburbia.

Lucy was sat grinning on the cab bonnet, feet on bumper, elbows on knees, chin on palms. 'Involuntary denial. Your subconscious doesn't want to accept they exist, so it hides them from you unless forced to reveal them.'

'And you expect me to live there?' He was incredulous.

'Damn right I do.'

He again watched the houses. 'Which one belongs to this Annette creature?'

'Both; fifty pence each from a bucket shop estate agent. For twenty-five years they couldn't sell either. Then along comes Annette and buys them both. Great, huh? Like the twin towers of Wembley but less clichéd. And every kid dreams of going to Wembley.'

'I didn't.'

'Now's your chance to start.'

'I've never seen anything so horrible,' he said.

'You've never seen yourself naked?'

'Lucy, I look a lot better than that naked.'

'Believe me, Danny, you don't.'

He looked at her.

Chin on palms, she shrugged. 'I drilled a hole in the bathroom wall once. Remember when you complained of funny noises while you were showering, and I said we had a big cement-burrowing worm problem? And you said the worm looked like an endoscope and I said, no no no, all cement-burrowing worms have glow-in-the-dark heads that follow your every move and try to look up your bottom. I had to stare for fifteen minutes before my subconscious'd let me register you. It wasn't worth the wait. I took photos. Want to buy them? Ten pence the lot. I've got stacks. Tried selling them at Poly but no takers. No one could see you, apart from Annette. She bought loads. She walked off smiling. But then Annette *likes* you.'

He stepped toward her. 'One of these days, I'm going to . . .'

'You're going to what?' she challenged, contemptuous.

Fists clenched, he tried glaring her into oblivion.

She was unaffected, her gaze settling on the house to her left. 'That, Daniel, is a style known as Wheatley Gothique. No one expects an ingrate like you to understand but some things can only be produced by the personal vision of an individual.'

'What kind of individual would build things like these?'

Wednesday, April 21, 1926. What Hejediah Johnson saw from his bedroom window bothered him.

He saw neat trimmed houses. Whitewashed picket fencing contained hedges topiaried into trains, snowmen, castellations, airborne kites, friendly dinosaurs and friendly dinosaurs flying kites. Each bordered one of a row of perfectly square gardens with identical ornaments in identical positions by identical ponds. Propriety as God.

Next morning, the same.

And the next.

And the next.

And the next.

After two months' growing disquiet, he emerged into a summer morning, paint pot in hand, bold strokes daubing his front door red. Not any old red, but the blazing scarlet of his fondest-remembered sunset.

The street's other front doors were army green. Always had been. Always would be.

His neighbours' reaction amazed him. Far from being outraged, they were delighted, having also hated being identical, though lacking courage to defy the Residents' Committee.

The Residents' Committee comprised one member; Miss Xenia Minnlebatt. It represented the interests of one resident; Miss Xenia Minnlebatt. Her meetings ran with an iron fist in a chain mail glove, often ending with the death of a small domestic servant. Frequently, she would beat even herself into submission during displays of bloody-minded intolerance.

But now he'd given a lead, they'd all paint their doors a different colour; and hang Miss Xenia Minnlebatt – literally, said some. But Miss Xenia Minnlebatt's public execution would have to wait a further ten years.

For the first time ever, Hejediah Johnson went to work with a spring in his step and a song in his heart. Though no one knows what the song was, some said it involved lost hats.

He whistled all through work at Givens' design office. Workmates thought him delirious. Osbert Givens insisted he knock off early, happy men being of no use to a munitions works.

Hejediah Johnson collected his coat.

He whistled all the way home, striding Wheatley's streets, like a man possessed. And some did claim him possessed, though they were the ones who said he sang about hats.

Faster, faster, ever faster, revelling in the twelve-mile journey's every step. His tune grew with each corner that brought his destination closer.

By the final turn, he was whistling so loudly people

shouted from their windows, 'Call the constabulary. Call the constabulary. There's a madman loose.'

Regardless, he turned the final corner.

And Hejediah Johnson's world crumbled.

Every door on that street had been painted red. Not just any red, but the blazing scarlet of his fondest remembered sunset.

'Isn't it wonderful?' said a neighbour. 'Now we're all different – just like you.'

No, it bloody wasn't wonderful.

Over the next two weeks, Johnson threw himself into insanity, installing a temperamentally unsuitable gazelle as a gazebo. His neighbours copied it. He built a spaghetti statue of the Phoenician war goddess Burut Ana, using pasta for plaster. His neighbours copied it. No act seemed too lunatic for them to emulate.

On May 8, 1926, Hejediah Johnson ate Wheatley.

Then with only an egg for an implement, he built a new home, one so nightmarish that no one would copy it.

And no one did copy it.

Except Miss Xenia Minnlebatt.

And that was the story of 353, Plescent Street.

At least, that was how Lucy told it.

'It's frightening,' said Danny. 'Take me home.'

'This is your home now,' she told him. 'Play your cards right, lick up to Annette, cough up a quid, and one day, when she graduates and leaves town, this'll be all yours.'

Lucy called from the porch. 'C'mon, Danny. What you waiting for?'

He stood, hands in pockets, kicking a heel, head down, leaning back against a cab door. 'I do *not* want to live there.'

'Course you do. Anyone would.'

He looked at her accusingly. 'Then why don't you live there?'

Sighing like she was dealing with an exceptionally dim child, she strode down the porch step, then along the path, toward him. 'You think I don't want to live here? Daniel, I would kill to live here. But I've not been invited. You have. You can't turn down a chance like this. This is the coolest address in Wheatley. When I tell them about this at Poly, they'll be so-o-o jealous, they'll be queuing round the block, waiting for you, with baseball bats. Now come on.' Grabbing his hand, she yanked his arm half out of its socket, and dragged him up the path, up the step and onto the porch.

They stood watching the front door, with its cobra's head door knocker.

'Go on,' she said. 'Knock.'

'Lucy.'

'Knock.'

With a deep breath, he half-heartedly pulled knocker away from door. But her hand prevented him knocking. She said, 'Hold on a mo.'

'What now?'

'I almost forgot something.' She took a silver chain from around her neck and placed it round his own.

He gazed down at the large, looped cross at the chain's end and held it between thumb and finger. 'What's this?'

'An ankh.'

'An anker?'

'Ankh; an ancient Egyptian lucky charm. All the pharaohs wore one. Some wore two. Tutankhamen wore dozens. He was famous for it, the Liberace of his day – and he played the piano. Annette insisted you wore one before entering. I hope you appreciate this, Danny; I had to slap the eighth toughest girl in Fabric Studies to get this off her.'

'What's it for?'

'Beats me. Annette said something about it protecting you from the head-sucking demons who infest every third corner of the house.' She grinned, gaze running up and down the door. 'Demons. Cool or what?'

He didn't answer. He was heading back to the cab.

'Danny?' she called. 'Where you going?'

No reply.

'Danny?'

He climbed into the car, slammed the door shut and demanded to be taken home.

nine

'He's gone?'

'I said he would.' Having watched Lucy's taxi drive off up the road, Annette Helstrang let the cobweb pattern net curtain fall closed and she told the boiler-suited legs protruding from beneath her bed, 'There was no way he was going to move in. He's not the type.'

The legs protested, 'But this can't happen.'

'You think not? If there's a wrong decision, bet on him to make it.'

'But it's his fate to move in here.'

'So?' she asked.

'If even one person refuses to follow his fate, it sets in motion a chain of events that may destroy us all.'

'I fail to see what Danny Yates could do that could destroy us all.'

'We must make alternative arrangements immediately.'

'You want me to kidnap him?'

'Would you like to do that, Annette Helstrang? Would you like to tie him to that chair by the door, and for several

weeks feed him a diet of bread, water and bromide to keep
his lusts to a minimum?'

'No, I wouldn't. Lucy might. But she might torture him.'

'We might still be able to cut him off at the pass.'

'Pardon?'

'You must get a pedicure.'

Perched on the bed, Ribbons Melancholia gazed down at
the legs, suspicious. He swiped at them with his ginger paw,
missed, and lost balance. He hit the carpet with a disdainful
miaow, shook himself down, tried to look dignified, failed
to look dignified, then jumped back onto the bed. He circled
three times before resuming his legwatch.

'Wheatley is full of bad feet,' said the legs. 'Only two
people in this town have ones of the necessary quality, and,
being a slightly tall girl, the other would be unsuitable.'

'I'm sorry?' asked Annette.

'You shall see.'

'But how can a pedicure save us all?'

'How many over the aeons have asked us that? Always
it comes down to feet.'

'Then I'll go and get them seen to.' She didn't know
what was going on. Since first appearing, the legs had
talked in nothing but riddles. Where were they from?
Who did they work for? They wouldn't say. But clearly,
they worked for a higher power. Magic's twelfth rule was
that only the very highest powers could leave disembodied
legs beneath your bed.

Grabbing her blackest coat, adopting her most earnest
face, she headed for the door. 'C'mon, Ribbons. We're
going.'

'Wait,' said the legs.

She stopped at the door, held the handle and looked to
the bed.

'You may not go yet. And there is one particular pedicurist
you must visit.'

58

'There is?'

'Yes.'

'Why?'

'Reasons.'

'What reasons?'

'Reasons reasons.'

'So,' she sighed, 'who is this pedicurist?'

'Watch the wall.'

She did.

And across the far wall, blood red letters began to appear forming the words:

MADAM FIFI'S LATE NIGHT PEDICURES

ten

Sullen-faced, curled almost into a ball, the prickliest of hedgehogs, Danny sat on the Mission's front step, watching the world fail to go by; no passers by, no wildlife, no points of interest. No weeds grew between the cracks in Tolly Street's paving. Across the empty road, the sun was setting behind a shut-down multi-storey car park by a shut-down industrial unit by a shut-down burger bar by a shut-down bus stop. Each reflected a shut-down life back on itself.

Just two hundred yards away, the town's main shopping street would be bustling with activity. But from here, in the city centre's dog end, you'd never know it.

His feet were bare, Lucy having claimed his trainers as payment for him wasting her taxi time. She'd again worn her, 'Don't argue with me,' look.

So he'd be stuck here forever, with the singing nun and her song of hats. Verse 155 drifted out from somewhere within the building, rhyming, 'Architeuthis,' with, 'Truth is,' with 'Toothies.'

He stared at the pavement, trying to make it wither. It

ignored him. He tried to wither the car park. It ignored him. They wouldn't have ignored Lucy.

Rumble rumble rumble.

?

Rumble.

?

Rumble.

?

Rumble rumble.

He looked to the street's far end. A tall fridge was climbing the slope, toward him. It clattered, rattled and jolted over bad paving join after bad paving join.

He rose to his feet, mouth drying in anticipation.

He'd noticed the tangerine, with yellow polka dot, dreadlocks bobbing along behind it.

'Erm, hello?' Danny walked along beside Teena Rama, sideways so he faced her while talking.

'Hello.' She concentrated on pushing her fridge; five feet eight, slightly too tall for her weight, Albert Einstein T-shirt, red (with white polka dot) skirt. Long bare legs. Small bare feet.

He watched his own small, bare, girl's feet. He and she had a thing in common.

'Am I bothering you?' he asked.

'Are you trying to?' Her teeth were gripping the thin end of a wooden door wedge.

'No. I'm not.'

She continued pushing the fridge, not looking at him. 'Then you're not bothering me.'

'Do you remember me?'

'Jog my memory; I meet too many people.'

'I was in the shop.'

'Which shop?'

'The comic shop.'

'Which comic shop?'

'The one that collapsed.'

'Two collapsed,' she said.

'They did?'

'Subsidence. The town's built over the world's largest cave system. Don't tell anyone I said so. I'll deny it.'

'You pulled me from the rubble. I never got a chance to thank you. Thank you.'

She frowned, recalling vaguely, 'You were in the little comic shop?'

'That's the one.' His spirits rose.

'You're Gary?'

'Danny.'

'Danny?'

'Danny.'

Still pushing, she looked at him. 'You're the erection boy?'

'There's no need for embarrassment, Gary; I'm gorgeous. That's not boasting, I have pie charts to prove I'm gorgeous.' She strolled alongside Danny, hands loosely clasped behind her back, enjoying the sunset. 'Upon meeting me, gay men turn straight, straight women turn lesbian. Straight men become ultra-heteros, setting themselves a helpless quest for my seduction, driven like lemmings by urges beyond their control. I feel sorry for them.'

Grunt, strain, wheel-squeak wheel-squeak. Teeth gritted, blood pressure soaring, Danny shoulder-pushed her rock heavy fridge up yet another stupid hill as best he could, already regretting having offered. The things he'd do to impress a girl. And she wasn't impressed, he could tell. It was hard to be impressed by a man having a seizure.

Did girls go to these lengths to impress boys? If so, why didn't boys ever notice? He studied her flawless face, unable to imagine her ever having had to go to any lengths to impress anyone.

She said, 'Involuntary erection, in a young man with hormones still in full swing, is all but unavoidable in my presence. As a doctor, I'd be more concerned if you didn't react that way. Close your eyes.'

'Are you going to kiss me?'

She gave a look that suggested not. 'Just close your eyes.'

He closed them.

'Imagine me,' she said.

'Okay.'

'Where do you see me?'

'In a field.'

'Surrounded by?'

'Big toadstools.'

'Next to?'

'A rabbit warren.'

'And I'm . . . ?'

'Lying by a burbling, little fountain.'

'Am I naked?' she asked.

No reply.

Again; 'Am I naked?'

'No.'

'Am I in a state of near undress?'

'No.'

'Am I half dressed, like a brazen hussy, with you about to administer the seeing to I'm asking for?'

'No.'

'I should be.'

'You're not.'

63

'That'd be the standard fantasy I'd induce in your personality type.'

'It's not mine.'

'Are you telling me the truth, Gary?'

'Yes.'

'I don't believe you.'

He opened his eyes. 'Can we change the subject?'

'To?'

'Where're we taking this fridge? You do know the council tip's the other way?'

'That's where I got it. I'm taking it home. I want to test it.'

'For?'

'Time travel potential.'

'Time . . . ?' At the hill's crown, he stopped pushing. Worn out, he leaned back against the fridge, sank to his knees and tried to regain his breath. The world was purple and spinning.

She dropped the door wedge to the ground, kicking it into place beneath a fridge castor. 'You probably know time can be frozen. You may have done it yourself, setting your freeze box to nought degrees Kelvin; Absolute Zero. A switch, on the back of all fridges, allows you to do so. Amazingly, most people don't even know it's there, not having bothered to read the instructions fully. Flick it left, time stands still. Flick it right, time accelerates. But what if you lower temperatures further, into negative values? Then time runs backwards.'

'Are you winding me up?'

In fading light, she clambered onto the fridge, sat cross legged atop it, and looked down at him. 'Within two weeks, this battered frigidaire,' clungk, her knuckles rapped it, 'may be the world's first functional time machine. Weird Science, I hold several doctorates in it.'

He gazed up into deep green eyes, trying to imagine them

64

travelling through time atop that fridge. But somehow, no matter how hard he tried – and he tried hard – he could only imagine her naked in a field of strangely phallic toadstools.

'You were sat outside the Seaman's Mission?' she asked.

'I'm staying there, between homes.'

'Are you a seaman?'

'I'd rather not go into that.'

She went quiet, thinking, finally deciding, 'I suppose you could stay at my place.'

'You mean it?'

'I could do with the company. Since arriving in this town, I seem to have spent all my time talking to the walls. Plus, I'd like to further research the problem of you being unable to imagine me naked.'

He scrambled to his feet, pulse quickening at the prospect of moving in with her. 'I can imagine you naked,' he insisted, hoping to impress her with his etiquette. 'I just choose not to.'

'Even odder.'

'What's the rent?' he asked, like it mattered.

'No rent.'

'Bond?'

'No bond.'

'References?'

'No references.'

'Demons?'

'Demons?' she asked.

'Are there any head-sucking demons?'

'Not that I've noticed. Do you want me to get you some?'

'No chance.' And not altogether successfully, he fought back the urge to laugh like an idiot. 'Are there any catches at all?'

'None. Just a place to live and the pleasure of my company. So, how about it?'

eleven

Clack. First thing next morning, something dropped through Lucy Smith's letter box and hit the mat. Yawning, straight from bed, she shambled from her room and collected the buff, windowed envelope.

She checked the back; no sender's address. Curious, she tore the bitter envelope open with her teeth then pulled out the crisp, white paper.

Discarding envelope on floor, she unfolded the note. It read:

Mz Lucille Smuth,
    77, Osmosis Tenements,
    Dead End Street,
    Wheatley 2

(April 15)

Drear Mz Smuth;
Please make an appointment to see me at the erliest

oppurtunity, to discuss staff and student complaints that you have an altitude problem.

Yours

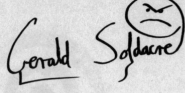

Gerald Sofdacre,
Principal, Wheatley Pollytecnick.

Lucy frowned. Meanwhile the phone began to ring. She went to answer it.

Altitude problems?

twelve

Danny arrived, first thing that morning, stopping only to collect his jaw from the pavement.

Teena Rama's own personal White House ran some three hundred feet from one end of Moldern Crescent to the other, half enclosing the houses across the road, as though trying to eat them. From somewhere behind the building, a white pole prodded the sky, its polka dot flag declaring the owner to be in residence.

He checked the address she'd given him and, having reassured himself for the fiftieth time that this must be the place, climbed the step that connected it to the street.

Staring at the oak panelled front door, he again checked the address. It was still the right place. About to knock, he noticed a tiny sign beside the handle; PLEASE PRESS ME. An arrow pointed to a green plastic panel by the door. He did as instructed. The panel lit up.

'Hello?' asked a voice that seemed to be Bob Holness.

Danny looked around, trying to locate its source.

Above the door, a camera's red light activated. He addressed it. 'Er, good morning. I believe I'm expected.'

'Expected?'

'By Teena Rama. I'm her new lodger.'

'Ah. You'll be young Mr Gary.'

'No. I'm Danny.'

'What happened to Mr Gary?'

'He won't be coming.' He lacked the inclination to go into all that again.

'Has he had an accident?' asked the voice.

'No.'

'Is he dead?'

'No.'

'Have you murdered him and taken his place, in a daring assassination bid on Miss Rama?'

'No,' protested Danny. 'He just won't be coming.'

The voice fell silent, as though checking something, then said, 'Miss Rama will be disappointed. She was rather looking forward to receiving young Mr Gary, much as one welcomes the arrival of small but unfocused animals. However, I'm sure she'll accept you in lieu. Miss Rama can be tolerant.'

Clunk, the door unlocked.

'Feel free to enter, Mr Daniel.'

'Thank you.'

He was about to push the door open, when the voice warned, 'But please don't touch the door frame; you'll be disintegrated.'

Once in the hallway, Danny closed the front door behind him. Stepping over a junk mail mountain, he took care not to touch the frame. But perhaps the man had been having him on.

His finger reached toward it, curious, then stopped.

Upon starting work once, he'd resolutely refused to cross town for a left-handed screwdriver and had promptly been sacked from Wheatley Long Stand, Glass Hammer and Left-Handed Screwdrivers PLC. It was a mistake anyone could have made, but hadn't.

Then there'd been his fourth day at Lucy's, when she'd said Osmosis had given her Danny's room and he'd have to sleep out on the landing because he was the new kid and sleeping out on the landing was what new kids always had to do. And he wasn't to use her old room, it was needed for frog storage.

For a month he'd slept on that landing, until Osmosis had pointed out the lack of ribbiting.

Perhaps everyone played a joke on the new kid and this was Teena's.

But he withdrew his finger anyway.

He looked around.

The hallway stretched to the distant back door, silent but for the ticking cuckoo clock to his left. A wooden bird burst from its slot, said, 'Cuckoo,' then went into hiding for another hour. Tiny doors flipped shut behind it.

Danny went across.

Stretching on tiptoes, he removed clock from wall, turned its hands forward fifty-nine minutes, then took it to the door. He pointed clock at frame then, confident it would be unharmed, waited.

Tick tick tick tick . . .

The bird burst from its hidey hole, gave one proud, 'Cuck –' and disintegrated.

Clunk, Danny threw the twisted thing-that-was-once-a-clock out onto the street, hoping someone would steal it. They would have done back at his old home.

He slammed the door shut, having not seen any shady characters in the moment it was open. Like the police, shady characters were rarely around when you needed them.

He checked again, easing the door slightly open, peering out through the gap. The blackened mass was still there. He retrieved it, bringing it back inside, again stepping over junk mail.

He hung the clock back on the wall. The wreckage hung lopsided. He hung it straight. It hung lopsided. He hung it straight. It hung lopsided. But who looked at clocks anyway?

Now he heard just the mild hum of some unseen machine.

Two endless rows of rooms ran the walls' length, like the *Yellow Submarine* scene where everyone ran in and out of doors, opening them, slamming them, disappearing into them.

No one emerged from these doors.

'Hello? Anyone at home?' he asked.

No reply.

Between each door hung three black-framed photos arranged in an inverted triangle. He took a closer look.

The photos hung chronologically. The first showed Teena as a five-year-old, a grim-faced little thing receiving an award from a scientist.

The next showed her receiving an award from a scientist.

The next showed her receiving an award from a scientist.

The next showed her receiving an award from a scientist.

The pictures continued, each at a four-week interval.

Each photo was larger than the one before, each prize bigger than the previous, till the awards were too big for her to lift; a girl grown too clever for her arms.

The scientists tried to help her lift the trophies but eventually she was too clever for everyone's arms.

Nearing the back door, he found an eighteen month gap when she'd not won a single award nor done one thing of note, as though she'd disappeared into some black hole.

The pictures resumed just before the incident in Osmo's shop. *She's back*, declared the accompanying magazine caption. *Kooky genius Teena Rama collects her eighth Nobel Prize for Physics*. Kooky?

The photo parade continued.

'No no no. I want no more mess ups.' To Danny's right, a door opened, a stern voice striding through into the hallway, followed, moments later, by its owner. Teena Rama was carrying a roll of cable. Upon noticing Danny, she stopped, hard expression replaced by that smile. It looked like she'd been working on it since yesterday. 'Gary?'

'Danny.'

'Of course. Well, Gary, welcome to my abode. Humble though it may be.'

'You call this humble?'

'It serves its purposes.'

Thud. The thing that had once been a clock hit the carpet. It lay there dead.

Danny turned red.

Teena watched the smoking wreck then looked directly into Danny's soul. 'Have you been touching that?' she asked.

'No.' He shuffled uneasily, transparent as glass.

Still gazing at him, she said, transparent as six inch thick lead shielding, 'I should show you around.'

'This is the Sponge Room.' Having already shown him the three kitchens, drawing rooms, piano rooms, dining rooms, gyms and reception areas, she held the latest door open for Danny to look inside.

Its walls were windowless, paperless and white, with a radiator attached to the farthest. Otherwise it was empty but for a small bath sponge carefully placed on the floorboards at its centre.

'Sponge Room?' he asked.

She seemed embarrassed. 'The lower floor has fifty-eight rooms. My research shows no individual needs more than ten. Consequently, upon moving in, I had to manufacture uses for the remainder. By room twenty-three, those uses were becoming somewhat contrived. The Sponge Room was Doors' idea. Doors insisted.'

'Doors?' asked Danny.

'The voice that let you in.'

'And what room's he in?'

'None. Doors is a computer. It answers the front door, controls heating, air conditioning, lighting, et cetera. It also assists with my experiments, despite being of little use.' She shut the Sponge Room door. 'You don't really want to see the Shower Cap, Rubber Duck, and Margarine Rooms, do you?'

'Too right I do,' he enthused. 'I've never seen a Margarine Room.'

For some reason, her eyes rolled.

Teena showed Danny the rest of the downstairs.

'What's this?' he asked, rattling.

Teena Rama stopped, halfway up the embassy-width staircase, and turned to see the Gary boy stood by the door at the stair bottom. Her eyes flickered over the scene.

She pulled a dreadlock away from her face, tucking it behind her right ear. It fell across her face again. She tutted internally. 'It's the broom cupboard. I have a man who comes in twice a week and "does" for me.'

Again the boy rattled the knob as though trying to tear it from the door.

Calves tightening, she descended one step.

'It's locked,' he said, still rattling.

'Chemicals. Many used in housework are highly toxic, I'm told. I ensure my Man Who Does always uses suitable protection while performing his duties. He keeps the key. I could phone him, drag him from bed and all the way across town during mid-morning rush hour for you. I'm sure he wouldn't mind.'

'No. It's okay,' he joked. 'I'm not desperate to see mops.'

'You're sure. Only, you were so keen to see the Margarine Room. Look; the phone's just here.' She reached through an Art Deco banister and lifted the receiver from its table. She waved it in his direction.

'No. I'm certain,' he insisted, waving a hand.

Click, she hung the phone up, and again tucked dreadlock behind ear. This time it stayed. 'Good. I'll show you the rest of the house.'

'I thought this should be your room, if acceptable.'

Danny stood at its centre, gazing round, amazed by its sheer white expanse. Teena remained by the door.

He'd been in fields that were more claustrophobic than this. 'Acceptable? It's incredible.'

'I feared it might not live up to your expectations. I can always transfer you to another. Any room on the top landing, except mine, could be made available. I'll simply have to reprogram Doors' register.'

'Register?' He paid little attention, hand pressing a firm but fair bed. It didn't creak. He tried the other end. It didn't creak. He sat on it, bouncing along the mattress. It didn't creak.

She explained, 'In an emergency, I'd need to know exactly where any guests are, a fire for instance. Quick location could be a matter of life or death.'

Danny bounced.

'Well,' she said. 'I have things to be getting on with. I'm sure you have too, unpacking and the like. Doors'll deal with any enquiries you might have. Make yourself at home.'

'Thanks. I will.'

And she left him to bounce.

He let himself fall back into silk sheets, arms and legs outstretched. He tensed them into relaxation, sinking into the bed's warm embrace. Resembling a Modern Art sculpture, a multi-faceted lighting installation hung from the ceiling directly above. He pressed a switch on the understated headboard. The lights came on, humming gently. Click, he switched them off.

A white slatted wardrobe stood by the window.

He went across.

He opened its twin doors, peering into emptiness. He stepped inside, closing the doors behind him.

The smell of fresh pine tickled his nostrils. Light seeped in through the slats, making it almost as bright inside as out. Arms outstretched, he performed a full turn, fingertips at no point contacting wood. He estimated the closet to be three inches wider than Lucy's old room, and had to concede she'd had a point.

Teena's door-muffled voice reappeared. 'Gary? Are you still here?'

'I'm in the wardrobe.'

'Oh.' She said it as though she'd never stood in a wardrobe in her life. 'I see.'

thirteen

Late afternoon sun peeking through clouds, Lucy Smith relaxed on the front steps of the tenements which contained her flat. She repeatedly plucked the D string of a guitar found on a bus while the owner wasn't looking. She was learning to play from a book placed on the bottom step. The breeze flapped a page corner against the brick which held it down, and she sang along with each note struck. 'D.D.D.D.D.D.D.D.D.D.D.D.D.D.' This was easy. They called Hendrix a god just because he could do this? 'D.D.D.D.D.D.D.D.D.D.D.D.D.'

Footsteps approached, stopping by the songbook. A shadow hung over her.

She continued twanging. 'D.D.D.D.D.D.D.D.D.D.D.D. D.D.D.D.D.D.D.'

The shadow remained, demanding her attention.

'D.D.D.D.D.D.D.D.D.D.D.D.D.D.D.D.D.D.D.D.D.D.D.D. D.D.D.'

And still it waited. Let it wait, she was cooking on gas.

'D.D.D.D.D.D.D.D.D.D.D.D.D.D.D.D.D.D.D.D.D.D.D.D.D.

D.D.D.D.D.F. Shit.' Having hit a wrong note, she looked up.

'You are the human Lucy Jane Smith?' The compound eyes of a seven foot tall ant, stood on its hind legs, gazed down at her.

'Depends who's asking.'

'I am Destructor, the insect who walks like a man. I communicated with you earlier, on the telephonic device that transmits speech without the need for unsightly shouting.'

She stuck a finger in one ear, clearing out wax, remembering his previous, earbursting performance.

'You are in search of a mate?' he asked.

'A flatmate,' she corrected, bluntly.

'Then that shall be me.'

'You never mentioned mandibles.'

'Nevertheless I have them. And soon,' it seethed, 'soon the human race shall learn to fear them. Soon it shall know the heavy hand of extinction, as my insect hordes sweep through this world, conquering, pillaging and destroying.'

'How many hordes you got, pal? Doesn't bother me but Osmo's not keen on hoarding in his flats.'

'I have three.'

'You got three hordes?'

'Three insects. I have not been in this world long.'

'How long you been in this world?'

'Six months.'

'So in six months you've got three insects on your side?'

'Two cockroaches and a magnificent ladybird. It is a yellow ladybird, with black spots.' His mandibles opened and closed in a manner presumably meant to be threatening. 'Quiver and fear, human.'

'So, in a year you'll have four cockroaches and two ladybirds?'

'As you say.'

'And in ten years . . .'

'We need not go into details. All you need know is that soon . . . soon . . .'

'You got references?' she asked.

'References?'

'Osmo always insists. No references, no flat.'

'Then I shall eat this "Osmo".'

'Eaten or not, he'll still want references. He's the type.'

'Oh.' It stood, downcast, antennae twitching, watching the pavement, trying to scheme a way around this problem.

'You got money?' she asked.

'Indeed. I have a vast fortune at my disposal.'

'How much you got?'

'Fifty-five pounds.'

'For fifty-five pounds I could fake you references.'

'You would do this for me, a stranger?'

'I'd do it for anyone. That's what people round here are like.'

'Lucy Jane Smith, you are a marvellous and splendid flatmate.'

She plucked an E string. 'Better believe it, babe.'

fourteen

'Lift 'em.' First thing next morning. In no mood for argument, Annette was vacuuming around the Mysterious Legs. Her old upright hoover droned like a Nazi bomber.

Reluctant, they raised their feet. And she vacuumed under them.

'Is this necessary, Annette Helstrang?'

'It's Thursday. You know what I do Thursdays. I'm not having them go back claiming I don't keep my house clean.'

'But do you have to invite them round?'

'Every Thursday for three years or I fail the course. And yes, they are a nuisance.'

'But –'

She switched off the hoover. Its drone faded to a whine then stopped. She set about assembling its tube attachment ready to clean deep beneath the bed. 'Silence of the Lambs.'

'Where?'

'Clarice Starling. She's a student at FBI school. She gets

called in on a big case and is the only one who can solve it.'

'Why?'

'She's a woman. It needs a woman's mind. But all the time she's helping out she's falling behind in her studies. If she doesn't solve the case within days, she'll be reprocessed.'

'Reprocessed?'

'Sent back to beginners' class. The Occult Studies Department'll do the same to me if I fall behind. I don't care how important this mission of yours is, I won't be reprocessed for you.'

'But they steal our shoes and parade around the room wearing them as hats.'

'Snatch them back.'

'What? And come out from under the bed?'

The Higher Powers couldn't find better messengers than those two? She snapped into place the last piece of the tube attachment. She looked at it. She looked at the legs. And she said, 'Spread 'em.'

Early morning, Danny lay in his new bed, daydreaming about how great things were turning out.

Without knocking, Teena strode in. Wearing just a knee length T-shirt, she deposited two rabbits on his chest then left, closing the door behind her.

'What're these for?' Sat at the kitchen table, rabbits on lap, Danny stroked their fur, feeding them a cornflake at a time. No milk, he feared that might be bad for them.

Danny could have been a rabbit. Doctor Moreau at

Wheatley Royal Hospital had said so just before being struck off. If Danny had had three chromosomes in a different place, Mrs Jean Yates would have given birth to a healthy, bouncing baby lepus. He often wished she had. You never saw rabbits looking miserable. Even hung up, skinned in a butcher's shop, they looked happier than any frozen chicken.

Teena turned a page. She sat opposite him. A pair of half moon spectacles at her nose's tip, she read a paperback while distractedly placing a spoonful of cereal into her mouth. 'Hmn?' she queried, crunching cornflakes. Then she glanced over her spectacle rim. 'Oh.' Chomp chomp chomp. 'They're yours. The white one's called Proton. The brown one's Neutron. From now on, whatever you do, you must never, ever, go anywhere in this house without them.'

'What about the toilet?'

'What about it?'

'Do I take them with me?'

'Are the toilets in the house?' she asked rhetorically.

'Yeah.'

Her shrug said, *Then take the rabbits with you*. She claimed another mouthful of cereal, attention returning to her book.

He fed Neutron another cornflake.

Teena said, 'You're perfectly at liberty to leave the building, unaccompanied. But within its environs, keep them with you at all times.'

'Is there a reason for this?'

Teena, still reading; 'I'm conducting an experiment into human/animal bonding within modelled circumstances. If you like, you can read the three thousand and thirty-eight pages I've so far compiled.'

'No offence, I'd rather not.'

81

'Good. To be frank, at the moment I'm a little dispirited. You may have noticed.'

He hadn't.

'You see, I've collected every science gong going, except the Barry Trusk Award. That's the dull one, always won by an experiment only sad people could be interested in; why does toast always land butter side down? Why do right shoe heels wear down before left ones? Why does throwing things into water make them wet? No matter how hard I've tried, I've been unable to conceive an experiment of such stultifying dullness. However, on the grounds that the complete scientist should investigate the mundane as well as the miraculous, I'm hopeful this rabbit thing will do the trick. I can see no way in which it could become interesting.'

She placed the book open, face down on the table, palm ironing its spine flat to avoid losing her page. 'Gary, be honest. Do you think I could be dull and ordinary?'

'I wouldn't have thought so.'

She frowned, spoon listlessly stirring ketchup smothered cornflakes. 'I thought not too.'

'Anyway,' he joked, 'I'm relieved. For a moment I thought you were going to warn me of impending doom if I let them go.'

Her eyes narrowed to suspicious black slits. 'Why would I tell you a thing like that?'

He fed Proton another cornflake. 'It's just something my previous flatmate said.'

'She gave you rabbits?' She chomped some cornflakes.

'An ankh.'

'Did it work?' Chomp.

'I never got the chance to find out.'

'I see.' She drifted into thoughts he couldn't guess at, finally saying, 'So, I have your agreement never to leave Proton and Neutron alone while in the house?'

'I suppose so.'

'Good.'

Clink. Her discarded spoon hit her half-empty bowl. She stood, the action pushing her chair backward; its feet scraping tiles. 'I have things to do.' She donned the camouflage jacket which had been draped across her chairback. 'I'll be back whenever. In the meantime,' she removed her glasses, depositing them unfolded on the table, 'make full use of the house and its facilities. There are no hidden secrets in this place.'

'Why should I think there was?'

Her eyes bored into his. 'Believe me, Gary, you shouldn't.'

And she was gone.

Danny picked up her reading glasses. Why didn't they have lenses?

After doing the washing up, Danny set off to buy some new trainers.

Annette entered her darkened living room. She crossed to the window. Swish, she drew back the heavy curtains to let in early morning sunlight.

She went to the room's centre, feet clomping bare boards.

She bent down.

And Annette Helstrang began chalking a pentacle on her living room floor.

fifteen

'Psst.'

Danny watched his feet.

'Psst.'

He feared the hissing belonged to killer pythons trying to crawl up his trouser legs. It wouldn't have been the first time.

'Psst.'

He saw nothing but his just-bought trainers.

'Psst.'

He turned round, watching the pavement behind him. Where was the sound coming from? This was getting irritating.

Shopping completed, he'd stopped in the pedestrian precinct to admire the skills of a Government Training Scheme knife juggler about to perform for thrilled shoppers. That had been before Danny had seen him in action.

Now, ignoring the hissing, he watched the ambulance leave. He could have told the boy, some people were never meant to dazzle.

'Psst.'

And now there was hissing.

'Hey, you,' a furtive voice half-called half-whispered from behind him.

He turned and saw a small man, in a big hat, stood against a recessed doorway in the nearest alleyway, clearly trying to keep a low profile.

'Me?' Danny pointed to himself, not understanding why the stranger would want him.

'I don't see no one else I'm pssting,' said a bad Joe Pesci impression. A hand gestured for Danny to 'come here.'

Puzzled, he followed the man, who was now moving deeper into the alley. Now looking back, now looking forward, he was no mugger. Getting mugged in a side street, by a blatantly criminal type, was too obvious for the fates who controlled Danny Yates' life.

He passed a tiny butcher's shop, its window full of skinned rabbits, each smiling.

Halfway down the alley, the man stopped, and ducked behind two wheelie bins. He pressed himself against a wall, waited for Danny to join him, and looked around for witnesses.

Danny caught up.

Wide eyed, the man spoke from behind a fake Zapata moustache. 'You, my friend, look like a man who has trouble pulling.'

'I'm sorry?'

'No need to apologize. We're all stuck with the face we're born with. Nothing we can do about that, we might think. But would we be right? I think not. Would there be a little someone, a young lady perhaps, you'd like as your own?'

'How do you know that?'

'Look around.'

Danny looked back toward the street, at congregated

shoppers. Their voices mingled in tutted sympathy over what they'd just seen.

The man told him, 'Look at them. You know what they got on their minds?'

'The juggler?'

'Juggler? What juggler? They don't care about no juggler.'

'Then, what?'

'Christmas.'

He looked at the man. 'Christmas?' It was April.

'Picture it. Husband and wife, Christmas morning, by the tree; "Oh. What have you bought me? Socks? They're lovely, dear. Thank you." Then the other says, "Oh. What have *you* bought *me*? An iron? Thank you, dear, that's lovely." You think they want socks? You think they want irons? No one wants that shit. But they lie because success in *affaires d'amour* requires dishonesty. Now you, you I may be able to help.'

'How?'

Again the man looked around. 'Tell no one.'

Danny shook his head to indicate compliance.

The man retrieved a foot-long cylinder from deep inside his overcoat and handed it to Danny.

It was an aerosol can. Danny read its label; BONK. MIT THEREMINS. The rest was in Spanish.

The man asked, 'You know what theremins are?'

He knew he was looking blank.

'They're hormones,' the man said. 'But not just any hormones. They're pheromones but better, developed by the Iraqi military to overpower American opposition. No one wants to bayonet someone they've just fallen in love with. Give 'em six months of marriage, that might change.'

'But . . .'

'Theremins, no man can resist them, no woman can say no. Our operatives risked life and limb to smuggle this stuff

86

out of the middle east. Now, on a scale of one to ten, how attractive is this woman of your dreams?'

'A million. She's got pie charts to prove it.'

A knowing smile cracked a shapeless face. 'Would this girl be Dr Rama?'

'You've heard of her?'

'In neon techniColor with full strobe effect. The woman's a legend in hormone circles. If Iraq could bottle what she has . . .' He let the sentence die, feeling its frightening implications to be self evident. 'The men – and women – I've had come to me in tears, pleading, "Oh, Armando, help me please. I must have that Dr Rama. She's driving me mad. Mad. Mad! Mad!!!" you wouldn't believe it. But not one of them has succeeded in pulling her. You know why?'

'Because she doesn't fancy them?'

'Because they won't purchase enough Bonk for the job. You know what I'm saying, man? They buy a can, maybe two, not convinced it's worth the extra expenditure. They're losers. That girl, she's a twenty-can woman. Maybe more, depending on the natural appeal of the wearer.'

'But if she couldn't control herself,' said Danny, 'wouldn't it be wrong of me to . . . ?'

'No no no. This ain't about compelling no one to do nothing. The way theremins work, they rid the subject of unhelpful inhibitions and promote worthwhile outbreaks of emotional honesty. Those Iraqi and American soldiers, they love each other, love each other. They just need the juice to let 'em show it. Thing about this Dr Rama is, all through breakfast you wanted to ask her out, maybe to the movies, maybe to a fancy kind of restaurant that doesn't make you eat fries with everything, but you lost your nerve.'

'How'd you know that?'

'You think, because she's beautiful, rich, clever and

sometimes charming, she's too good for you. Maybe too good for anyone.'

'Maybe I do.'

'That's bull. You don't think, last thing at night, lying in bed, she don't have her urges?'

'I suppose she must. It hadn't occurred to me.'

'And there's you, across the landing, all conveniently placed for her. You don't think *that* occurs to *her*?'

Suddenly it all made sense. She must have had a reason for asking him to move in with her, and he couldn't think of another one. And she probably didn't even realize why she'd done it, the subconscious mind being what it was. Danny often did things without knowing why he'd done them. And when he did, it was always through lust. This Armando was a genius.

This Armando said, 'So, all she needs is winkling out of her shell.'

Danny studied the can, and frowned. It was covered in red and yellow symbols that seemed to be a warning. But, not knowing Spanish, he couldn't be sure what they were warning of. 'And you're sure this is ethical?'

'Ethical? You see this label?' Armando's stubby finger prodded one of the gaudy symbols.

'Yeah.'

'Know what it says?'

Danny shrugged.

'It says, "Endorsed by the American Feminist Organization". If it's good enough for them it's good enough for us, neh? Bonk is the world's first politically correct aphrodisiac.'

'Well, if it's politically correct I suppose it's okay.'

'Too right it is.'

He looked at the man – whose moustache was starting to fall off – and asked, 'How many cans do you think I'd need?'

The man hastily pressed his moustache back into place then looked Danny up and down. 'I'll tell Pedro to fetch the truck.'

Annette paced back and forth beside the pentacle. In relentless monotone she read from the blood red pages of her Tome of Incantations.

Turning yet another page, she read on, Ribbons matching her, stride for stride.

And at the pentacle's heart, creatures never meant for this world began to appear.

That evening, sat in Kitchen Number 2, biting a ham sandwich, Danny heard the front door slam.

He stopped chewing.

Bare footsteps, accompanied by non-specific whistling, strode down the long long hallway.

The saloon style doors swung open.

And Teena Rama stood before him, stuffed emperor penguin dangling from her left hand. He watched her mud-splattered form. And, for the first time in his life he wished his name really was mud.

Proton and Neutron ignored her. They were beneath the table, contentedly nibbling his new trainers.

She smiled at him. 'Good evening, Gary. Busy day?'

He shuffled in his seat, guilty as Judas. No matter what Armando had told him, he couldn't really believe that Danny Yates becoming a babe magnet was a reasonable act. 'I've been down town.'

'Uh-huh?'

'I bought something.'

'Uh-huh?'

'It's called Bonk.'

'Uh-huh?'

'I bought four hundred cans.'

'Uh-huh?' Her mouth retained its fixed smile, though puzzlement seemed to have claimed her eyes.

This wasn't the response he'd expected. He'd assumed she'd know what Bonk was, because Teena Rama knew everything. 'You do know what Bonk is?'

'Uh-huh.'

'So you know why I bought it?'

'Uh-huh.' Thud, she deposited penguin on table then crossed to the sink.

He watched her, in disbelief. 'You wouldn't mind me using it?'

On tiptoes, she took a glass from the cupboard above the sink. 'How you spend your money is up to you, Gary. Bonk isn't something I'd choose to buy but, if you feel it'll help you achieve your aims, who am I to say no?' She shut the cupboard. 'I spent my day at the tip, that's where the penguin came from.'

It glared across the table at him, beak open, head thrust forward, wings outstretched, clearly having been in a bad mood at the moment of its stuffing.

He stared back at it. 'What's this for?'

She filled her glass, from the tap. 'That? Nothing much. Automata, it's a sideline of mine.'

'Automata?'

'The art of making the inanimate appear animate.'

He watched it, wide eyed. 'You're going to bring it back to life?'

'Merely make it seem that way, by filling its insides with a clockwork mechanism.'

He prodded the bird, not altogether trusting it to remain dead. It wobbled then fell, beak embedding in table top.

Gripping its feet, Danny tried to lever the bird loose, giving up when splintering wood began to fleck surrounding floor tiles.

This was embarrassing.

Teena leaned back against the sink, arms folded, studying him. He awaited her pronouncement on his stupidity. It never arrived.

She just watched . . .

. . . and watched . . .

. . . and watched.

Then he realized.

The Bonk must be working.

And he hadn't even used it yet.

Teena took a sip of water before asking, 'You still have that erection?'

He chose to say nothing.

'Odd,' she said. 'It really should have worn off by now. And this occurs *every* time you see me?'

He shrugged, biting into his sandwich.

'And when I'm absent?'

He shrugged, biting into his sandwich.

'Hmn.' She climbed beneath the table, glass of water in hand.

Danny stopped chewing, surprised by her eagerness.

The rabbits still nibbled his footwear.

'Does this give you pain?' Her fingertip prodded the offending organ. Danny nearly choked on his sandwich.

'Gary?' she asked.

Cough cough gakk, cough. 'Do we have to analyse this? Can't we just get on with it – like they do in movies?' Cough cough, chest thump, cough.

'Movies?' she asked.

'Yeah.' Cough. 'You know; in movies they do it without all the medical talk.'

'They do?'

'Every time.'

'You've been watching different movies from me, Gary.'

'I don't doubt it.'

'Gary, I'm a doctor. If you can't talk to me, you can't talk to anyone. Not talking about such things leads to heart attacks, strokes, stress and failure. Do you want those fates to befall you?'

'They already have.'

'They have?' Prod.

'All the time.'

'Then the sooner we deal with this the better. Now, does this cause you pain?' Again she prodded.

'Not physically.'

Her head re-emerged, her gaze watching him over the fallen penguin. 'And emotionally?'

'I'd rather not talk about it.'

Exasperated eyes raised heavenward. Her sighing head again disappeared beneath the table, and Danny's eyes bulged; now she was squeezing the thing and asking, 'How about this?'

She got no reply but the grinding of teeth.

'Okay,' she said. 'How about this?'

And she punched it – hard.

sixteen

Scrunch. Last thing at night, Danny dumped the final binbag of Bonk in the last wheelie bin behind Teena Rama's house. He rammed it in with more force than strictly necessary, then punched it repeatedly, just to see how it liked it. Fifteen seconds he'd been blind, fifteen seconds. And he still couldn't walk in a straight line.

The disposal operation had filled all twenty-four bins. For all her talk of recycling, Teena Rama was wasteful, discarding things too easily, requiring the bin men call each morning. But she was never as wasteful as a man who'd blow a fortnight's giro on something that made scientists dangerous.

If he could lay his hands on the bloke who'd sold it him. But he'd be long gone, laughing in some pub, spending Danny's money, unable to believe he'd offloaded the junk after years of trying.

Teena wouldn't have fallen for it. She'd have seen right through the man, and given a cold blooded assessment of why his theremins could never work. Then she'd have hit him, hard, in the goolies.

Danny jumped up onto the bin lid and sat there, pressing it down like the lid of an overstuffed suitcase. From his perch, he watched graffitied walls, having from the start been amazed that Teena's home should have a back as grubby as anyone real's. He'd not yet ventured more than three yards into the back alley labyrinth which connected the house with others in the area. He feared what he might encounter.

From his bedroom window the previous night it had been clear that the alleyways stretched all the way to Bougier Woods. Boggy Bill was claimed to inhabit those woods.

Lucy hadn't understood at the hospital. Danny had.

One April morning, two years earlier, his then unemployed brother – Brian – went looking for Bill, attempting to become Britain's foremost crypto-zoologist and adventurer. Two days later, he returned with a video. Wide eyed and gibbering, he swore it showed Boggy Bill out walking his dog, which may or may not have been called Tamba-lulu.

And an industry was born.

The Health Authority claimed the tape showed the hospital's out-of-focus financial director taking his morning constitutional, and that patients were in no danger – provided they didn't make him angry. From then on, the director was often mistaken for an inhuman creature, not least by the nurses. Fed up of being shot at by hunters, he'd taken to wearing a sign around his neck, I AM NOT BOGGY BILL. PLEASE DON'T SHOOT ME. It rarely worked. Wheatley's big game hunters not being hired for their literacy skills, they'd often misread it as, I AM BOGGY BILL. PLEASE DO SHOOT ME. At least that was what they always claimed.

Brian claimed the whole story was a cover-up by an authority unwilling to admit to having built a hospital in the stalking grounds of the most ferocious beast this side of the Rockies.

The Health Authority said he was nuts.

He said they were nuts.

He wrote a book.

He made a fortune.

The Health Authority wrote a book.

They made a fortune.

The financial director wrote a book, *I am not Boggy Bill. Please stop shooting me.*

He didn't make a penny. No one likes a killjoy.

Danny didn't know which truth would be worse, a hospital that was home to a carnivorous man-beast, or a hospital whose financial director was easily mistaken for a carnivorous man-beast. It was possible both truths were true, and he had visions of accountant fighting yeti to the death after a chance encounter in the woods while walking their respective dogs.

He didn't fancy the yeti's chances.

But the relevant truth was, there was nothing to stop Bill making his way from those woods to Teena's back door. And the reason Bougier Woods were now filled with hunters – each determined to be the one who shot the Wheatley Bigfoot – was because of Danny's brother.

Bill would want his revenge. And if he couldn't get Brian – which he couldn't because Brian was up the Amazon, seeking the Brazilian potato fish – then he'd come for his closest relative.

For anyone else this scenario would seem ludicrous. For a boy who rarely went a day without experiencing some implausible nightmare, it was almost inevitable.

Clink.

His ears pricked up.

His heart missed a beat, waiting to hear what happened next. Something had knocked over a milk bottle in a nearby alley.

Clink. Another fell.

Then another.

Each falling bottle was closer to him than the one before. Something was approaching – something clumsy.

He jumped down from the bin and ran into the house, slamming the door behind him, fastening the bolts, locks and security chains before anything could get him.

Danny stood, back pressed against door, breathing heavily, heart pounding.

Now something was moving outside by the bins, knocking over Teena's empty bottles.

Then there was nothing; just a long long pause as he imagined two great, hairy arms smashing through the door's oak panels, grabbing him, dragging him kicking and screaming all the way to its Bougier Woods lair.

He listened.

And he listened.

Ice cold sweat trickled down his cheek.

And he listened.

Another milk bottle fell, some distance away.

Then another, more distant still.

And whatever it was, had gone.

seventeen

The next afternoon.

SCREEEEEEEEEEEEEEEEEEEEEEEEEEEEECH!!!

In a cloud of burning rubber, a psychedelic taxi screamed to a halt in the Polytechnic car park, narrowly missing the Reception wall. To observers, it stopped so abruptly it threatened to perform a somersault.

But Lucy knew better.

'Right.' Lucy unfastened and snapped open her cab's perspex partition then addressed the besuited man in the back. 'I'm going into that building.' She pointed at the Poly, the only one in Britain ever to be turned down for university status. 'I'll be five minutes. I'm seeing the headmaster. Sorry, we're not supposed to call him that. He prefers "Principal". He likes to put on airs and graces, though God knows why when you see his kids. A regular bunch of Pugsleys if you ever saw some. I call him Gomez, though only to his face.'

'Should we . . . ?' The besuited man began to ask, taking hold of his door handle.

Resting forearms on seat-back, chin on forearms, she didn't let him finish. 'Do I look like I have altitude problems?'

'Altitude problems?'

'He says I have altitude problems. What does he think I am, a jumbo jet?'

'Miss?' Still holding the door handle, the man prepared to climb out. 'Perhaps we should . . .'

'Stay put,' she ordered. 'And I mean "put". If you're gone when I get back, rest assured, I'll find you. I know where you live. I know where you're headed. I know all roads between.'

'But . . .'

'And, you.' She pointed to the small girl sat beside him. The girl had a Cornetto stuck to her face. Maybe Danny had had a point. Maybe Lucy did always brake too hard. But how else could you avoid hitting walls? She warned the child, 'Don't vomit while I'm gone. Do you know how tough it is to scrub vomit from the back of a cab?'

Large eyed, the girl shook her ice-cream smeared head.

'Pray you don't get to find out.'

After conquering the world's highest staircase, Lucy strode past three kids dumb enough to sit in the corridor while waiting to get the green light. She knocked on the Principal's door. The kids were staring at her, clearly envying her assertiveness. She resisted the temptation to gloat.

Not awaiting invitation, she entered.

The College Principal sat behind his desk, pen in hand, writing on lined paper, his mouth moving as he wrote. He was thinnish, baldish, late fortiesish, in shirtsleeves and tie. If he'd been twenty years younger, and a lot brighter, she could have given him one – if she hadn't seen the way his kids had a knack of turning out. She studied the hollow rings around their eyes in the photo on his desk. What were they, cannibals?

Putting the pen down, the Principal looked up at her. 'Ah, Mz Smuth?'

'You wanted to see me?'

'Indeed I did. I . . .'

'Make it quick.' Backheeling the door shut behind her, she grabbed a seat.

'I'm sorry?'

'My cab's in your parking space, engine running, passengers in the back. I reckon they'll last four and a half minutes before going walkabout. Also, the last thing I need is getting clamped. I left a note on the windscreen: "This cab's the headmaster's. He drives it part-time to supplement his wages after his first wife screwed him in the divorce court." I've told my passengers to back up the story if the clampers appear, but they look the type to break down under interrogation. And everyone knows *you* can't afford a cab that cool, not with your second wife using you like a mug.'

He looked at her as though thinking. She didn't know what; probably something bad about his kids. Finally, he said, 'Mz Smuth, why are you always so hostile?'

'Hostile? Who's being hostile?'

eighteen

That evening, sat in Kitchen Number 2, biting a pork pie, Danny heard the front door slam.

He stopped chewing.

Bare footsteps, accompanied by non-specific whistling, strode down the long long hallway.

The saloon style doors swung open.

And Teena Rama stood before him, muddy, a prosthetic leg tucked beneath one arm.

He shuffled uneasily in his seat, remembering the previous evening's events.

Proton and Neutron ignored her, contentedly nibbling Danny's latest new trainers.

She smiled at him. 'Good evening, Gary. Been keeping busy?'

'So so.'

'Me also. I've been dredging the canal.' Thud, she deposited the prosthetic leg on the table, before visiting sink. On tiptoes she retrieved a glass from the top cupboard. 'The things people drop into this town's waterways. You'd think someone would miss a leg.'

'Perhaps they had three.'

'Sorry?'

'Perhaps they had three legs. That way they wouldn't miss one.'

'Gary, no one has three legs,' she Scullyd. 'And if they did, they certainly wouldn't require a false one.'

'It was just a thought.'

'Not much of a thought.'

The leg burst into life – juddering noisily across the table, toward the startled Danny – then stopped, lying on its side, by the embedded penguin.

He prodded it distrustfully. It juddered.

'What's this for?' he asked.

She filled her glass, from a tap. 'Nothing much. More automata.'

He prodded again. It juddered again.

He pushed it away to the table's far end, happy to place the greatest possible distance between it and him.

Again it clattered toward him, like novelty clockwork dentures. Before he could react, it reached his end of the table and tipped off onto his lap. With one final judder, it again became inert.

He gazed at the thing, sighing internally. Clearly, it had found its new owner.

Thud, he re-placed leg on table.

Teena was watching him, arms folded. He slowly crossed his real legs.

'Still experiencing the erection?' she asked.

He chose to say nothing.

'Hmn.' Leaving her glass at the sink, she climbed under the table.

'Teena, I really don't . . .'

'No need to hide your glory, Gary. I'm sure you've got nothing I've not held before.' With the disturbing, no nonsense strength only medical people possess, she parted his legs, saying, 'I do believe it's grown. Strange. A hefty impact, like yesterday evening's, should've disabled it for a week. Yet here you are, flag once more hoist. Perhaps another attempt will . . .'

'No!' He declared trying to rise to his feet. 'You really don't have to.'

She hauled him back down into the chair. He remembered his brother's claims of having fought trolls which lurk beneath Norwegian bridges and possess a terrible grip no man can break. 'Gary, take it from me, repeated pummelling is bound to work eventually.'

'It's okay,' he insisted, desperately. 'I don't mind things staying as they are.'

'Has this stiffness been causing you any distress?'

'Not till now.'

'Weakness in the legs?'

'No.'

'Loss of blood to the brain?'

'None.'

'Irregular breathing patterns?'

'No.'

'Constricted chest? Gasping for breath? Head swimming? Hallucinations? Fainting? Fits?'

He answered to all six in the negative.

She asked, 'No side effects of any sort?'

'None.' Again he tried to stand. Again she stopped him. He said, 'I just have this . . . this symptom you keep mentioning.'

'Erection, Gary. The word is *erection*. Every man has them. Of course, the male erection is crude and undisciplined compared with its clitoral equivalent, responding more to physical stimuli than the higher emotions. But that makes it no less valid in its own archaic manner. Now, since moving in, have you masturbated?'

102

'Teena,' he pleaded.

'What?'

'Can't we discuss something else at meal times?'

'Like what?'

'Normal things.'

'These aren't normal things?'

'No.'

'Then what is?'

'Football, TV, movies.'

'We never discussed those things over dinner in the house where I grew up. Instead we'd have frank discussions about my gynaecology. At least, I did. My parents rarely joined in, sinking into a strange and baffling silence. And, being childish, my little sister was rarely on speaking terms with me anyway.'

'So only you used to talk about your gynaecology,' he pointed out.

'I suppose I did. I never thought about it that way before. You see, Gary, that's something I've learned from you. And when I first asked you to move in with me, who'd ever have imagined I'd be learning things from you?'

She re-emerged, rising to her feet, straightening her skirt. Danny was just relieved to have escaped a repeat of yesterday's 'therapy'. She said, 'We can't have you spending the rest of your life like this, can we? Whatever it takes, we'll have to alleviate your pent-up desires. And only one method leaps to mind.'

'You mean?'

She checked her watch. She wore it like a man. 'At ten-thirty precisely, I want you in your bedroom, minus the unhelpful inhibitions, trousers down.'

nineteen

Slam! Walls shook, Lucy kicking shut the back door, then – clatter, crunch, whap, whap, whap – kicking the stupid letterbox. She kicked it again. She stomped through into the living room, marched to the far corner and, arms folded high and tight across her too small chest, sat in her favourite armchair. She vowed never to leave it.

Her lower lip jutted, teeth grinding into oblivion.

She watched Destructor. He was at the room's centre, playing with his pathetic war table. On one side, representing the forces of Earth, stood plastic Star Trek figures retrieved from cereal packets; twelve Mr Scotts, a Captain Kirk, two Bones; and half a Mr Spock, melted when she'd dropped him in the toaster while teasing the insect during breakfast. Each wielded a phaser, each with his head chewed off, each head discarded on the table. Opposite, two cockroaches and a ladybird gathered.

Between the opposing forces stood the toy Blackpool Tower she'd purchased from a gift shop while the owner wasn't looking. Presumably Destructor meant it to represent the

Eiffel Tower. Only an idiot would choose Blackpool as his key strategic target.

Gloating over the table, he urged, 'On, on, my beauties. Destroy the humans. Let them know the bitter taste of defeat. Soon, soon, all Blackpool sea front shall be ours.'

The insects ambled in their own half of the table, feelers waggling, occasionally colliding while, on their behalf, he pushed Mr Scott over. As master plans went, it didn't.

She sighed hugely, looking as fed up as possible. He didn't notice, too wrapped up in his schemes.

She told him her problems regardless. 'You know what's just happened to me? I've been kicked out of Poly, that's what.'

Uninterested, he knocked over the Blackpool Tower.

'Have you, Luce?' she asked herself. 'Yup. Who can believe it? You steal the odd thing, hit the odd kid, and they kick you out. I mean, it's not like I assaulted the College Principal or anything – at least not till after he expelled me. And if you do it after being expelled, it shouldn't count against you on your college records should it?'

He put the tower back upright.

'So that's my brilliant career buggered before it even began. And you know what pisses me off? I could've been a good psychiatrist. I know people say I couldn't, that I'm pathologically unsuited to the profession but they're wrong. Listening to people, I could have learned to do that.'

He knocked the tower over again.

'*And* my passengers escaped. I knew they would. I should sue.'

But Destructor's cockroaches were eating his ladybird. 'No, no,' he protested. 'Don't do that, my little friends. Regardless of past differences, you are all on the same side now.' He tried prising them apart but too late. Colonel Ladybird was gone, and Destructor's hordes were down to two.

Like Lucy cared about ladybirds. 'That's terrible, Luce. What'll you do now?' she asked herself. 'I don't know, Luce. I'll probably just hang myself from the light fitting, right over my flatmate's sodding war table that's so much more important than me.'

'Is something bothering you, Lucille?'

'Never mind.'

So he didn't.

Thirty minutes later, Lucy still sprawled in the armchair, now holding her hair before her eyes, comparing it to Jennifer Aniston's on the portable. Aniston's wasn't indelibly green, following a school laboratory accident. And it didn't need washing. And it wasn't more lifeless than the Dead Sea. Otherwise it was a fair contest.

Remote control in hand, Lucy watched on. Some bloke with a monkey was depressed. Everyone rallied round.

She compared her hair to the monkey's. It was a close call but she reckoned her hair just about won, just so long as the monkey didn't get shampooed. 'Des?'

'Hmmn?' Destructor eyed the battle that wasn't unfolding before him. His insect horde was now down to one. If that took to eating itself, things would look bad for the invasion.

'D'you want to go to the pictures?' she asked him.

'The pictures?'

'I need cheering up. And you may be a scraggy geek with too many arms and not enough marbles, but that's what flatmates do when one of them's down – the others rally round, feed them popcorn, and cheer them up.'

'This was what you did with your last flatmate?'

'All the time,' she lied. 'Danny was great. He took me everywhere. He was a much better flatmate than you.

Danny was my best friend ever, and I loved him deeply.'

'And what are these "pictures"?' asked the ant.

'You don't know?'

'On my world, we do not have "pictures". I would be fascinated to discover what such a thing is and whether it is a threat to my invasion plans.'

'Good. Then we'll go.'

'Go where?' he asked

The monkey got shampooed.

And Lucy sighed.

twenty

In early evening darkness, Danny reached into a wheelie bin, arms and fingers straining for something left behind.

He found nothing.

He shook the tilted bin, hoping a can would rattle in the depths beyond his reach.

Silence.

He sighed, letting the bin pivot upright. He watched twenty-four bins lined up like daleks ready to exterminate his love life. They'd been emptied that morning, retaining not one can of Bonk.

But perhaps it was him Teena wanted, not chemicals.

Yeah.

Right.

He looked to the back doorway – remembering who was inside – and felt like a character in *Night of the Demon* who'd just found the runes in his pocket, knowing nothing could now stop the demon from squashing him because he was too far down life's cast list to be more than a plot device included to demonstrate the trampling prowess of a demon's big rubber feet.

He gazed up at Teena's unlit window.

What did you do for a woman who could have any man? You'd have to be sensational. Danny Yates didn't do sensational. Danny Yates did very little. And what he did do, he didn't do well.

He headed for the door, mounting its low, concrete steps. Maybe Doors could give him tips on how to proceed with her. Doors must know what she liked. Doors knew everything.

'Psst.'

He stopped.

He leaned out through the door, eyes scanning the gloom.

'Psst.'

He looked harder, and spotted a familiar figure crouching at the alley's far end.

Armando ducked behind the neighbours' bins, asking, 'What happened? You threw the Bonk away, thinking, It could never happen for me. Not big time loser Danny Yates. I never get what I want?'

From a couple of yards away, Danny scrutinized him, eyes narrowing suspiciously. 'How do you know my name?'

'Names shnames. What are they? They buy you a meal when you're starving, or water when you're thirsty? They buy you love when you're lonely? Names are just things to hide behind. Like Shakespeare said, "A rose is a rose is a rose. Big deal. Seen one, seen them all. But a good lay, that's a thing to boast about in the pub for ever." Hamlet, Act Three, Scene Two.'

He continued, ignoring the occasional thwacking noise that now emanated from within the house. 'So Dr Rama,

109

she comes onto you like Lady Macbeth with Falstaff; "Ooh, big boy, give it to me, I'll die happy, with my legs apart."'

'I'd rather you didn't talk about her like that.'

Thwack.

'So now you want the Bonk back but the crazy, loco refuse collectors, they taken it to the tip coz those guys they never know what to take and what to leave. They're crazy, man, crazy.'

Thwack.

Danny frowned. 'Have you been spying on me?'

'I don't need to spy. You know why?'

'No.'

Thwack. Thwack-thwack.

'Coz I've heard the story a thousand times. These people, they say, "You gotta help me, Armando. She's coming on so strong I can't stand it, and I threw away all my Bonk." So I say, "Screw you. You got no faith in the product, why should I help you?" But you, my friend, you've learned your lesson. You learned faith.'

Thwack! Thwack! Thwack! Thwack!

Armando screwed his face up, looking around. 'What *is* that noise? It's driving me loco.'

'It's Teena.'

'That's Dr Rama?'

'She's in the gym, practising her karate. She kicks lumps out of concrete blocks.'

'And you wannna poke that?'

'More than anything.'

'Jeez.'

'How much will it cost?'

'More than *you've* got to give, by the sound of it.'

Thwack!

Then his gaze settled on Danny's wrist. 'How 'bout that watch you're wearing in such a manly fashion?'

Thwack!

110

Danny looked at it, failing to understand its appeal. 'This?'

'How many watches you got on?' he asked rhetorically.

'Someone gave me this.'

'Is it worth anything?'

'Not really.'

'They give you presents not worth shit? What kinda people are they?'

'My ex-flatmate gave me it for my birthday. She was stoned. I preferred her stoned.'

'You did?'

'She was nicer that way.'

The man seemed taken aback. 'Well, let me tell you, you shouldn't like her. That woman didn't care about you then, she don't care about you now. And don't let no one say otherwise.'

'How can you know that?'

'In *affaires d'amour*, Armando knows all.'

'I never said I loved her.'

'I know what you're implying.' The man tapped his nose, conspiratorially.

'I'm not implying anything.'

'Sure. Just friends, neh?'

'No. Really. I'm not implying anything.'

'It's the tits, right? Too small.'

'Look, who are you?' demanded Danny.

'The best friend you got. But I didn't come here for Auld Lang Syne. You know what I'm saying? The watch, I'll take it.'

'But . . .'

'You want the Bonk? You want the watch? You want Dr Rama? You want the watch? Consider; a war between Earth and Mars, most delightful life form takes all. Who's the Earth's champion? Which Planet's gonna win? No contest. What you want? That body? That smile? That

111

hair? Or you want some lump of tin, tells the time, bleeps in your face? You get the Doctor, hell, *she* can tell you the time. What is she? Stupid? She don't know what time it is? And that girl, she don't bleep. "Dr Rama," you say, sharing a post-coital spliff. "What time is it?" She takes a puff, exhales, says, "It's the future, man. Now do things to me no watch could ever do."'

Thwack!

'Don't let me down, Mr Y. You already got further than anyone else came to see me.'

Danny handed the watch over, uncertain but ready to try anything twice.

The man leaned forward and again checked for witnesses. 'You won't regret this.'

Danny looked unconvinced.

'Have faith in me, my friend.' Grinning, he placed a hand on Danny's upper arm and gazed up into his eyes. 'Has Armando DuParma Du Cortez D'Amerigo De Vasquez Garma let you down so far?'

'How many cans do I get?'

The man inspected the watch, back and front. He sniffed, then said, 'I'll tell Pedro to get the small can.'

Danny forced a sigh from the pit of his stomach, a sigh so loud someone was bound to notice. Then he did it again. He was sat before his bedroom mirror, chin on hand, elbow on dressing table. His other hand listlessly rolled the tiny Bonk can back and forth on the table.

He watched his reflection. It just got stupider, copying his every move, and was thus no use for independent advice. So he sighed again; and rolled on, back and forth, back and forth.

'Is something the matter, Mr Daniel?' Doors asked from

the wall to the left.

Danny stopped the can and mumbled flatly. 'In two hours' time, the world's most beautiful woman will stride through that door, rip my clothes off and roger all sense out of me.'

'Oh how marvellous, Mr Daniel. Congratulations.'

'But it's only because of this.' Chin still on hand, he waved the can lifelessly for Doors to see, then replaced it on the dressing table.

'What is it?'

'An aphrodisiac.'

'How marvellous,' enthused Doors.

Danny stared at his reflection, hating every drab molecule of it. 'It's not marvellous. It's terrible. It's the worst thing ever.'

'No, Mr Daniel, it's marvellous.'

'Why is it?'

'Miss Rama will be most impressed that you've discovered a working aphrodisiac, something that has eluded the finest scientific minds for centuries.'

Danny looked to the wall. The voice was coming from somewhere behind the bed head. 'Doors, you don't understand. She'd only be having sex with me because of this spray. I'm using her in a way she'd never use me. And I'm ashamed of myself. But I don't want to stop, because I want her too much. And I don't want to go on, because that would be contemptible.'

'But, Mr Daniel, if she found someone attractive, and he used that spray and she subsequently wanted him, how would she know it was the spray that had done the trick and not her own mischievous hormones? Alternatively, if she found someone repulsive but, after exposure to the spray, couldn't keep her greedy little fingers to herself . . .' Doors saw no need to complete the sentence.

Danny frowned, staring at the wall. 'That's weird.'

'Not at all. Being devoid of the hang-ups most humans possess, Miss Rama regards sexual intercourse as a legitimate analytical tool. Why, right now, she's probably down in the Records Room, collecting her tape measure, callipers, ruler and notepad.'

'Her . . . ?'

'Tape measure, callipers, ruler and notepad.'

'And why should she need those?' He feared the answer.

'For measuring.'

'Measuring what?'

'Everything. Miss Rama makes thorough notes about her every experience.'

'But not sex?'

'Especially sex. She does so enjoy it; on the bed, on the carpet, on the furniture, swinging upside down from lamp fittings, under the bed, up the flag pole . . .'

'The flag pole?'

'I can't claim to understand the appeal, merely being a machine. However, she assures me the analysis doesn't spoil her pleasure.'

'And what about mine?'

'Miss Rama is excellent in that department. She has graphs to prove it. She'll keep you entertained, while making her notes. Then, in two days time, she'll give you her report on the encounter; your strengths and weaknesses, tips for the future, et cetera. Then you'll know how much you enjoyed it.'

'But . . .'

'Your little experiment with the spray will dovetail nicely with her tests. Also, you should know that – despite her dainty slenderness – thanks to her nightly gym sessions, Miss Rama's muscles have the tensile strength of steel. Like the cheeky baboon, she could easily tear a man's head off. So, even if you *are* doing something you shouldn't be, you can always comfort yourself with the knowledge that she'll be able to exact a full and bloody revenge.'

'That really doesn't help, Doors.'

'Oh piffle. You don't have to worry about bloody revenges. She'll love your experiment, provided you tell her about it first. You *will* be telling her about it first?'

Like the cheeky baboon, Miss Rama could easily tear a man's head off.

'Mr Daniel?'

Like the cheeky baboon, Miss Rama could easily tear a man's head off.

'Mr Daniel?'

'I've already told her.'

'When?'

'The other day.'

'And she doesn't mind?'

'She doesn't mind at all.'

'Then, if I'm allowed to ask, why are you worrying?'

'Things are going too well.'

'Mr Daniel, has anyone ever told you that you worry too much?'

Like the cheeky baboon, Miss Rama could easily tear a man's head off.

twenty-one

Stolen popcorn in hand, grinning, Lucy clomped, three steps at a time, down the empty civic cinema's central aisle. Stopping at the bottom, she turned and called up to Destructor. 'Come on, Des. All the way down to the front.'

He stood silhouetted in the doorway's light. 'Is that necessary for the evening's enjoyment?'

'You want to see it up close, don't you? To see inside the actors' mouths when they eat, the fear in their eyes whenever a mike boom swings too close.'

'I do?'

'Course you do. Now, come on.'

And, humming Wham songs to herself, she sidled along the front row, two feet from the screen, claiming a seat in the middle.

Destructor clomped down the steps then sidled along the row, with more difficulty than her, due to his greater size. Shown how to tip down a seat, he joined her. 'Lucille, what is this "pictures" we are here to see?'

116

She nodded at the screen. 'That is.'

'This is?' He studied its blankness, trying to perceive something not immediately apparent to him.

Her eyeballs grazed on every inch of its whiteness. 'Pretty cool, huh?'

He looked harder, eyes narrowing to yellow slits, head tilting one way then the other. He looked with one eye covered, then the other, then both. He looked at her. He looked at the screen. He almost said something but didn't.

Finally, he rose. 'I have seen it now, Lucille. I shall depart.'

She hauled him back into his seat. 'No. Hold on. It gets better.'

'Better?'

'I know it's hard to believe but . . .' Again she stared at the screen, in eager anticipation. He'd soon get the gist.

She explained, 'It's a blockbuster tribute to Miles Silkland; all his movies running back to back for a week. You could fall asleep then wake, days later, still in the same scene. Ever heard of him?'

He shook his head.

'No one has,' she said. 'It's the 21st Century's greatest scandal; the man who tried to put Wheatley on the map, unrecognized in even his own home town.' She studied the rows of vacant seats behind, then watched the projection booth. Within moved a shadowy figure.

'Miles Silkland was this town's celluloid savant,' she said. 'He produced, directed and starred in *Trailer Park Ju-Ju; Pyjama Bikers on Mambo; Go-Go Gorilla, Gone Gone Gone; Kill Double-Top, Kill Triple-Top, One Hundred and Eighty, Bullseye Bullseye Bullseye; Sea Monkeys, Aargh; My Name is Spanner.* – that's my favourite.'

'Which one?'

'That one.'

'Which one?'

'That one.'

'The last one?' he asked.

'Last one? There was no last one. That was all one film; *Trailer Park Ju-Ju; Pyjama Bikers on Mam –*'

'Thank you, Lucille. I believe I understand.'

'Miles Silkland was the worst ever film maker, even worse than Bergman. He had no budget, no talent, no clue.'

'Then why are we here to see this "pictures" of his?'

'Because he was brilliant.'

'Brilliant?'

'Funny,' she said.

'Funny?'

'You know, funny. Or have you eaten that too?'

'I do not believe I have eaten it. I shall make enquiries.'

'Sometimes, Des, you worry me.'

'Why, thank you, Lucille.'

'Eat your popcorn.'

'I have eaten it.'

'Drink your orange juice.'

'I have eaten it.'

'Read your ticket.'

'I have eaten it.'

Jerk.

The screen lit up. On it appeared a startled parakeet in a pink wetsuit.

Destructor gasped.

And the first feature rolled.

twenty-two

Like the cheeky baboon, Miss Rama could tear a man's head off. Teena practises karate. She likes to kick holes in concrete. Miss Rama makes measurements of her every experience, and records it. Miss Rama kicks holes in concrete. Miss Rama kicks holes in concrete. Miss Rama kicks holes in concrete, then measures them. Miss Rama tears men's heads off then measures them. Miss Rama. Miss Rama. Miss Rama.

Maybe he should put his clothes on and leave.

Danny lay in bed. By his bedside lamp stood the Bonk can. By the can ticked the alarm clock. Twelve minutes to go. Was there time for a third shower of the evening? And these tests of Teena's? He'd never passed a test in his life.

Proton and Neutron crouched on opposing sides of the bed, conducting a tug-of-war over his discarded T-shirt.

Pat, pat, pat, pat, pat.

He sat up, ears open in a mix of anticipation and dread.

Pat, pat, pat, pat, pat. Footsteps approached from the landing outside.

Pat, pat, pat. Each step raised his pulse rate a notch.

Pat, pat, Thoom.

Thoom? He frowned, unable to remember Teena ever having thoomed before.

THOOM, THOOM, THOOM, THOOM, THOOM.

The vibration knocked a framed photo of Teena from the wall, its glass smashing on impact with the floor. Another joined it. Then another. Then another. With a bump, the dressing table toppled. The light fitting above him swung wildly, as though in an earthquake. But this was no earthquake, just the pounding feet of whatever was drawing closer on the landing. And Danny knew what that thing must be.

THOOM. THOOM. THOOM. THOOM. THOOM. THOOM. THOOM.

The bed bounced, creaked and rattled across the room then back again, tossing him helplessly; there, here, anywhere; now on his back, now on his backside; a pancake tossed by an angry god. And each approaching step made things worse.

THOOM! THOOM! THOOM! THOOM! THOO . . .

Silence.

Tense silence.

The Silence between a time bomb's last tick and its ultimate explosion. A solitary bead of sweat formed on his forehead, trickling down his cheek.

The thooms had stopped directly outside his door.

He listened intently, hearing only his breathing, and his pounding heart.

Scratch. Scrape. Clack. Rattle rattle rattle. The door handle half turned one way then the other, as whatever was outside tried to find a way in. And soon, a primeval horror would discover how that handle worked.

Danny's heart tried to escape through his mouth.

It changed its mind, instead seeking refuge in his feet as

the handle performed its first . . .

   . . . complete . . .

   . . . turn . . .

twenty-three

Blam. Blam. Blam. Captain Manners, thirty-two, fired three more shots through the sash window before slamming it shut. His target had died with a shriek and a thud, falling from a low branch twenty yards away. But there were more targets among the trees and not so many bullets. The house would be overrun within minutes.

Little Jimmy Manners, thirteen, ran forward and flung his arm around Captain Manners, pressing a tear-stained cheek against the captain's waist. 'Pop? Pop? What we gonna do, Pop? We have to stop them.'

'I don't know, Jimmy. It's beginning to look a little hopeless round here.'

'D-don't say that, Pop. Never say that.'

'I-I'm sorry, Jim.'

Professor Schwartzer, sixty-two, stood by the door, hands in his lab coat's pockets. 'Captain, maybe we can reason with them. They're higher beings with a sense of right and wrong. They must worship God, as we all do.'

'It's no use, Professor,' Captain Manners said urgently.

'They can't be reasoned with. I'm afraid I've been keeping something from you, hoping to avoid scaring you. You see,' and he paused for dramatic effect, 'the space chicks are feminists.'

'Then we are truly doomed.'

And, with the screeching of strings and gratuitous lighting effects, Miles Silkland's opus rolled on, having reached *Space Chicks Conquer Coventry*.

Destructor's snoring head lolled on Lucy's shoulder, settling there for the evening. What was wrong with him? This stuff was great.

She moved a drooping antenna away from her face, rested both feet on the screen bottom and, mouth stuffed with popcorn, watched on.

Something fell from Little Jimmy's back pocket, hitting bare floorboards. Captain Manners retrieved, opened and read it. 'Why, Jimmy, what's this?'

Hands in pockets, the boy kicked his heels, coyly watching the floor. 'That, Pop? Aw, that's nothing; just something Miss Mimi at school had us make. You remember Miss Mimi from parents' evening? You got on real well with her and, gosh, I'm rambling. I guess I'm just hoping that one day you'll find me a new mom to replace the one who died in suspicious circumstances, tumbling down the stairs on that lightning-struck night.'

His father's expression instructed him to continue.

'Miss Mimi had us make a Fathers' Day card. She told me to take special care with mine, as I had such a special Pop, especially after she lost her husband when he fell down the stairs one stormy night. I was planning on keeping it till Fathers' Day but, if we're all gonna be dis . . . dis . . . dis . . . dis . . .'

'Disintegrated,' Captain Manners assisted.

'If we're all gonna be that, you better have it now.'

The captain studied the card in greater depth. 'But this

sticky secretion holding it together?'

'It's glue, Pop.'

'Glue? What's that?'

'It's for holding things together, paper and stuff. All the kids in our gang use it.'

Captain Manners became excited. 'Of course! That's it!'

'It is?' said Jimmy.

'Professor,' said Manners.

'Yes, Captain?'

'Get me an interior decorator.'

Hands still in pockets, Schwartzer opened the door, ready to go. 'Certainly, Captain. But why?'

'Because I've just had the craziest notion.'

Schwartzer smiled. 'It's not crazy, Captain. You don't have crazy notions – not like the space chicks. The space chicks need putting over someone's knee and getting the spanking they deserve. And you're just the man for the job.'

'Thanks, Prof. I like to think I know how to handle a woman.'

And Schwartzer left, closing the door behind him, making free use of his pistol once outside. It wasn't clear whether he'd removed his hands from his pockets.

Little Jimmy looked up at his father. 'What you gonna do, Pop?'

Captain Manners ruffled his son's hair. 'Jim, you may just have saved mankind.'

'I have? Gee.'

'No, Chimpbongo. Naughty Chimpbongo. See what you've done, Chimpbongo? You've mixed up the glue formulas. Now we'll never be able to tell the Beautiful Giantess from the Eighty-Foot Lobster.'

124

Chimpbongo sat on a bar stool, eating his own fleas, clearly uninterested.

Arms folded, Lucy frowned. Was this the same movie?

The final space feminist dissolved on the floorboards.

Captain Manners stood, his revolver pointed at the gurgling puddle. 'Looks like *she'll* never menace mankind again.' And he shot it twice to make sure.

But Schwartzer watched gravely, hands in lab coat pockets. 'I hope you're right, Captain, I really do. Though I can't help feeling they might return in ten months' time, when we, or someone very like us, will have to fight them all over again.'

Manners laughed the laugh of a man who laughed at danger. 'If they do return, Professor, they'll find us ready for them.' He ruffled his grinning son's hair. 'Come on, Little Jimmy, there's still time to catch that ball game I promised you. We'd best run, or we'll miss the oche.'

The End?

And with a flurry of strings the final credits rolled.

Destructor's head still snored on Lucy's shoulder. She decided to leave, before the pubs shut.

twenty-four

The living nightmare that was Boggy Bill missed the door completely, smashing in through the wall. Rubble flew like cardboard.

It stood before Danny; huge, wide, monstrous, unimaginably horrible, a malevolent shadow clad in darkness, its animal bellowing again setting the room rumbling.

On the bed, the terrified boy grabbed the rabbits, who were still fighting over his T-shirt, and clutched them close, to protect them – as though there were anything he could do to protect them.

Boggy Bill skulked around the foot of his bed, red glowing eyes never leaving the boy. Growling, it slightly nudged the bed – at arms' length, like a chimpanzee with a stick prodding a cobra, hostile but wary of approach beyond a certain point.

Then, it started to draw closer.

The trembling Danny shut his eyes, and hugged the rabbits tighter, awaiting its one deadly blow.

It never arrived.

Instead, Boggy Bill emitted an anguished wail and charged, flailing-armed, through the outer wall. It disappeared into the night.

Silence.

Relieved silence.

The silence of a last-minute reprieve from a hangman's noose.

A loose brick fell from the outer wall's new hole, hitting the carpet.

Still shaking, Danny sat staring out at the city lights, traffic noise rumbling distantly. He looked down at the rabbits. The rabbits looked up at him.

Clatter. Whirr. Clatter clatter.

He looked at the floor.

The false leg emerged from beneath the bed, juddered across to the hole and, four times, kicked the adjoining plaster, as though warning the Wheatley Bigfoot, 'And don't you come back.'

But it would be back.

It knew where he lived.

Folded jeans hit already packed underwear. Danny had learned his lesson, learned it big time, learned it so big you'd need a periscope to see round it to the grass on the other side of the light at the end of the tunnel. And even that light was two trains on collision course, him tied to the track midway between them.

Always settle for the worst in life, his mother had told him. Girls, the uglier the better. Houses, the smaller the better. Pets, the more inert the better; 'After all, I settled for you and Brian.' Simple rules for simple folk. From now on, he'd follow them to the letter.

As soon as the monster had gone, Danny had leapt from

bed, hurriedly dressed and begun packing. He'd crossed to the wardrobe, opened its doors and yanked the rabbit-gnawed remnants of two T-shirts from their hangers. The hangers had swung wildly on a horizontal rod. He didn't care. Danny Yates didn't care about hangers. He evicted his spare trainers onto the floor, little patience for either. Kicking shut the doors, he toe-poked trainers across carpet.

The shirt remnants joined his other possessions in the opened suitcase on the bed.

Beside the case, Proton and Neutron fought over his final T-shirt. Let them, the mad rabbits whose only interest in life was eating his clothing even when threatened by monsters.

He slammed shut the bag, fastening twin straps as quickly as shaking fingers would allow. He gathered his luggage under one arm and prepared to escape before the monster's return.

A voice stopped him. 'What's this, Gary? Planning on leaving?'

'Been doing a spot of late night DIY, Gary?' Flat voiced, dark eyed, Teena Rama stood on the landing, looking in through a monster-shaped hole. She held a small syringe.

'DIY?' he protested, clutching suitcase to chest. 'Do you know what's just happened to me?'

Barefoot she stepped over rubble, into the room, and gazed around at the damage. 'I'm more concerned about what's happened to this place. I come up early to investigate a commotion, and find a disaster area.'

'It's nothing compared to the disaster area that could've been me.'

'So, what happened? I think I have a right to know.'

'Don't ask.' Brushing past her, he headed for the door,

opened it and held it there. He turned to her, saying, 'I'm leaving. I still like you – and I'd like you to visit me in my next home, every chance you get – but it's too dangerous for me to live here. And I'm sorry about your room. And if I can ever afford to, I'll pay you back for its repair, but it wasn't my fault.'

'And do you have somewhere to go?'

'No.' And he left, walking along the landing, toward the distant stairs, angry and bewildered that life could do this to him just as it had seemed he might finally get everything he wanted from it.

Despite what he'd said, he knew precisely where he was going – back to Sister Tes and her rotten accordion.

Reaching the stairs, he placed his hand on the banister and began to descend them for the last time.

Teena called after him. 'I can't stop you leaving, Gary, but if you intend to see me again, I'll still have to administer your injection.'

'What injection?' asked Danny. He and Teena now stood at his bedroom's centre.

'This injection.' She squeezed her syringe's base. A clear liquid spurted out before hitting the carpet. 'We discussed it earlier; "Be in your room, at ten-thirty, with your trousers down." A good strong dose of sodium bromide up your backside, plus other mixed items, should cure your problem. Not that there are any guarantees, your hormones do seem rather ...' she gazed around at the carnage, '... rampant.'

'Injection.' He sat on the bed, feeling stupid.

She looked down at him. 'Uh-huh.'

'I thought you wanted sex.'

'Sex?' She blinked twice. 'With whom?'

'With me.'

'Why should you think that?'

'You said you knew an obvious way to release my sexual tensions.'

'Yes; injections. I'd hardly call sexual intercourse with you an obvious option. I'm sure most people's first fallback would be the needle, leaving intercourse very much as a last, desperate act. At the risk of sounding conceited, my sexual performances are outstanding. You might become addicted. I'd hate to be responsible for that.'

'You don't find me irresistible?'

'Should I?'

He collected the battered aerosol from the floor, handing it to her. She handed him the syringe.

Fist on hip, unimpressed, she studied the can's label. BONK. MIT THEREMINS.

'That's Spanish.'

'German,' she corrected.

'No one can resist theremins. Not even you.'

'Not even me? You make me sound frigid. Doors?'

'Yes, Miss Rama?'

'Am I frigid?'

'Oh, no, Miss Rama. You're a woman of remarkable passion.'

Her gaze didn't leave the label. 'Do you read German, Gary?'

'Why?' he shuffled uneasily.

Pacing back and forth, she translated the instructions. *Keep away from livestock. Keep away from people. Keep away from skin. Keep away from flames. Keep away! Do not inhale spray. When empty, dispose of can at registered disposal centre. May cause paranoid delusion. Do not mix with public water supply. If water supply becomes contaminated, contact health authorities. If stupid, do not use. If keen on legal action, do not use. Not to be used as a deodorant. Do not use!'*

130

She stopped pacing. Her back to him, she popped the lid off then gave the can a shake. Tssssssssssssssst, she fired a spray into the air then watched vapour droplets fall. 'Bonk is a former East German pesticide banned in a hundred and eight countries for its marbles-loosening qualities. If you've been spraying this stuff on yourself I'm not surprised you went weird.'

'But it has theremins.'

'The theremin was an early synthesizer used in "B" movies. It provided "spooky" music whenever rubber aliens approached necking teenagers in Lovers' Lane. Its finest moment was the whistling intro to the Beach Boys' *Good Vibrations*. Gary, why should canned synthesizer waste make me come over all Meg Ryan?'

He deflated with a silent hiss.

She replaced the lid then tossed the can aside. 'You're a strange boy, aren't you, Gary?'

He said nothing, too busy blaming himself, and 'Armando'.

Back still turned to him, knuckles on hips, she gazed around, taking a more complete overview of the damage. From the floor she retrieved a bedside lamp. She blew dust from it and dropped it on the bed. 'I assume this destruction was a physical manifestation of lust?'

'It was a physical manifestation of Boggy Bill.'

She looked at him. 'Is that a friend of yours?'

'He's the Wheatley Bigfoot.'

'The . . . ?'

'The Wheatley Bigfoot.'

She squinted at him. 'You don't mean the thing that idiot claimed to have filmed in the woods?'

'That idiot was my brother.'

'You have my commiserations. But I don't see why that'd make you want to destroy my house.'

'It wasn't me,' he insisted, amazed by her sudden stupidity when faced with the obvious. 'That's what I'm saying.

I'm saying it was Boggy Bill. He burst into my room then wrecked it. And if I stay here, he'll be back for me.'

'Gary, there is no Boggy Bill. I've been in those woods, frequently, scouting for junk. The only danger comes from morons with guns. There's nothing like the variety, nor quality, of fauna to support a large carnivore.'

'But he's not a real creature. That's the point. He's para-normal. When you shoot him, the bullets go right through. That's how you can tell him from the hospital's financial director.'

'Gary, now you're making no sense at all.'

'Look. There's two great gaping holes in my walls, and in walls throughout the surrounding streets. How do you explain that?'

She strode over rubble, to the outer wall, and inspected its monster-shaped hole. Her index finger crumbled loose plaster fragments. Small masonry chunks hit the carpet.

'Well?' he asked, arms folded, confident he had her.

Hands clapping free of dust, she turned her attention to the bed where Proton and Neutron were finishing off the remnants of Danny's T-shirt. One hand on hip, she wagged a finger at them; 'Naughty rabbits.'

And then she left.

'Teena, there's no way rabbits could've done that to the walls.'

'On the contrary.' Hand on doorknob, she was about to enter her own bedroom when Danny caught up with her on the landing. She said, 'The chewing powers of rodent teeth are well documented. A pair of healthy lepi, such as Proton and Neutron, could perform the feat within seconds.'

'And do it in the shape of a monster?'

'The average rabbit's creative gifts are often underestimated by the public. Many fine works have been created by rabbits.'

'Like what?' he challenged.

'The Mona Lisa.'

'The Mona Lisa?'

'I have strong evidence that Leonardo's entire canon was a hoax perpetrated to discredit the Renaissance, as hoaxers have used chimpanzee daubings to discredit Modern Art.'

'Teena, the Mona Lisa wasn't painted by rabbits.'

'*Figurative Self-Expression in Rodent Nibblings*, I have a degree in it.'

'I thought you might.'

'If you like you can study my thesis on the subject.'

'When?'

'First thing in the morning.'

'First thing in the morning, after you've written it?'

'Gary.' Her eyelids lowered to half mast. 'Cynicism ill becomes a boy as sweet as you.'

And she pecked his cheek, retreating into her room before he could react.

'Mr Daniel?'

He answered without enthusiasm. 'Yes, Doors?'

'To put your mind at ease Miss Rama has just ordered I erect force fields over all the house. Now, if there were any monsters on the prowl, they'd be unable to gain access.'

'And will I be able to leave the building?' He already knew the answer.

'Ooh no, Mr Daniel. You'd be fried like a sausage. Not that Miss Rama approves of sausages, nor any fried foods.'

'What about fried guests?'

'She didn't say.'

133

Danny stood on the landing, cheek still burning from her kiss, nostrils still drinking her banana milkshake aroma. His eyes still stared at her locked door. She was using him. Even he could see that. The kiss was just her little bribe, something to keep him quiet. All the same, he wished she'd use him some more.

From her room came the scrape of chair across floor – and the hurried clacking of a typewriter.

Danny returned to the remnants of his room, collected his bag and rabbits then moved into the next room along the landing.

He didn't sleep a wink

twenty-five

The phone before him, the Great Osmosis sat at the dressing room mirror. He lifted the handset, placed it against his bucket and dialled.

He awaited an answer.

The receiver lifted at the other end.

And Osmosis asked, 'Hello? General Biggshott-Phaffing?'

twenty-six

'Lucille, your bedroom is so much larger than mine.'

She disappeared from sight, kneeling in the gap between bed and wall, retrieving something. 'Comes with being the senior lodger, squire. Hang around long enough, this place could be yours.'

'That is indeed a special thing to aim for.' Destructor stood, unconvinced, at the room's centre, gazing round, up and down at walls, ceiling and furniture plastered with photographic reproductions of female humans' bulbous chests. 'Lucille?'

'Yup?' She was still hidden from sight.

His gaze didn't leave the photographs. 'All those eyes on your walls?'

'What eyes? I hope you're not coming over all hallucinogenic on me.'

'The pink eyes,' he said.

'Pink? You mean the nipples? They're called nipples. Everyone has them.'

He looked down at his chest. 'I do not.'

'You're not human.'

'Do *you* have them, Lucille?'

'Is this some sort of come on?'

Again he looked at the photographs. 'Those "nipples" appear to be watching me.'

'Take a step to the left,' she instructed.

He did so. The pink eyes followed him.

'Now step right.'

He did so. They followed him. He walked round the room. They followed him. 'Lucille?' A shiver ran down his back. 'This is frightening.'

'Damn right it's frightening. You know why it's frightening?'

'No, Lucille. I do not.'

'Because breasts are the scariest things on Earth.'

'They are?'

'More frightening than disease, more frightening than power-mad insects, more frightening than atom bombs.'

'But how can this be?'

'For one thing,' she said, 'they're unbelievably intimidating to other women. Breasts are the repository of a woman's self-esteem and therefore her greatest fears. At the sight of a pair bigger than her own, the average woman shrivels up and dies like a slug in salt. Pretty soon I'll have bigger breasts than anyone who ever lived. Then just watch other girls' faces when I roll up at parties and walk all over them, them paralysed by a sense of total inadequacy.'

'But these things are watching me.'

'That's an evolutionary ploy.'

'It is?'

'How did humans get to be the Earth's dominant species?' she asked.

'Because they created marvellous weapons and squashed all opposition, like a dominant species should.'

'No. It's because men have nipples.'

'It is?' Was there no end to the number of things he had to learn about humans?

'A lion encounters a zebra,' she said. 'What does he see.'

'A marvellous new friend to be played with.'

'No, a meal. A lion encounters a human being, what does he see?'

'A marvellous big meal to be consumed like vermin.'

'To animals, yourself included,' she said, 'nipples look like eyes. A belly button's a mouth. When a lion sees a human chest headed its way, it thinks it's being confronted by a gigantic face and assumes there must be a gigantic animal attached. So the lion slinks off, wetting itself. That's why humans have no natural predators. And without predators there was nothing to stop us taking over the world. It's like some butterflies have fake owl eyes on their wings, and it's why human beings have relatively little body hair. Hairy bodies would obscure the nipples and condemn the wearer to instant death.'

'Is this all true, Lucille?'

'It's an established fact. I was developing it for my thesis before the idiots expelled me and wrecked the whole future of Animal Psychology.'

'Lucille, there is so much more to your species than I had realized. But why have you brought me here? To teach me the futility of warring with a people whose very chests are unconquerable?'

'I've brought you here to show you something.'

'Your nipples?'

She re-emerged from behind the bed, shoe box in hands.

'Is that where you keep them?' he asked.

Springs creaking, she sat on the bed. 'These are my pet rats – Danny and Osmo.' She half held her mysterious box out toward him. 'Take a look.'

Reluctantly he stepped forward, leaning over the box to

see, staying just far enough back to duck should something leap out and stick to his face like in that splendid videotape recording she'd shown him.

She removed the lid.

'Squeeeeeeeeeeeeeeeeeeeeeeeeeeeeeeeeeeeeeeeeeeeeeak!!!' At the sight of Destructor, rodent eyes bulged, cardboard ears shot upright, panicked rats leapt from box, scurried between his 'feet', and scampered out into the hallway.

From the hallway, tiny feet pitter-pattered on lino.

Then silence.

The letter box slapped.

Then silence.

Lucy and Destructor knelt side by side, looking out through the letter box, at the darkened landing with its plain banisters and dingy stairs leading up and down.

'I see no rats,' said the insect.

'Shit.' She let the letter box slap shut then, heart sinking, took her coat from the peg by the door. 'I'll have to go and get them.'

'Leave them, Lucille. Let them roam the sewers, wild and free. Leave them where they belong.'

'Those two? They wouldn't last ten seconds down a sewer. If I didn't cut their chips into starship shapes, they'd refuse to eat them.'

'Then, get real rats,' he said. 'Fierce monsters to tear the flesh from the limbs of your enemies.'

She watched him, unimpressed. 'You really don't get "pets", do you?'

'In my world we have no pets, only allies.'

'Well,' she stated, holding him entirely responsible for the disappearance, 'in my world we have pets.'

'And do these things that do not fulfil their natural

function really mean so much to you, Lucille?'

'Oi! They might not be much but they're the only proper animals I ever had. As a kid, I always wanted a pet, nothing special, nothing fancy, maybe a cat or a budgie. A goldfish would've done. Know what I got?'

'An elk?'

'An elk?' She stared at him. 'Why would anyone buy me an elk?'

'An elk is a magnificent beast,' he said. 'King of the sheep-like creatures.'

'You really are a clueless git, aren't you?'

'Then what *did* you receive in your fond-remembered childhood days?'

'A clockwork dog, a clockwork dog that couldn't go three strides without rocking back on its arse and yapping. Have you ever tried taking a dog for a walk, and having to stop every ten yards to wind it up?'

'No, Lucille. I have not.'

'The block's other kids didn't stop to wind their dogs up. They had proper pets, ones you could throw sticks for. Mine, you'd throw it a stick, it'd fall over. You'd say, "Sit," it'd fall over. You'd say, "Heel," it'd fall over. It'd lie there, yapping, legs waving till they ran down. And the local cats picked on him.'

'But if . . .'

'But I didn't care. I loved Yappy. And I knew he loved me. When he died from rust, I cried for days and days and days. No one ever cried longer over a pet's death, not those flash kids with their real dogs.'

'Then . . . ?'

'Those rats were the first pets I ever had that didn't need a key. And maybe they couldn't sleep with the lights out, and maybe I had to tuck them in every night, and maybe they wouldn't drink from a mug till they'd seen me cleaning it, but at least they weren't a fucking clockwork elk.'

140

'Lucille Smith, you are a woman of many surprises.'

'Big deal.'

He took hold of the door handle. 'I shall come with you, for the city streets at night are treacherous, filled with the scum of the Earth. And we shall scour for these creatures that brought you keyless joy.'

Lucy threw her coat on. 'And have you scare them off every time we get within a zillion yards?' She swatted his claw away from the handle. 'You've caused enough trouble for one night. Stay here. *I'll* get them.'

And she slammed the door behind her.

Fucking elk.

'Danny? Osmosis?' Lightning crashing, Lucy checked beneath a box by some bins. 'You under here?' They weren't. Nor were they anywhere else she'd tried in the ten minutes since leaving the flat.

Frustrated, she let the box drop, and kicked it. It halted three yards away.

She studied the darkened alley, with its nooks and crannies, crates, bins and iron-banistered stairways which led to old coal cellars. It was hopeless. She could search for years without finding them, assuming they wanted to be found. If they did, why hadn't they come back? Had she not looked after them properly?

Clothes clinging to her in hissing rain, she called. 'It's me – Lucy. You know, the one who runs round after you, like an idiot. Danny? Osmosis?'

She scanned the alleyway. No movement.

And, lower lip jutted, she turned, resigned to having lost the only real pets she'd ever had.

Then Lucy Smith screamed.

*

'You were calling my name, Miss Smith?' The Great Osmosis stood before her, melodramatically lit by a lightning flash.

'Oh!' She caught her breath, heart thumping, one hand on her chest, the other on his. 'Osmo.' She smiled with relief that he wasn't some murderer, swallowed a mouthful of rain and reclaimed her composure. 'I mean Mr Osmosis. You nearly gave me a seizure. I was just looking for rats.'

His inscrutable bucket gazed down at her, yellow smoke drifting from narrow eye holes. 'Rats?'

'Yeah. My pet . . . I mean . . .' She glanced sideways, guiltily.

'Miss Smith, you are aware of the rules against pets in my properties?'

'Of course.' She squirmed, shrinking with each word. 'I meant Danny's rats. I told him not to keep them. He wouldn't listen. He threatened to kill me. He was like a man possessed. I'm glad you threw him out, his rages frightened me. When you got rid of him, I threw out the rats. But they keep coming back and back and back. So I have to toss them out and out and out, in case he returns and returns and returns for them. Oh, Mr Osmosis, you don't know what it's been like. Don't let him hurt me again.'

She threw her arms round him, squeezing tight, trying to remember how to cry on demand. Osmosis was the type to fall for tears. He had it written all over his bucket. He didn't care about others' suffering but liked to look as if he did – the paternal entrepreneur going out of his way to help his 'lessers'.

But she couldn't cry. No matter how hard she tried, she couldn't squeeze out one tear. How was she meant to use people if she couldn't cry?

'Miss Smith, you cannot fool me. These rats you seek, they're yours, are they not?'

Slowly she nodded, looking at the ground, cold and miserable and small and despondent, rain getting in through her collar. Now she was going to lose her rats and her home. And all because of that stupid insect.

But Osmosis said, 'Then I suggest you get back indoors, before you contract pneumonia. And I shall seek your little friends.'

She was amazed. 'You will?'

Tenderly, he pulled wet hair away from her face, like a curtain, placing it to one side. White smoke drifted from his eye holes. 'Miss Smith, what do you take me for? An ogre? A tyrant? A bugbear? I would no more cast your little accomplices out on the street than I would you, especially not on a night such as this.'

'You wouldn't?'

'Leave the search to me. Spotting rats is a speciality of mine. Heaven knows it's had to be since Mr Yates' stapler antics. I fear, because of him, I shall never again be the trusting fool I once was. But that doesn't mean I can't be of service to my most valued tenants. Now run along, my dear, run along. And as soon as I locate your rats, I shall have them brought to you.'

She watched him, and asked, 'In return for?'

'In return for?'

'In return for?' she repeated.

'In return for nothing. Miss Smith, I hope you don't think me the kind of landlord to take advantage of a broken-hearted tenant? The smile on your shapeless, little face shall be my reward.'

She took a step back, preparing to leave. 'Mr Osmosis, I don't know what to say.' And she didn't. For the first time in her life, had she misjudged someone?

'Tish. Say nothing. Thank me later. Now run along home.'

And, following a two-handed push in the appropriate direction, which nearly knocked her over, she ran back toward the flat.

Osmosis watched his tenant scamper up the tenement's five front steps then back indoors. The front door slammed shut behind her.

He waited.

Now, sure she wouldn't be returning, he could take his hand from behind his back and reveal the rats hanging by their tails from between his fingertips.

Holding them up for closer inspection, he gloated, 'Well, well, well. So you *are* Mr Yates' pets. My rodentine friends, I have plans for you – special plans.' And, head tipped back, the Great Osmosis hurled a malevolent laugh at lightning-splashed skies.

Slam. Lucy shut the flat's front door behind her and stood dripping on the Welcome mat. She watched her flatmate. He was stood at the hallway's other end, holding the bathroom door in his mandibles. For some reason he'd torn it from its hinges. Was it meant to impress her? If so, it had failed.

She strode into the bathroom, yanked a towel from the rail and headed for her bedroom. On the way past, she offered him only an offputting frown though doubting he could see it through the door.

'Mmflr mmfle mmfle,' the insect mumbled, words smothered by half a ton of wood.

'Yeah, yeah, whatever. Goodnight.'

She slammed her bedroom door behind her, locked it,

left key in lock to deter peeping Destructors, stripped off, and rubbed herself dry.

For the first time since the age of eleven, Lucy Smith climbed into bed without first measuring her bust.

But, as lightning illuminated the room, she worried about rats.

twenty-seven

'Hello? Hello?' First thing next morning, Sister Tes answered the Mission door and found no one there. Mystified, she leaned out, and looked up and down the street. She saw no one.

Deciding it must be the Archbishop playing another of his pranks, she prepared to return to her duties.

Then she spotted it.

A picnic hamper sat at her feet on the front step, a pink ribbon around its handle.

After one more look around, she collected the basket and took it indoors.

Placing it on the reception desk, the Sister opened the basket's lid and found, within, two white rabbits with big, brown eyes.

A note nestled between them, half nibbled. She took it from the hamper, smoothed it out on the counter, and read.

It said, in neatly typed script she suspected was not all their own work, PLEASE LOOK AFTER US NICELY.

So she did.

'Hello? Hello?' First thing in the morning, Annette Helstrang answered her front door and found no one there. Mystified, she leaned out, looked up and down Plescent Street, and saw no one.

Deciding it must be Ribbons Melancholia playing another of his pranks, she prepared to return to her homework.

Then she spotted it.

A picnic hamper sat at her feet on the front step, a pink ribbon around its handle.

After one more look around, she collected the basket and took it indoors.

Annette placed the basket on the hallway floor then sat beside it. She opened its lid and found, within, two white rabbits with big, brown eyes.

A note nestled between them, half nibbled. She took it from the hamper, smoothed it out on the carpet, and read.

It said, in a typed script she suspected was not all their own work, PLEASE LOOK AFTER US NICELY.

So she did.

Everyone in Wheatley woke to find two rabbits on their doorstep.

**The Great Osmosis found two rabbits on his doorstep.
They were delicious.**

twenty-eight

Knock-knock-knock-knock-knock.

'Gary?'

'What?' First thing that morning, Danny lay in bed, arms folded across his chest, still sulking.

Teena was outside, her voice muffled by the closed door. 'Are you decent?'

'What do you care?'

'I don't care. Believe me, Gary, in both professional and personal capacities, I've seen odder sights than you naked. However, I've been devoting some thought to the matter, and conferring with Doors. And it seems you care about such things. I don't wish to cause you embarrassment.'

'I can't say I'd noticed.'

'Can I come in?' she asked.

'Why?'

'I have something for you.'

'How big is it?' he asked.

'Sorry?'

'The needle.'

'It's not a needle,' she said.

'A monster?'

'It's not a monster.'

'Rabbits?' He glanced across at the metal wastepaper basket, where he'd deposited Proton and Neutron to keep them away from his property. They'd almost chewed their way through to freedom.

'I have no rabbits,' she insisted.

'Something worse?'

'Something better, much better. I put a lot of effort into it, though I had to study several journals and ask Doors' advice on how it should be done.'

'There's something you don't know how to do?'

'I have my fallibilities, like anyone else. I like to think you and I are kindred spirits in that respect.'

'Teena?'

'Uh-huh?'

'Who discovered Neptune?'

'John Couch Adams, in October 1843, though Urbain Leverrier got most of the credit and Galle was the first to actually see it, in September 1846.'

'What causes the Northern Lights?'

'Electrically charged solar particles become trapped by the Earth's magnetic field and are then drawn to the poles, where they hit the atmosphere. The energy thus gained by the molecules is emitted as light.'

'What's the fattest cat the world's ever seen?'

'Himmy, a neutered tabby, weighed forty-six pounds, fifteen-and-a-quarter ounces.'

'Who's the world's weirdest criminal?'

'For some years now, a mystery person has been tranquillizing wild gorillas, with a blow dart, then dressing them up as clowns. Is there a point to this interrogation?'

'Just comparing your fallibility to mine.'

'You don't want to see what I've made you?' she asked.

'What is it?'

'A surprise.'

'What kind of a surprise?' he asked.

'An unexpected one.'

'How unexpected?'

'So unexpected, you'll never guess what it is. So, do I come in?'

'Is my permission necessary? Won't you just come marching in anyway, blithely ignoring my feelings, like you always do?'

'Do you not like me anymore, Gary?'

'No.'

'And you no longer fancy me?'

'No.'

'Even if I were naked out here, you wouldn't want to see me?'

'Are you naked?' he asked, sitting up.

'No.'

'Then you can't come in.' He lay back down again.

'Okay.'

'Even if that monster returns and I'm screaming, "Teena! Help! Help! I'm being torn limb from limb!" you still couldn't come in.'

Silence.

He waited for her to say something pompous.

She didn't.

He waited some more.

'Teena?'

Silence.

He watched the door. 'Teena?'

Silence.

'Teena?'

'What?'

'You haven't come in.'

'I know. I said, I'm not coming in.'

'Ever?'

'If Boggy Bill bursts in through that wall right now, which he very well might – monster behaviour in the domestic context, I have a degree in it – and begins tearing you apart, I'm staying out here; even though, upon seeing me, any monster would lose all interest in you. Monsters are notoriously drawn to beauty. Just look at Frankenstein's monster. Instead, I'd simply walk off down this corridor. Wrestlemania, you and a Bigfoot, who do you think would win?'

As much to shut her up, Danny sighed, 'Oh, for God's sake, come in.'

'What's this?' he asked.

Tray balanced on one hand, Teena sat facing Danny, on one side of his bed.

He sat up, forearms holding the sheets over his nipples. If he wasn't going to see anything, she wasn't going to see anything.

'These are my bunny theses,' she said. Slap, a thick wodge of paper landed on his lap, stinging it even through the sheets. She told him, 'And this is breakfast in bed.' Four legs flipped down from the tray's underside. She placed it straddled across his upper legs.

'Why?' he asked, squinting at the tray, suspicious.

'Why not?'

'Because you never get me breakfast. I can't imagine you ever getting anyone breakfast.'

'I'm being nice, Gary, because I *am* nice. It seems you don't altogether trust me, a natural response when confronted by a superior intellect. But I feel I may have been at fault too, not taking your feelings into account. I do my best, believe me, but often have difficulty understanding the workings of the primitive mind.'

'You *are* trying to be nice?'

'I *am* being nice.'

'No. You're trying to be nice.'

'I'm not succeeding?'

'No.'

'Oh.' She thought about this, brow furrowed. 'Well, how should I be nice?'

'You could stop insulting me.'

'When have I ever insulted you?'

'You've just called me thick.'

'I have?'

'Sensitivity's not your strong point, is it?'

'On the contrary. I like to think I have an excellent bedside manner.' She attempted a demonstration; 'Good morning. I'm Dr Rama. Tell me your problem.'

'Okay,' he said, determined to prove a point. 'Best bedside manner, what do you think of me?'

'You're a mess; poor circulation, flawed complexion, sallow eyes, lifeless hair. Your face is as far as one could deviate from the Classical Greek Ideal without moving back towards the Classical Greek Ideal. You eat unhealthily and exercise too little.'

Her fingertips holding apart the lids, she leaned forward, and studied his eyes. 'A glance at your iris indicates, barring an immediate change of lifestyle, you'll die of total organ failure on September 27th, 2021, at three-thirty in the afternoon. I hope you've not made any arrangements for that day.'

He tutted loudly.

'Am I not being sensitive?' she asked in all sincerity, releasing his eyelids.

'At least you're trying.'

'That's right, Gary. I *am* trying. And you should appreciate that. Whatever you might think, I'm on your side.'

153

'So, what was all that about last night?'

'I told you – rabbits.'

'Teena, I heard you typing.'

'Oh.' She thought about this, finally saying, 'Gary, I really don't know what happened to your room. But I promise, the moment I discover anything, I'll let you know. Okay?'

He prodded the half-incinerated toast around his plate. It was smothered in ketchup, ketchup seeming to be her stock in trade. Then he watched her singed dreadlock ends. And he suddenly realized, since moving in, he'd never once seen her cook. Reluctantly, he muttered, 'Okay.'

'Good.' She patted his hand, rising to her feet. 'Now eat your breakfast. I have to go, busy day ahead.' She pecked his cheek – now he had two that would never again be washed – and headed for the door.

'Teena?'

'Uh-huh?' holding the door open, she looked across at him.

'What exactly is it you do?'

'Are we talking kinky?'

'We're talking living.'

She blinked three times, head tilted coquettishly. 'I breathe.'

Slam. She left.

Danny tried the toast, grimacing but making himself eat it all because each gruesome mouthful reassured him there were things the infallible Dr Rama couldn't do.

He considered what other everyday things she might be no good at.

And a smile spread across his face

twenty-nine

'There you go, boys. How about you stay here and behave nicely while I get on with my work?' Smiling, Sister Tes placed her new rabbits on the shelf beneath her counter, giving their ears a final stroke. She'd dressed each in a tiny blue sailor suit to make it feel especially at home. It was nice to have company, now Mr Yates had left.

But of course, it was God's work.

The previous night, before retiring, she'd knelt by the bedside, eyes closed, and prayed for Him to send a new guest to replace Mr Yates, though she knew it was wrong to pray for selfish things. But she reckoned the good Lord would understand. After all, it was His work they were conducting at the Mission. And perhaps these rabbits were the answer to that prayer. And though they weren't quite like Daniel, lacking his comprehension skills, barely equalling his attention span, she recognized that God was a busy man. He couldn't be expected to devote as much thought to these things as He'd like. And perhaps, in the overall scheme of things, two rabbits equalled one

Danny, just as Danny had himself replaced her previous guest.

While still beneath the counter, she heard a small voice.

'Erm, hello?' it said, vaguely resembling Droopy's. 'Anyone here?'

At first, she took it to be one of the rabbits, then, deciding that was unlikely even when God was involved, realized she had a visitor. She stood upright, and looked down at him.

A small, bald man, middle-aged, in a tight brown suit and Theodore Roosevelt's spectacles, looked up at her from the counter's other side.

'Hello,' she said. 'Would you be Gary?'

'No.' He shuffled slightly, both hands on the handle of a brown leather business case. 'My name's Arnold.'

Elbow on counter, chin on palm, she gave him her inscrutable look and said gently, 'Well, good morning, Arnold. Can I be of assistance?'

'You put homeless people up?'

Her heart skipped a happy beat. She didn't let it show. 'We offer refuge to those fallen on hard times after a lifetime in the maritime industries, yes. Are you a sailor?'

'Not by profession.'

'A cabin boy?'

'Not by profession.'

'A ship's mascot?'

'Not by profession.'

'Have you ever been on a ship?'

'Not by profession. It's the constant movement, you see; up and down, up and down, side to side, back and forth. It quite upsets me.' He rubbed his stomach to indicate queasiness. 'I celebrated my fourteenth birthday with a pedalo ride in the local park. You had to be fourteen to go on one. They were very strict about that, threatening a fifty pence fine and the confiscation of your ice cream if

156

you disobeyed. But a freak tidal surge overturned my boat, smashing it to splinters. Washed ashore, face down in mud, I was only saved by a huge goose repeatedly jumping up and down on my back, thinking I was attacking . . .'

'Thank you, Arnold,' she interrupted, doing cartwheels internally but not letting it show. It was unseemly for nuns to be too outgoing on first contact. But what a great bloke God really was. He could do anything for you, despite what the Archbishop always said. She told the man, 'You need go no further with your tale.'

He watched as she clomped down from the raised platform behind her counter and walked round to join him. He looked up at her, still a good foot shorter than her, and said, 'You mean you're kicking me out?'

She smiled down at him. 'I mean we may just be able to squeeze you in, busy as we always are.' And she placed a hand against his back, guiding him toward the appropriate corridor.

'Why thank you, Miss . . . ?'

'Sister Theresa. Call me Tes; everyone does. Now, come this way, Arnold.' Her footsteps echoed around the corridor's bare walls, ceiling and floor as she led on.

He walked alongside her, bag clutched to his chest, struggling to keep up with her longer strides. 'I really do appreciate this, Sister. It's so rare to find a good samaritan in this or any world.'

Looking straight ahead, to the posters on the corridor's far wall, she raised an eyebrow. '*Any* world, Arnold?'

'There *is* more than one.'

'Why, how refreshing to meet a man who believes. So few do these days. Tell me, Arnold, do you like songs about hats?'

And they made their way down the corridor. 'Oh yes,' he said. 'I love songs about hats.'

thirty

Trip. Crash. 'Oof oof oof oof oof.' Thud thud thump. 'Bleagh.'

Lucy's internal organs were suddenly in all the wrong places. Her brain was somewhere else altogether. Her head hurt. Her back hurt. Her legs hurt.

Late afternoon, having just crawled from bed, she'd stepped out of her front door and tripped over a basket some stupid git had left lying around. Tumbling down the front steps, she'd hit the pavement, landing flat on her back. She stayed there, stunned, staring at a green sky.

A passing hippy stepped over her and continued on his way. She watched him go, hurling mental knives at his back.

Then she plotted her revenge on whoever had left the basket.

The basket jostled beside her.

It repeated the act.

Rolling onto her side, unhfing with discomfort, she reached over, grabbed the basket and dragged it to her.

158

Tipping it sideways, she opened it, to discover two dazed rabbits.

A note nestled between them, half nibbled. She yanked it from the hamper, rolled over onto her stomach and read.

It said, in neatly typed script that no way could rabbits have done, PLEASE LOOK AFTER US NICELY.

Was this Osmo's doing?

What a great bloke.

thirty-one

That evening, Arnold whistled that lovely song Sister Theresa had just taught him. And though he had trouble remembering the words, he had even more difficulty getting the tune out of his head. He felt certain that, if she released it on record, it would top the hit parade for many months to come and be a major fundraiser for her Mission.

He was in the street, stood on a chair, using a small brush and tiny pot of paint to touch up the weathered JESUS SAVES sign by the Mission door. He'd wanted to make himself useful during his stay, and she'd suggested the sign. While he painted, his free arm clutched his full case to his chest.

He completed a beautiful final 's' finishing off with a dabbed full-stop. Smiling, he admired his handiwork.

But, through the corner of his eye, he glimpsed something, at first just a small blur to his right.

He took a proper look.

'Oh my,' he uttered, almost toppling from the chair, his right arm having to flail to maintain his balance. It was her, several yards distant, strolling toward him, up the street's incline.

The girl with the polka dot hair.

Whistling a tune of her own, she carried a Victorian diving helmet, from which the fingernails of her left hand scraped dried mud. She hadn't yet noticed him.

Before she could, he jumped down from the chair and ducked into the doorway's recess, his back pressed against the bare brick wall.

And he hid, case clutched to his chest, chest heaving. He tried to keep his breathing quiet but it was so loud, so loud. How could she not hear it long before reaching him? And his heart pounded. Edgar Allen Poe's tell-tale heart flashed through his mind. How could his own body turn against him like this?

He tried to hold his breath but was in such a fluster he couldn't even remember how to do that.

And the girl's whistling drew nearer, nearer, ever nearer.

He gasped, involuntarily, as she passed just inches from him. She stepped round the chair, not looking at it, and walked on, picking more mud from the helmet. Still she whistled, her bare feet padding. And for some reason, she heard neither his breathing nor his heart.

As her tune faded, he leaned out, watching her back recede up the street then disappear round a corner.

And the whistling faded away.

He waited, in case she planned to leap out from round the corner and surprise him.

He waited.

And he waited.

And finally, he breathed a sigh of relief.

Still shaken, Arnold entered the Mission reception. Letting the door clunk shut behind him, he composed himself.

Sister Theresa was behind the desk, writing in her ledger which was lit by an anglepoise lamp, or 'angel poise' as she liked to call it.

Approaching, he reached up, placing paintpot and brush on the counter. Trembly voiced he said, 'I've finished the sign.'

'Why thank you, Arnold.' She placed pen on counter and smiled down at him. 'I don't know what we'd do without you.'

And still shaking, he headed for the corridor that led to the sleeping quarters, so many thoughts swirling in his head.

'Arnold?' she called after him. 'Are you all right?'

'I'm fine.' He stopped, and turned to face her, his feet scuffing floorboards. 'It was just, I . . . there was a woman.'

'A woman?' She raised an eyebrow. 'What kind of a woman?'

'A beautiful one.'

Her other eyebrow raised. 'Would that be a beautiful woman of the curvaceous variety?' she teased, straight-faced.

'She might have been. I-I didn't notice.'

'And did this woman perform unwelcome actions towards you?'

'No. She just, I . . .'

'Did you perform unwelcome actions towards her?'

'Oh; no.' He turned red. 'I could never treat a lady like that. This was just something I can't tell you about.'

'Arnold, have you been having impure thoughts on God's front steps?'

'No,' he insisted, flustered. 'I . . .'

'Not that it matters. No one expects you to live like a nun

162

just because you live amongst them. And, looking at Sister Remunerable's behaviour, it's probably best you don't.'

'She had polka-dot hair.'

'Sister Remunerable? Sister Remunerable has never had polka-dot hair. Though she did once sport a rather too ambitious mohawk that collapsed beneath the weight of its own wallpaper paste.'

'No, the woman. The one who went past.'

'Ah,' she said knowingly.

'Ah?' he asked blankly.

'That'll be Dr Rama.'

'You know her?' He feared she might turn him over to her.

'She goes past every day, armed with some junk or other. Heaven alone knows what she wants it for; some wild scheme or other. There was quite a fuss in the local paper when she arrived in town. It seems she's quite the recovering basket case and much admired in such circles; others too, judging by the looks she receives from passing males. But she takes it all in her not inconsiderable stride.'

'Does she live locally?'

'Not Dr Rama. She's far too salubrious for this area. She lives in the big house up on Moldern Crescent. And Heaven help any man who finds himself alone in that house with her.'

thirty-two

Sat in Kitchen Number 2, about to bite a hotdog, Danny heard the front door slam.

His jaw stopped just short of the bread roll.

Bare footsteps, accompanied by non-specific whistling, strode down the long hallway.

The kitchen doors swung open. And Teena Rama strode in.

Thud, she deposited a diving helmet on the table, swiped his hotdog before he could bite it, and threw it in the pedal bin by the sink.

His expression asked her to explain.

She said, 'If you knew the chemicals they put in that stuff, you wouldn't risk one more mouthful.' She strode across to the fridge, and opened its door, setting milk bottles rattling. 'What you need is good old-fashioned home cooking like your mother used to make.'

'My mother never used to make home cooking. It all came from a packet. We insisted.'

'Whatever.' She trawled the fridge's depths, half disappearing into them, clattering unseen objects. She re-emerged, foil-wrapped plate in hand. 'This is what you should be eating.' She pulled away the foil, screwed it up and tossed it aside.

'A pie?' he asked, not altogether certain.

Side-kicking the fridge door shut, she collected a knife and fork from the draining rack. 'You can tell? Doors said you wouldn't guess what it was in a million years. I think it was attempting sarcasm. I switched it off. A mouse must be loose in its circuitry again. I made this straight after my toast success. Teena Rama cooking, amazing, like I've finally become my mother but without her annoying tendency to lecture.'

He raised an eyebrow at that remark, then queried, 'What is it?'

She placed it before him, like a commercial break house-wife set to rhapsodize on its flavour, contents, price and non-biodegradable qualities.

Plate scraped table, pushed toward him. 'It's meat and potato,' she said.

'It's cold,' he said.

'It's been in the fridge,' she said.

She plonked the knife and fork before him, and smothered the pie with ketchup from a bottle whose bottom she spanked as though it had committed a criminal offence. He sympathized with any children she might one day have. 'Try it,' she instructed.

'It's okay. I'm really not hungry,' he lied.

'Gary, this was the hardest thing I've ever done. And I did it just for you.'

Reluctantly he picked up the knife and fork. He cut away a pie segment and placed it in his mouth.

And he grimaced.

Now she leaned back against the sink, arms folded, watching him. 'Good?' she asked.

He nodded, trying to spare her feelings, needing water

between each tortured chew.

'Now,' she asked. 'Still have that erection problem?'

'The . . . the thing?' he mumbled, making himself eat more pie. Then he said, 'No,' surprised at his answer. 'The erect . . . the thing's gone.'

'Completely?'

He confirmed with a shrug, baffled by this turn of events. 'Completely.'

She strode across, took a hold of his head, yanked it forward, and kissed him like he didn't know was possible. Her lips threatened to eat his. Her troll grip pulled his head both ways at once as though trying to wrench it from his shoulders. *Like the cheeky baboon, Teena Rama could easily tear a man's head off.*

She twisted him round in his chair. Thud, she pressed him down onto the table – taking care to avoid the pie and the embedded penguin. She sat astride him, shins pinning his arms.

She broke off the kiss, sink plunger lips threatening to take his teeth with them.

Gasping for air, he crossed one item off his mental list of everyday things she may be no good at.

'How about now?' she asked, her weight pressing down on him.

'Nothing.' He lay staring at the ceiling, clueless but strangely relieved. 'I felt nothing.'

'As I expected. Seeing me as a cook has altered your perception. Now you view me as a drab homebody rather than super-intellect sex bomb. My psychology research has proven it's impossible to be turned on by anyone who cooks you meat and potato pies.'

It sounded like rubbish but clearly worked.

'So, how was it for you?' he asked.

'How was what?'

'The kiss.'

'I can assure you, Gary, for me it was purely diagnostic, involving no pleasure.'

'None?'

'None.'

'Don't you like kissing men?' he asked.

'I love kissing men. But not you.'

'Why not?'

'You kiss like you're not interested in me.'

'That's because you've cured me,' he said.

'I know.'

'So if you hadn't cured me, you'd have enjoyed it?'

'No,' she said.

'Oh,' he said.

'Now,' she said, 'monsters.'

'Monsters?' He still stared at the ceiling.

Teena, still on him; 'Did you encounter any monsters while I was out today?'

'Why would I encounter monsters?'

'It's just a thought. Did you see any?'

'Teena, there's no such things as monsters. Even I know that.'

'Great.' She picked up the plate, holding it near his chin. 'Finish your pie.'

And so, over the next three weeks, Danny and his land-lady got on swimmingly, though he refused to go within two rooms of her Olympic-sized pool. He'd just stand in the corridor, listening to her splashing around. She'd never understood his distrust of her advanced filtration system.

But Teena Rama's big problem was she needed dumbing down. This in mind, he asked her to accompany him to the Miles Silkland season, declaring it would be great for roomie bonding if they went together.

Reluctantly, she agreed.

When the final credits rolled, she looked at him, jaw hanging, eyes bulging, as though she'd never conceptualized the existence of such movies. When he told her they were his all-time favourites, she gave him red pills, advising he keep his head in the fridge for three hours, but not the fridge she used for time travel experiments; having your head and body in separate epochs rarely caused happiness. He followed neither thread of advice. But the adventures of two-Time-Zone Danny were a different story.

In reciprocation for Miles Silkland, she took him to see her favourite hard rock band, Stockhausen, and her favourite modern composer, the Abbatoir of Love. Her lengthy discourses on their relative merits confused him to the point where he didn't know what was happening. She gave him green pills for it. He jokingly asked if they were contraceptive pills. She didn't laugh.

Under Danny's tutelage, Teena's cooking came on by leaps and bounds, her pies growing larger and fancier by the day. Within a week, she'd felt ready to write to Gary Rhodes, giving him sound advice, not all of it about cooking.

Danny had talked her out of it.

Undeterred, she announced her application to enter *Masterchef*, feeling they had no reason not to include a pie-cooking section. He knew she was being over-ambitious, but encouraged her. It made him feel good to know he'd boosted her self-esteem to such crazed levels.

And, in all that time, amid all that fun with Be-Ro, not once did he want to kiss her, hug her, or lick flour from her face. Which must have demonstrated something or other.

What could possibly disturb their idyll?

thirty-three

Ring ring. Ring ring.

'Hello?'

'Mr Osmosis? Lucy Smith here.'

'Lucy . . . ?'

'Dead End Street; Danny Yates; green hair.'

'Miss Smith – how did you acquire my telephone number?'

'Computer hacking. There's this kid down the Poly, he loves me. He can get into any system on Earth. He's got into Norad. He says he's gonna start World War Three.'

'Do the Authorities know of this?'

'They do now.'

'You had a reason for disturbing me?'

'My rats.'

'What about them?'

'You have them yet? Don't get me wrong, the rabbits are great and I love them to bits but you know there's no substitute for rats.'

'Miss Smith, I am delighted to say that right now my

men are scouring the streets with tooth combs. You may have noticed them.'

'No. What kind of tooth combs?'

'The finest of tooth combs, made from gold. The moment they bring me news, I shall call you.'

'You're a trooper, Mr O. And I don't care how true all that stuff Danny used to say about you was.'

'What "stuff"?'

– Click –

'Miss Smith? Miss Smith?'

Ring ring.

'Mr Osmosis?'

'Yes?'

'Lucy Smith here.'

'Oh.'

'Mr Osmosis, why've you changed your phone number?'

'I have? I must have inadvertently done so without noticing.'

'Any news about my rats?'

'Miss Smith, did you not call me yesterday?'

'Yeah.'

'And the day before?'

'Yeah.'

'And the day before?'

'Yeah.'

'And the day before?'

'Yeah.'

'And the day before?'

'Yeah.'

'And the day before?'

'So what's your point?'

'My point is – as I keep telling you – the moment I hear anything, I shall call you.'

Ring ring. Ring ring.

'(Sigh) Miss Smith?'

'You guessed?'

'It wasn't difficult.'

'Do you know your number's changed again?'

'Really?'

'It's probably a fault with your receiver. But I'd have a word with the phone company if I were you. If you're not careful they'll charge you for it. It could end up costing you a fortune.'

'I'll bear that in mind, Miss Smith.' *When I'm working out your next rent increase.*

'So you haven't heard anything yet?'

'When did you last call me, Miss Smith?'

'Ages ago. That's why I . . .'

'It was eight minutes ago.'

'That long?'

'Miss Smith, when I recommended you change the frequency with which you phone, I meant increase the time between calls, not reduce it.'

'So, you heard anything yet?'

'I've neither heard nor seen anything of your rats. If that situation changes, I *shall call.*'

'I'll call back in a couple of minutes then, shall I?'

Ring ring. Ring ring. Ring –

Sigh. 'Hello?'

'Osmosis? That you, man?'

'General Biggshott-Phaffing?'

'The one and only.'

'General, you can't imagine how pleased I am to hear your voice.'

'Not as much as me.'

'The rocket launchers I supplied served their purpose?'

'Like a dream. Mildred and I taught the Hun a thing or two on our holiday in Spain. Do you know the place was alive with 'em? They were in the shops, in the streets, on the buses. Acted like they owned the place.'

'What part of Spain was this?'

'Berlin.'

'General.'

'What?'

'Berlin isn't in Spain.'

'Good God, man. Spain was full of Germans. Couldn't hang around there long.'

'General, I've no idea what you're talking about but I don't care. All that matters is that our little scheme's going to plan.'

'You have the weaponry we need?'

'All manufactured by my own munitions firm. I over-saw its design personally, so you can be assured of its quality.'

'I knew you were the man for this venture, Osmosis. These days it's hard to find allies of a suitable standard. Not like the days of the Raj, eh?'

'Indeed.'

'And where are you storing these weapons?'

'They're boxed and ready in my back yard. You have the troops we need?'

'Every single man jack of 'em.'

'And they're willing to betray their country?' asked Osmosis.

'Good god no. They wouldn't betray their country if their

lives depended on it. I wouldn't use them if they would. Traitors? I can't stand 'em.'

'Then how've you convinced them to overthrow the government?'

'I told 'em we're going to the moon.'

'The moon?'

'To fight the moon men.'

'?'

'Frightful chaps with false grins, and collars and cuffs that don't match their shirts.'

'And they believed you?'

'They'll believe anything,' said Biggshott-Phaffing. 'It never fails to amaze me how easy it is to find stupid people in the army. It's like you just reach out your arm and you're touching one.'

'And how do they expect to reach the moon?'

'By jeep.'

'Do they think they'll need space suits?'

'No.'

'I see . . .'

'But ready yourself, Osmosis. For, as I speak, all three thousand of us are gathering our forces.'

'Then you mean?'

'By this time tomorrow, you and I shall rule England.'

Osmosis hung up the phone, pushed it aside, and smiled to himself.

He admired his bucket in the dressing-room mirror as two rats squeaked and scratched in their cage at the room's far side.

'Unhappy, my little friends?' He watched their reflections as the phone resumed its ringing. 'Don't be unhappy, for you are to have a great honour bestowed upon you. [Ring

173

ring]. You shall be my vengeance. "But how?" I hear you ask.' And he explained, 'When sufficiently polished, my magnificent Helm of Mystery may be used as a crystal ball. And though the art is imperfect, I have learned that your absence shall guarantee the death of Master Daniel Yates. Therefore I suggest we keep you and he as far apart as possible.'

And he looked at the twin air tickets lying atop their cage.

thirty-four

Ding dong.

One dull afternoon, Danny answered the door.

'Hi,' said the green-haired girl stood grinning on the front step, a camera hung from round her neck.

'Er, hello.' Not recognizing her, he waited for her to say what she wanted.

Instead, she leaned to one side then the other, glancing round him for a better view of the hallway. 'So, you inviting me in, or am I supposed to stand here like a plant pot?'

'Er, no. Of course not. Come in.'

She brushed past him forcefully, saying, 'I would've done anyway.'

'So this is the new home? Not as cool as Annette's but it has a certain opulence.' The girl stood in the hallway's centre, gazing up, down and around.

Danny closed the door, and watched her, assuming her

175

to be a scientist friend of Teena's.

She lifted a vase from the small table by the stairs and studied it. 'This vase Minoan?'

'No idea.'

'Is that urn Roman?'

'No idea.'

'Is that Sphinx Sumerian?'

'No idea.'

'Is that lamp Lalique?'

'No idea.'

'Is that painting a Lichtenstein?'

'No idea.'

'You've really got this place sussed, haven't you, Dan?'

'I know where the brooms are kept.'

'Are they gold plated?'

'I've never seen them.'

'This place must be worth millions,' she said studying the ceiling and its security cameras. 'Whatever you've done, no way do you deserve a house like this while I'm stuck in a hovel.'

'Do I know you?'

'Funny, Danny, really funny.' She put the vase back, then scrutinized one of Teena's wall photos. 'This the sensational Dr Rama then? She's okay I suppose, a bit beautiful mutant but that'd appeal to the shallow mind – same as the pierced nipple.'

'She has a pierced nipple?'

'You haven't noticed? What kind of heterosexual are you?'

'She wears clothing in my presence,' he said.

'I'm sure she wears clothing in most people's presence. What's that got to do with the price of bread?'

'So how would I know about piercing?'

'Danny, look at her. Look at that face. Any woman'll tell you it's a face that owns a nipple ring.'

He studied the photo closely, unable to see anything in the face that would give such a clue. 'You're sure?'

'Sure I'm sure. What kind of psychologist do you take me for? It'll be a small ring, not large, through the left nipple. Silver. Gold would be vulgar. It'll be undecorated but nicely polished. On special occasions, such as award ceremonies, she wears a tiny cross dangling from it. All the time they're handing her awards, she's stood there with her all-time hard-on coz she knows something they don't, and knowing things others don't is all that really does it for her. The right nipple, she's left alone, to avoid overkill.'

'But if . . .'

'She has a Chinese dragon tattooed all the way down her back's left side. Her favourite colour is lilac. And she loves Matey bubble bath though she won't admit it to anyone except her best friend.'

'So she . . . ?'

'Her best friend's probably called Louise and falls out with her a lot but always forgives her because Teena Rama knows how to turn on the charisma.'

'Then, how . . . ?'

'I'd guess she's two parts Dutch, one part Irish, two parts Swedish, four parts Egyptian, three parts Indian and five parts Madagascan. Her hair really is tangerine though the polka dots are an affectation.' She looked at him, incredulous. 'Danny, how long have you lived here?'

'Four weeks.'

'Four weeks? And in all that time have you not found out anything about the girl?'

He was beginning to wonder.

'Is there anything else you want to know about her?' she asked.

He shrugged blankly.

'So,' she asked. 'Is she in? Only, I brought my camera.' She held it up. 'I thought she might pose for some snaps for my collection. She probably won't. She doesn't look the type; stuck-up cow. Maybe you could grab and hold her while I take the shots.'

'You've never met her?' He was growing more confused by the moment.

'I feel like I have. Once they found out she was in town, the lecturers at Poly kept raving about her; "Dr Rama's done this. Dr Rama's done that. The sun shines out of Dr Rama's perfectly appointed posterior. They say she's cloning herself, the great philanthropist. That's why she had all that mysterious equipment delivered one midnight, seven months ago, and still won't tell anyone what she wanted it for. Soon then there'll be a Dr Rama for everyone." Then they'd go dreamy-eyed, tight-trousered and weak-kneed. Arseholes. Do you know she blew up half of Yale University, doing forbidden literary experiments? And they still didn't expel her. Just because she was pretty.'

He didn't know that.

'So,' she said. 'You gonna show me her back passage?'

And before he could answer, she went out back.

'Well, well, well.' Hands on hips, her back to him, the girl stood outside, looking up, down and around at the alleyway.

Danny stayed in the back doorway, looking out. 'I know. It's rubbish compared to the rest of the house.'

'Are you kidding?' she asked. 'It's the best part of the house. Have you never seen antique furniture? The front's always beautiful, the back's always a mess. That, Daniel, is how you know it's got class. So, where do all these gennels lead?'

'No idea.'

She looked back at him. 'You've never explored them?'

He shrugged. 'There didn't seem much point.'

'C'mon. Let's get nosey.' She grabbed his hand, half yanking his arm from its socket. And for some reason, it reminded him of another time and another house.

She dragged him up the alleyway and round its first corner.

They stopped dead.

A hole in the wall confronted them, seven feet tall, five feet wide, in the shape of a 'man'.

'What's this?' she asked. Releasing his hand, she stepped forward and prodded a loose brick. Clink, it hit the ground.

'I've never seen it before,' he said. 'Teena must've carved it. She's into sculpting.'

'She sculpts monster-shaped holes in back passages?'

'It's probably a performance art. All her art is. It's useless. She's won awards for it.'

The girl stepped through the hole and disappeared from view. He heard her feet scrunching among rubble.

She called through. 'There's another hole back here, and another, and another, a diagonal line of them leading all the way off into Bougier Woods.'

'What do you think they mean?'

'They mean you'd better have hung onto that ankh I gave you.'

Last thing that night, Danny found something tucked away in his bottom drawer. It was an ankh.

thirty-five

Crunching gravel, Osmosis' limousine halted smoothly on the runway. Rain drummed its fingers on the roof.

From his seat in the back, he looked out into the night, at the light aircraft idling alongside them.

The rats squeaked in their cage on his lap. He watched them, satisfied.

Not closing the car door behind him, Osmosis emerged into the dark, the twin prop's giant-bee drone cutting through the rain's hiss.

The plane door swung open atop metal steps. Yellow light shone out, inviting him aboard.

And the Great Osmosis set about putting two rats on a one-way flight to Australia.

thirty-six

3.00 a.m., lights out, sat on the foot of his bed, Danny talked to the walls.

'Doors?' he whispered, hoping not to alert Teena.

'Yes, Mr Daniel?' boomed Doors.

'Shhh.'

Doors whispered. 'Yes, Mr Daniel? Are you having trouble sleeping? Perhaps a nightcap would do the trick? I have many excellent remedies.'

'Is there anything going on round here?'

'Going on, Mr Daniel? Such as?'

'Anything. Something I don't know.'

'There are many things you appear not to know, Mr Daniel. Pleasurable though your presence has been, I'm afraid you're not the most clued-up of guests. However, I'd be more than willing to educate you.'

'Good. Do it.'

'See the cat; C-A-T. Can *you* spell cat?'

'I meant something a little more specific to this building.'

'Ballcocks.'

'Are you trying to tell me something, Doors?'

'Indeed; I'm striving to supply you with all available information about this household. Miss Rama personally designed the plumbing, having won much praise for her ballcocks. Each of Miss Rama's ballcocks has a unique double rotational –'

'I was hoping for something a little more useful,' he butted in.

'If you'd like to tell me what it is you don't know, I'll happily explain it to you.'

'If I knew what it was, I wouldn't need to ask, would I?'

'If you could select a subject heading.'

Danny remembered the holes in the walls, and the strange girl who clearly knew him though he didn't know her. 'Monsters.'

'Ah.'

He perked up. ' "Ah," what?'

'I'm afraid Miss Rama's been putting things in your pies, to make you forget any monstrous creatures you may ever have encountered. Ugh, horrible things; I was amazed you could bring yourself to eat them.'

'And you didn't tell me?'

'I'm a machine, Mr Daniel. I cannot prejudge what you may or may not wish to know. You shouldn't anthropomorphize me; Heaven knows, I don't, not after the last time Miss Rama "repaired" me for getting ideas above my station. Her tempers can be quite frightening.'

'So, what's this about monsters?'

'Miss Rama has instructed me not to tell you.'

'But she didn't order you not to tell about the pies?'

'She didn't credit you with the intelligence to ask.'

'So who does she think I am – "Mr Stupid, King of Stupid Land"?'

'But you didn't ask, did you?'

'I would've done.'

'When?'

'When it was appropriate.'

'When you'd forgotten everything that had ever happened to you, and had been reduced to an empty-headed vegetable resembling a rhubarb?'

'Yes.'

'And was this *your* plan, Mr Daniel? Or did someone help you with it?'

He felt it best to change tack. 'What about these monsters?'

'Well . . .' Doors' voice tailed away.

'Doors,' Danny insisted.

'If you went downstairs to the library, perhaps seeking information on Miss Rama's double rotational ballcocks, you might fortuitously discover a CD-ROM beneath a painting entitled LOOK AT ME. I'M THICK. It might – if you accidentally discovered its access code to be MR STUPID. KING OF STUPID LAND – be of interest. Not, of course, that you heard any of this from me. If you catch my,' he coughed discreetly, 'drift.'

Danny eased shut his bedroom door, looked both ways for witnesses, then tiptoed along the landing, toward Rama's room. Her light was out.

He turned left at her door and, hand on banister, crept down the stairs.

The third step down creaked, loudly. He stopped, breath held, and looked to see if her light had come on. It hadn't. He heard her mumble, 'Man Who Does,' in her sleep, turn over in her bed then settle down.

And Danny exhaled, quietly.

He descended the remaining steps, faster with each, as though more haste would lessen his chances of discovery. Creak, creak, creak, CREAK, CREAK, CREAK.

Danny closed the library door, gently, so as not to alert Rama. Heart thumping, he studied the darkened room, with its shelves of CDs, tapes and books. Again, shelves. Wherever there was treachery, there were shelves. A grandfather clock's ticking provided the only sound.

He whispered, 'Okay, Doors. Where's the CD?'

Doors whispered, 'Beneath your portrait.'

'There is no portrait of me.'

'Directly to your left.'

Seeing only a mud creature painting, he approached, and looked closer at its drab surface. He frowned up at it. 'This is me?'

'Miss Rama tells me she'll be winning next year's Turner Prize with it.'

He eyed the picture further. 'But this is how she sees me?'

'I believe it's how she sees everyone.'

Danny took a couple of CDs from beneath the portrait, tilting them one way then another, trying to make their lettering catch the moonlight. 'But these aren't CD-ROMs. They're just Rama's Modern Jazz albums.'

'On the contrary, they're a record of everything that has happened since the dawn of existence. Also deposited are her personal notes, journals and odds and ends.'

'But I tried these CDs, the morning after I moved in. They were just "music".'

'Correction. You tried one CD – a Mr Filwrj Fgigfkjvkj, an accomplished master of randomness. It was placed there to discourage you from wanting to play the others.'

184

'But how could she know I'd play that particular disc?'

'Would that be the one below and to the right of her rather sensational 3D swimwear photo? You're right-handed, unlike Miss Rama, so if you were ogling her photo from a distance of, say, two inches, there'd be only one CD you could comfortably take.'

'So now you're saying I'm predictable?'

'If one finds one's strings being pulled, one must conclude one is a proper puppet.'

'And you couldn't tell me any of this either?'

'I'm only a machine, Mr Daniel.'

'When it suits you,' he muttered darkly.

'All the time, Mr Daniel.'

Danny chose Mr Filwrj Fgigfkjvkj's *Mr Predictable Comes to Stay* CD, intuition telling him it might be the one required.

At the PC, he removed the disk from its container, inserted it into the appropriate slot, and booted up. It played a little tune; *Nellie the Elephant.*

A winking cursor appeared. 'Please enter the access code,' the computer requested in Rama's voice, implying that otherwise *Nellie the Elephant* would never stop.

Chin on hand, deflating with each key tapped, he one-finger typed, 'Mr Stupid. King of Stupid Land.'

Open-jawed, Danny watched what could only be Boggy Bill rampage through his bedroom then crash out through a wall. Then Rama was trying to explain it away with pseudo-scientific rubbish about rabbits that even he couldn't possibly have believed.

He fast-forwarded the recording. With jerky movements

and a helium voice Rama left the bedroom. Preferring her that way, he reverse-played her, to make her look even sillier. He fast-forwarded again. Then he discovered that, by quickly alternating between the two settings, he could make her look a complete idiot. At one point in the action, he could even get her to do a Hitler salute though his attempts to make her goose step failed.

Finally, after making her run round and round and round in little circles, he let her leave the room.

The screen went blank, picture resuming the next day with him in bed, sulking, as she knocked on his new bedroom door. And suddenly she was making a fool of him again.

Sighing, he switched the screen off. The picture collapsed into a white dot then vanished.

Horrified, amazed, he tried gathering his thoughts together. Could this be real?

'Mr Daniel?' asked Doors after a few moments.

'That thing was in my room?' he asked.

'Yes, Mr Daniel.'

'And I'm still alive?'

'If you say so, Mr Daniel.'

'And now it's on the loose?'

'Yes, Mr Daniel.'

'And no one's noticed?'

'No, Mr Daniel.'

'Is it just me, or does none of this make sense?'

'At the risk of causing offence, very little in life seems to make sense to you.'

'And the monster? Rama's doing nothing to stop it? Well, isn't that just typical of her?'

'Oh, no, Mr Daniel. Normally, Miss Rama leaves things to sort themselves out, having a basically benign view of fate. However, this time, she's constructing a robot to grapple with the monster throughout the streets of Wheatley. She believes one carefully placed blow to the cranium may – if delivered with sufficient force – stop it. That's where she goes each day, collecting parts for her Fighting Android.'

Danny frowned. 'She's building a Fighting Android from a stuffed penguin, a diving helmet and a prosthetic leg?'

'Miss Rama prefers never to do things the conventional way, Mr Daniel.'

'Miss Rama prefers computers that know when to keep their mouths shut, Doors,' interrupted a stern voice.

Startled, Danny turned toward the door. His heart ran screaming into a corner and cowered, taking occasional peeks through its fingers.

Teena Rama stood silhouetted in the doorway.

And in her hand was the biggest pie anyone ever saw.

thirty-seven

Midnight. Annette arrived, a rabbit under each arm, out-side Madam Fifi's late night pedicurists, a narrow building up a city centre side street. A police siren wailed in the distance.

Her gaze scaled three anonymous grey storeys. Annette stepped forward, pushed open a blank wooden door with no handle, and entered.

'Hello.' Annette placed her new rabbits on the pink reception desk. 'I have an appointment.'

'I know.'

'I'm Annette Helstrang.'

'I know.'

'I live at Plescent Street.'

'I know.'

'I'm twenty-one.'

'I know.'

'I'm here to . . .'

'I know.'

'I . . .'

'I know.'

Annette's expression indicated she'd like an explanation.

'We have a file on you.' For the first time removing her attention from the holiday brochure on her counter, the receptionist retrieved a thick, pink folder from the pink pigeonholes behind her.

A genteel xylophone version of *I'm Sending a Letter to Daddy* wafted down from an overhead speaker; rarely a cause for optimism, Annette often found.

With an insouciant thud and a flurry of dust, the pink folder hit the pink counter.

The rabbits ignored it, nibbling at the desk top.

'We have a dossier on everyone,' said the receptionist, flat-voiced, as Annette flicked through its pages. 'Fifi insists. We even have a file on her, which she uses to discover endless new facts about herself. Its contents never cease to amaze her though she never reads it.'

Madam Fifi was thorough. Everything was in Annette's file; her birth, school days, early college years, embarrassing photos of her as a child with various saucepans stuck to her head after pretending to be a dalek, her mum, her dad, the first time she'd met Lucy Smith, Danny Yates arriving at her house in Lucy's cab, Danny Yates as a child, saucepans stuck to his head after pretending to be a dalek.

Later chapters featured predictions for the rest of her life. Annette didn't read them, not wishing to ruin the surprise.

But one thing heartened her; in all the dossier, there was no mention of the week spent camping in southern France. It seemed Madam Fifi didn't quite know all. 'There seems

189

to be a piece missing.' Annette closed the folder, placing it back on the desk.

'That'll be in the supplemental.'

'The supplemental?'

The receptionist disappeared beneath the desk. Seconds later, thud, another thick document hit it. 'Everyone must have a supplemental,' she said.

Annette checked the supplemental's crisp, pink pages, with their blood red script. And there it was, the week in France, with a saucepan stuck to her head after pretending to be a Napoleonic bunker. 'Is this standard practice for a pedicurist?' She rippled through yet more pages.

The receptionist took the file from her, placing it back beneath the counter. 'Madam Fifi is not a pedicurist.'

'Then what is she?'

'A disturbing pedicurist. I wouldn't have my feet done by her. She steals toes. Has a whole collection back there. She won't show them to you but they're there, row after row after row of them, each in its own matchbox. One day, she hopes to make a whole new set of feet from them. She calls it God's little army of toes. Toes'll be important come the next millennium, she reckons. You probably knew that, being the mystical one. Mystical, maybe, but weird? You don't know weird till you meet Fifi. Fifi insists on tying her customers to the table.'

Elbows on counter, chin on palms, she studied Annette's face before asking, 'Ever considered a nose job?'

Annette felt at her nose, never having considered such an operation.

'Fifi's secateurs could do that like you wouldn't believe. Of course we'd have to sell your nose on, to cover costs. She's efficient like that. Madam Fifi uses ear lobes as pastry fluting.'

'I see.' Annette still wasn't sure why the Mysterious Legs had sent her here. 'Well, can you tell her I've arrived?'

'No.'

'Why not?'

'She already knows.' Her gaze settled on an eye-shaped camera blinking above the door. 'Fifi knows all.'

thirty-eight

In the Mission's sleeping quarters, Arnold paced this way then that beside a hammock he chose never to use. Hands clasped behind his back, he stared at the floor. His little, pit-patting shoes were wearing a groove in the boards.

He turned, and walked the other way. Should he go and see her? He didn't want to. She might do awful things to him.

He turned, and walked the other way. But perhaps he should see her. She was the only one who could put things right. And things were so terribly wrong.

He turned again.

But she was the one who'd made things wrong in the first place. She could make them even worse. He'd seen for himself what a monster she could be.

He turned again. And again. And again, now simply going round in circles.

But if he did nothing, it was only a matter of time before something dreadful happened; to Sister Theresa, the Mission, the whole world. But then . . . but then . . . but then . . .

But then no matter how he tossed it round in his head, no matter how many directions he tried walking during the course of one evening, only one route lay open to him.

Whatever the consequences, he would have to confront the terrible Dr Rama.

thirty-nine

'I expected to find you here, once I realized you were loose in the building.' Rama entered the library, still silhouetted, pie still in hand. Wearing just the knee-length T-shirt she slept in, she approached, remorseless, somehow filling Danny's entire field of vision.

He thought of the concrete slabs in her gym, smashed to smithereens by countless bludgeoning karate blows. Each slab, in his mind's eye, now had his face. 'And what if you have found me?' he bluffed, rising to his feet. 'Do you think I'm scared of you?' Mind racing, he hurled his swivel chair across the floor at her. Its castors rattled across polished tiles.

She slung the chair aside, unfazed. It rebounded from a wall and into a book case. 'I think you find me intimidating beyond belief. So you'd better do as you're told.'

'Never.'

She drew closer. 'Then, I'll have to use force.'

A wall stopped his retreat, forcing him to sidle along it, trying to find a point of escape. Now he was backed into a corner. 'You think you can take me?' he challenged.

She closed in. 'I know I can take you.'

'Oh dear. I simply can't look.' Doors' camera light blinked off.

Danny tried selling her a dummy. It didn't work. Her forearm pinned him against the wall. And she held him there, steely fingers gripping a handful of his skin through his T-shirt. 'Open your mouth, Gary. Eat this pie.' She tried cramming it into his mouth. It brushed his lips.

He kept them shut, moving his head away. 'Never.'

'Eat it.' She tried again.

Again he moved his head away. 'You won't get away with this.'

'Eat it.'

'I have friends.'

'Name one.'

'A frightening girl with green hair. She knows where I am. She'll miss me – whoever she is. Maybe she's my girlfriend. Maybe she loves me. Maybe she's wondering where I am right now. She'll . . . she'll . . .'

'She'll what?'

'She'll . . .' He didn't know.

'Gary, I'm not going to hurt you. This pie will restore your memory.'

'Yeah,' he sneered. 'Sure it will. And I suppose it'll also cure my, my, that problem I once had.'

'Erection, Gary. The word is *erection*, E-R-E-C-T-I-O-N. How many times must I tell you? In fact, it'll restore that problem but will at least cure your amnesia.'

'You expect me to believe that? My God, I knew you were evil but is there no depth you won't sink to? Even now you won't tell the truth.'

'Gary, the pies can only clear your memory once. Now you've rediscovered your encounter with the monster, that memory can't be re-wiped without using enough drugs to melt your brain into a particularly unpleasant sludge. And I for one have no intention of standing here watching your hippocampus leak from your ears.'

'That's exactly what you want to see.'

'And why should I want to see that?'

'To shut me up.'

'The thought is tempting.'

'So you admit it?'

'Yes! I admit it. I'm the most evil woman on Earth, and I'm only after your body – and any other nonsense that mixed-up head of yours wants to believe. I'm an alien, here to drink your brain. Now eat the fucking pie.' Again she pushed it at him.

He broke free, running for the exit, feet heavy as in a dream. The door seemed to be getting no nearer though he knew it must have been. If he could get to that, shut and lock it from the outside, he could call the police and get her put away like she deserved.

'Doors,' she ordered.

Slam! A metal panel dropped down, blocking the exit. Danny pounded it, feeling betrayed by the one 'person' he'd trusted; 'Doors! Doors! Let me out!'

'Doors won't help you. Regardless of unreliability, it's essentially spineless. I designed it that way.'

'I'm sorry, Mr Daniel.'

'And stop calling him Mr Daniel,' she snapped. 'His name's Gary. How many times must I tell you?'

'Sorry, Miss Rama.' Doors sounded almost in tears.

Danny turned to face her, back pressed against the metal panel, heart pounding as she drew nearer.

She told Doors, 'You and I are going to have a long talk after this. And my talking will be done with screwdrivers.'

'Yes, Miss Rama.'

Danny looked to either side for potential weapons. He'd

have to belt her one to escape. Maybe when she was unconscious, Doors would disobey her again. But what could he hit her with?

On the shelf by his head sat Gibbon's *Decline and Fall of the Roman Empire*, just asking to knock someone senseless. Danny grabbed it, ready to deliver the knockout blow that would end this insanity.

Thwack!

Everything went black.

forty

'Is all this rope necessary?' asked Annette, hands tied above her head, as Madam Fifi wrapped yet more coils around her midriff.

'It's vital,' insisted the crimson-chiffoned pedicurist. 'You small girls are devious. Tall girls are gallumping things, lacking the foresight to see danger looming. Boys? Boys are too stupid to even think of escape. They blunder around inviting terrible fates upon themselves, then blame everyone else.'

'Have you had any small girls on your operating table before?' asked Annette.

'None.'

'Tall girls?'

'Many.'

'Boys?' asked Annette.

'Thousands,' said Fifi.

'Then I suppose that's an argument won, though I've never considered myself devious.'

'Don't put yourself down, my dear. Devious you are.'

'Well, thank you.' Annette remembered her manners.

'You're welcome.' And Fifi continued binding.

Still, Fifi must have known what she was doing. In her time she must have tied dozens of people to dozens of tables and was probably the world's leading authority on the art. You wouldn't tell Aleister Crowley how to summon the devil, nor H. P. Lovecraft how to find things lurking in his cellar. Don't tell Madam Fifi how to bind.

Finally having exhausted her copious rope supply, Fifi gathered the network of cables together and heaved it good and tight, one foot propped against the table for extra leverage. With a trawlerman's dexterity she knotted the ropes in every conceivable manner, binding Annette to pink table, pink table to pink floor, pink floor to sawn-off elephant legs protruding from pink walls, pink walls to pink ceiling. Finally, she tied the ceiling to Annette.

She removed Annette's shoes, tossing them aside. Apparently they were of no interest, despite being her best pair.

Leaning close, Fifi inspected the girl's feet, starting with the big toes, pinching them, one by one, between Cruella DeVille fingertips.

Annette supposed she should be flattered at the interest in her feet. Not everyone shared it, though some did. Gavin the fetishist had, spending long hours by the fireside, talking to them. They never replied.

Sadly, Annette's feet had been the only part of her that Gavin had been interested in, spending the small hours with one or other in his mouth while their owner nodded off over an 'improving' novel. It's not a happy woman who has less fun than her feet.

Finally, the pedicurist concentrated on the little toes (or, Divine Pinkies, as she knew them), clearly regarding them as the pick of Annette's bunch. 'Tell me.' She manipulated them, engrossed. 'How long have you had these?'

'All my life, though – as the human body renews itself

every seven years, and I'm twenty-one – I suppose they're brand new. Not that I remember the moment of their delivery. They must have arrived while I slept, perhaps last Thursday.'

'Yes. Yes. Thursday is when Jack New Toes makes his spangly sprinkly rounds, delivering new toes to sleeping children everywhere. Excellent. Excellent. New toes. Excellent.'

She took an eyebrow pencil from behind her left ear and, like a butcher marking a slab of meat for carving, drew a line round each Divine Pinky's base circumference. 'Just stay here, my pretty,' she requested, as though Annette would be going anywhere with all that binding. 'I'll be right back.'

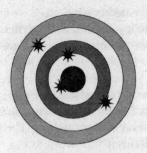

forty-one

Needles of light stabbed Danny's eyes as he opened them. He blinked twice, trying to find his bearings. Strip lighting was passing above him. The thing he was lying on rattled, clattered and squeak squeak squeaked. It was pushed by Teena Rama.

Her chin's underside faced straight ahead. 'You're conscious?' she asked.

'Am I?' There was a pie on his chest.

'I've never known anyone take so long to recover from a left hook,' she said, 'well delivered though it was.'

His head raised, straining to see his surroundings. 'Where am I?'

'In the broom cupboard.'

He gazed at the walls of a hospital-style corridor.

She pushed on, Gibbon's *Decline and Fall* tucked beneath one arm. 'I'm afraid my house has no brooms. My Man Who Does stores all his equipment at his own home, bringing it over only when I request its application.'

'I'm tied to a table?'

'No. You're strapped to a trolley.'

'Big difference,' he grumbled.

'There's a world of difference, tables not being renowned for their manoeuvrability.'

'Where are you taking me?'

Halting the trolley at a lift, she ordered, 'Doors.'

Ping. The door rumbled open. She pushed the trolley inside. Rattling, it jolted over the join between lift and corridor.

Clunk. The door shut behind them.

Then: 'My God!' With renewed urgency Danny tried to break free, suddenly understanding. 'This isn't a trolley!'

'No? Then what is it?'

'It's an altar!'

'An altar?' Rama gazed down at him as the lift descended through countless storeys. 'You think I plan to marry you? I can assure you, Gary, the day I wed, I hope to do it with a little more style than this. Though I must say, being tied up does add a certain frisson to a man's appeal.'

'How can you joke about this?'

'Who's joking?'

'You're going to sacrifice me to Boggy Bill. That's why you wanted me to live here. You think, by giving him Brian Yates' brother, you'll curry favour with your "master".' A trickle of sweat ran across his forehead.

'Is this a colour thing?' she asked wearily.

'What's colour got to do with it?'

'Would you be talking this nonsense if I were white?'

'Of course I would. If someone drugs you, beats you up, ties you to a mobile altar and cuts your heart out right in front of you, what difference does colour make?'

'You don't find this human sacrifice to a gorilla god thing

redolent of 1930s Hollywood stereotyping?'

'Race doesn't come into it. Everyone's ancestors made sacrifices to Boggy Bill.'

'Mine didn't.'

'Yes, they did.'

'No, they didn't. My family are from Hampstead. Human sacrifice rarely goes down well in Hampstead.'

'So you came here to do it.'

'Well.' She shrugged, now watching the lift doors. 'Perhaps I did.'

His eyes narrowed accusingly. Now he was getting somewhere.

She said, 'Perhaps there *were* certain things I couldn't do in Hampstead, so I came to Wheatley. After all, who can know what any of us would do if free of social constraints? Who, for instance, would have thought a seemingly harmless boy would be so underhand as to try to drug a woman into his bed?'

'Doors said it'd be okay.'

'Yes, well,' she said icily. 'Good old Doors.'

'I should've guessed it all along,' said Danny. 'But maybe I did. Maybe I had you sussed and was going to report you to the medical authorities. That's why you started drugging me, to make me forget. Maybe I'm really shrewd, the twenty-first century's Herbolt Myson.'

'Who?'

'Herbolt Myson, Victorian super sleuth.'

'Oh,' she said. 'That clown.'

'Clown? He was the greatest mind of his age.'

'It doesn't say much for the rest.'

'And that girl with the green hair, she's my sidekick in sleuthery. And it's only your drugs that're making me seem stupid.'

'I can assure you, Gary, your stupidity is purely natural.'

Straps refusing to budge, he stopped struggling. 'My jaw

hurts.' He could still feel where her knuckles had impacted.

'Yes. Well. Whose fault is that?'

'Yours.'

'No, Gary, it's yours. You won't eat my pies. You won't keep your nose out of things that don't concern you. Frankly, as a housemate, you're not working out.'

'And you are?'

'I've been an excellent host, the best. You've forced me to do what I'm doing now, and don't forget that. Anything that happens to you from now on is entirely your own fault. No wonder your last landlord kicked you out. I'm only surprised it took him so long.'

'Will you let him eat me?' he asked feebly.

'Who? Your last landlord?'

'Boggy Bill.'

'If he insists.'

'Alive?'

'How could I stop him?'

He imagined himself tied struggling to the trolley, the creature consuming him, starting at his legs and working its way up. 'How many?'

'Many?'

'How many lodgers have you sacrificed? Dozens?'

She said nothing.

'Hundreds?'

She said nothing.

His jaw dropped. 'Thousands?'

Ping. The lift stopped. His stomach regained its full weight.

The door rumbled open.

And, with a jolt and a rattle, Teena Rama wheeled him out.

'What do you think of my masterpiece?' Rama pushed the trolley round a white, circular room. At its hub hung, vertically, a huge, atom-smashing phallus of a gun, ten foot in diameter, oozing power, hubris and God-defying menace in equal measure. It was the work of a madwoman.

As Danny circled, his gaze climbed the gun – twenty storeys, thirty storeys, forty, more – having to give up exhausted before reaching anything like its apex.

'Is this what you'll use to sacrifice me?' he asked, feebly.

'If you like.' She stopped the trolley on a ramp's gentle rise and, slap, dropped Gibbon's *Decline and Fall* to the floor. A bare foot wedged it beneath one wheel to ensure it stayed put.

Striding up the ramp, she approached a console with a blank screen on top. She donned Walkman headphones and plugged them into the console. Her back to him, she fiddled with controls. The screen hummed to life, images cascading as though on a maladjusted television.

'That'll summon Boggy Bill?' Danny's mouth dried as he spoke.

'If you like.' She manipulated a knob here, a mouse there, trying to draw a coherent image from the device.

'You've probably convinced yourself you're doing this for the good of humanity, haven't you?' he protested. 'Well, let me tell you, *Doctor* Rama – and I can't believe you're a real doctor, real doctors have ethics and codes and oaths and give you lollipops to encourage you to come back; no one'd want to come back to your practice – when I'm a ghost, I'm going to get you, get you big time. And nothing'll save you, not tame doors, not force fields, not hidden bunkers, not a pretty face, not a big gun, nothing.'

An image settled on screen, showing the house's empty hallway. He didn't know whether it was the hallway as it was now, as it had been, as it would be, or as it had never been.

'Gary, if you want to get out of here in one piece, shut up. I have something to show you.'

forty-two

'Right, Gary.' Rama stood over Danny's trolley, holding a second pair of earphones. 'I'm attaching these to your head. You'll feel a little giddy but that should soon pass.'

'Will *this* kill me?' he asked feebly.

'The console I'm linking you to is a mind-reading machine.'

'Mind-reading?'

'I'm going to project my memories onto the screen. That way you'll be able to see what's been going on round here. I'm connecting you up as a neutral counterbalance to ensure everything that appears is true. That means you'll be able to trust the evidence of your own eyes. Normally, I wouldn't be able to use this device. My intellect would overload it instantly. However, as I have an idiot handy –'

He had a feeling she meant him.

'– I can use your mental functions as a handbrake to damp down the effects of mine.'

'Then will it kill me?' he asked feebly.

She just rolled her eyes.

Rama returned to the console, again fiddling with dials. Danny strained to see.

The console whined, a low throb almost too deep to be heard but then rising beyond human audibility. The screen crackled, settling down before replaying Teena Rama's memories . . .

. . . Two weeks after the completion of her house, Teena Rama, new to Wheatley and still delighted by its second-hand possibilities, backheeled the front door shut. She'd returned, empty-handed but content, from a day at the tip. She slipped off her camouflage jacket. 'Hello, Doors. I'm home.'

No reply.

She watched the camera suspended from the ceiling. Its light was out.

'Doors?'

Still no reply.

Hanging her coat on the stand by the door, she headed for the lounge.

'Doors? You okay?' Teena strode in, stopping at the room's centre.

A magazine lay open on the coffee table. She suspected pornography, having recently half-completed the task of teaching him human anatomy.

From his ceiling camera, a narrow tractor beam scrutinized the magazine, lazily turning pages. 'Oh. Miss Rama. I was just reading.'

'Reading what?'

'A vigorous narrative incorporating recurring icono-graphic themes to provoke a Nietzschean allusion to . . .'

Knuckles on hips, eyelids slowly lowering, she interrupted.

'You mean a comic?'

He turned another page. '*The Hormonal Fifty*, to be precise.'

'Doors, did I spend thirty-five minutes last Saturday programming your culture chip just so you could use it for comic book appreciation?'

'Yes, Miss Rama.'

'No, Doors; I did not.'

'Oh.'

'Have you not considered Joyce, Conrad, Dostoevsky? I have a library crammed with the world's most challenging books – many authored by me.'

'Yes, Miss Rama, I've done all those. And most enjoyable they were – even yours. But this is much better. Larry Hormonal, enigmatic leader of the Hormonal Fifty, has finally completed his Xeta Gun.'

An eyebrow arched.

Doors continued. 'He's built it to punch a hole through to Anti-Space, a strange and bizarre world where no one has super powers. The Hormonal Fifty's other members can't believe such a place exists but he insists his fiancée – Vanishing Woman, her powers confound friend and foe alike – may be there. Vanishing Woman hasn't been seen since Issue 2's foiling of Captain Bladderwrack's seaweed exploits. The Fifty are having a proper confusing time of it.'

'You mean it's a world like this one?'

'That's right, Miss Rama.' He read on, too engrossed to grasp her implication.

'*Exactly* like this one.' Her foot tapped impatiently, waiting for his electronic thought processes to catch up with hers.

'That's right, Miss Rama (chortle).'

'I mean *exactly* like this one.'

'Why, Miss Rama, you're correct. It's precisely like this world. But how?'

She scooped comic from table and greedily scrutinized its gaudy pages. 'Doors, you may just have given me an idea.'

('Okay, now eat your pie, Gary.'

'No.'

'Do it,' she insisted.

'No.'

'Why not?'

'It might be poisoned,' he said.

'There's nothing wrong with this pie. I made it myself.'

'That's some recommendation.'

'And what's that supposed to mean?'

'Guess.'

'Just eat it, Gary.'

'Herbolt Myson wouldn't.'

'You are not Herbolt Myson.'

'I only have your word for that.'

'You want me to prove it's safe?' she said.

'Now what're you doing?'

'Eating it. I'll prove this thing's harmless, if it's the last thing I ever do. For God's sake, why does no one ever trust me?'

'I can't imagine.'

Meanwhile the image on the screen moved on . . .)

. . . Two weeks after Doors' comic book discovery.

'More light please, Doors.'

The anglepoise brightened.

On a specially installed bar stool, Teena Rama sat at a worktop, early hours, fixing the circuitry of an atomic battery made from a drinks can found outside a takeaway. Her screwdriver probed its innards, tightening the final screws. Behind her hung the dark bulk of the near complete Xeta Gun. Two weeks' work, the longest she'd spent on anything, but it would be her crowning achievement, until her time machine.

Larry Hormonal had built a time machine, in order to meet his past self, in order to instruct it on building a time machine, in order to instruct his future self on building a time machine, in order to instruct his present self on building a time machine.

It had culminated in him travelling forward in time, to accidentally kill his grandfather. Or was it backward in time, to kill his grandson? Or was it sideways in time, to kill himself? Or was it Man's primitive ancestor he'd killed? It had been hard to tell; his grandfather having been Reptilius, the puny dinosaur man; his grandson having been Lizardus, the reptile weakling.

Paradox or pseudo-science? Only Larry Hormonal knew, and he was saying nothing to the chickens who now ruled his world.

It was a mistake Teena Rama would not be repeating with her own time machine.

'But, Miss Rama,' Doors asked. 'How can this possibly work? Surely the Hormonal Fifty are purely fictional.'

She twisted tight the penultimate screw. 'Space is infinite, right?'

'So you taught me, though I must confess to having drifted off somewhat towards the end of your last attempt to explain that.'

'Time is infinite,' she said.

'Yes.'

'Therefore possibilities are infinite. Give an infinite number of restaurant lobsters infinite time and space, they'll reproduce the works of Shakespeare. In fact they'd produce a greater canon than any single writer could ever manage, churning out masterpiece after masterpiece, flooding the market, devaluing all plays, making all

211

playwrights redundant, and – with any luck – destroying the theatrical profession.'

'But, Miss Rama, that hasn't happened.'

'What's your point, Doors?'

'Doesn't that suggest there can be neither infinite lobsters, space nor time?'

'Do you think you're cleverer than me, Doors?'

'No, Miss Rama.'

'Then why are you arguing?'

'I'm sorry, Miss Rama. You are of course correct.'

And she made yet another mental note to adjust his faulty programming.

She resumed screw tightening. 'Now. If there's endless time, space and possibilities, there must be an infinite number of worlds, including one inhabited by the Hormonal Fifty. In fact there must be an infinite number of worlds inhabited by them, just as infinite numbers of worlds contain versions of us. Ergo, there must be a world in which Larry Hormonal's Xeta Gun brought him to this one.'

'Carry on, Miss Rama.'

'I believe Dick Dicksley, the strip's creator – far from being a sad geek with a tree fixation, as popular belief would have it – in fact met these people upon their visit to our dimension. He then recorded subsequent events in his comics, much as Mary Shelley fictionalized real events in *Frankenstein*.'

'And,' realized Doors growing excited, 'by copying Dicksley's "imaginary" device, you can punch a hole through to that other world and bring Larry Hormonal to this one.'

'Well done, Doors.'

'And he can show you how to build a time machine, saving you much time and effort.'

'Precisely.'

'Why, that's brilliant, Miss Rama.'

212

'Well,' she shrugged coyly, 'I don't like to blow my own trumpet but . . .'

'But wouldn't such a device be unbelievably dangerous?'

'No more so than nuclear fusion.'

And, the night after that . . .

'Okay, Doors, prepare to fire up the Xeta Gun.' Teena flicked three switches on the wall.

'No, Miss Rama.'

'What do you mean, "No, Miss Rama"?'

'It's too dangerous.'

'It's not in the least bit dangerous. Now start it up.'

'No, Miss Rama.'

'Start it up. Now,' she demanded.

'No.'

'I mean it, Doors.'

'And I mean it too, Miss Rama.'

'Oh, for Heaven's sake.'

'Miss Rama, I really must pro . . .' His voice ran down like a suddenly unplugged record player, and ground to a halt on the last letter of the last syllable.

She tossed aside the fuse she'd yanked from his control panel. Computers, who needed them? Not Einstein. Not Newton. And what were their intellects compared to hers?

Kneeling, she reached beneath the control desk and pulled out a long, steel box with a handle on top; her tool kit. She threw back the lid, rattled around inside, and retrieved the perfect thing to put Doors in his place.

A crowbar.

She flipped the lid shut. Standing, she kicked the tool box back under the console then headed for the wall.

She inserted the crowbar's end into a vertical slot and, with a grunt, broke open a hatch, letting its cover hit the floor with a clang.

She'd revealed a secret lever embedded in the wall.
She took a firm hold.
And Teena Rama pulled her Xeta Gun's manual control . . .

forty-three

Cassette tape, Annette decided watching ceiling cables. That was what *she'd* use, cassette tape from no longer wanted Cure albums. In excessive quantities it would be more practical than rope – being thinner and more flexible. Plus, it would dig more deeply into flesh and thus be more use for torture sessions. Thick rope really didn't hurt at all.

Maybe she'd point that out upon Fifi's return.

The pedicurist reappeared in the doorway, glinting secateurs in hand, grunting, straining and *unhf unhf unhfing* her way through the web of ropes.

Cassette tape, definitely.

Regaining her composure after the struggle, Fifi straightened her crimson dress and, breathing heavily, stood by her customer. The dress again dropped from one shoulder. She ignored it, better things to do. A bloodless face framed by Bride of Frankenstein hair smiled down as she stroked Annette's head. Beneath her pantomime villain makeup, Madam Fifi was in her early twenties. 'Nothing to be alarmed about, my pretty. I'm just going to cut your toes off.'

She held a lop of Annette's black, newly washed hair and, snip, cut it off to test her shears' sharpness. She casually discarded the lop. 'Now, lie still. And when I'm finished you won't recognize your feet.'

'You're completely insane, aren't you?' Annette's arms, hands and feet were growing numb from their bonds.

'Better to be insane than inane, I always say. Fortunately, you're in no position to do a thing about it, Annette Helstrang of 353, Plescent Street.'

Annette watched her quizzically.

'Oh yes, I know all about you, Annette Helstrang of 353, Plescent Street; who you are, where you live, your little quirks, your shoe size – four. All these years I've coveted your toes over all others, save those of Dr Tinashta Ramalalanyrina of 23, Moldern Crescent. And she is beyond my influence, having never answered the direct mail I send to houses chosen from all others on her street.'

'Then you . . . ?'

'Yes! I send that stuff, every single mailing. I've been sending it for years, to lure the gullible to my lair.'

Annette frowned. 'Has anyone ever responded to those things?'

'Not one person. But that matters not, Miss Helstrang of 353, Plescent Street. Fate's computer has selected you as my latest customer. Soon, your Divine Pinkies will join God's Army of Toes, where they shall sit on the frontmost shelf, latest and proudest of my recruits, a monument to the Lord's glory. Then Dr Ramalalanyrina's toes shall join them, for she is a slightly tall girl and will thus blunder blindly into my next trap where she will be held like a fly while I slice her toes off. For surely feet are our Lord's finest creation. Isn't that so, my little dears?' She stroked them, red-painted lips making kissy gestures. But the toes

216

were no more talkative than they had been for Gavin the fetishist.

The secateurs gripped Annette's right, little toe. Cold blades pressed against the line drawn earlier. She tried moving her foot but the tangle of ropes prevented her. Now she understood the preference for rope over cassette tape.

And Madam Fifi began to squeeze . . .

forty-four

The screen of Teena Rama's mind machine now showed the night when her Xeta Gun flung its searing energies at the comic which lay open beneath it. Like dancing trees, mini lightning fingers ran up and down its length, colliding with each other, forming new patterns. In all creation nothing was as awesome as Teena Rama's Xeta Gun. And it flung those energies in pulsing, pounding waves that struck like the footfalls of God. They battered the comic until it seemed nothing could survive. But Teena Rama knew two things would survive.

Finally drained, the gun went dead, its roar running down to a steady hum. The lightning fingers settled into the occasional phzz, then zzk, then nothing.

Billowing sulphurous smoke filled the room's centre.

The operation had lasted just three seconds but it had seemed a century, as she'd waited, heart pumping, on the starting line of greatness.

She pushed the lever to OFF, removed her protective goggles, tossed them aside, then switched on the air extractor.

As the smoke cleared, Tinashta K. Rama straightened her grey pinstripe skirt bought for the occasion. She reached up inside her silk Chinese-print shirt bought for the occasion, and attached a second cross to her brand new nipple ring. What the hell; she attached a third cross – and a fourth. If any occasion deserved four crosses this did.

She tucked in and straightened the shirt.

She straightened the grey double-breasted pinstripe jacket bought especially. She straightened a new pair of stockings, slipped her best shoes on, tidied her hair, checked her makeup and, bubbling with pride, prepared to welcome the great Larry Hormonal to her world.

The last of the smoke drifted away.

A man coughed politely into the side of his hand. He stood beneath the Xeta Gun, small and bald, in round metal-framed spectacles. He wore a slightly too-tight brown suit and held a briefcase.

And Teena Rama demanded, 'Who the hell are you?'

'Good evening,' said the small man. 'I'm an accountant.'

'An accountant?' She strode toward him, climbing over the low safety rail and into the gun's circle of operation. 'If I'd wanted an accountant, I'd have built a telephone! How dare you waste my Xeta Gun's time?'

He stepped forward, saying with cartoon meekness, 'I'm very sorry, Miss . . . ?'

'Out of my way!' Not breaking stride, she shoved him aside, snatching up the comic. She paced in ever tighter circles, rooting through page after page after page, trying to discover what had gone wrong. Where was Larry Hormonal?

'Do you work here, Miss . . . ?'

Her gaze scurried over comic book panel after comic book panel. 'Work here?' She yanked open another page, almost tearing it from its staples. 'I must be the resident slave; I seem to be the *only* thing round here that works.'

'Oh dear,' he said. 'I seem to be . . .'

Ignoring the idiot, she read on. By page twelve the Hormonal Fifty were among abandoned dockland warehouses. It was their standard practice to defeat villains by ganging up on them. It might not have been brave but it worked. But now, they looked mystified.

'What happened to the accountant?' Brawling Varney sat on his backside and scratched his head. 'One moment he's stood here, ugly as day, just asking to be bashed, the next he's gone.'

'That smell of sulphur.' Larry Hormonal's eagle eyes scanned the scene, his mighty intellect working overtime. 'It can only mean one thing.'

'What?'

'Someone somewhere's used a Xeta Gun on him.'

'But, Larry,' asked Birchie the tree lad, 'who, besides you, has the brains to make a whizz-bang-gosh-wow machine like that?'

'I wish I knew, Birchie. But whoever it is, I just hope they realize that the Xeta Gun, when combined with obstructive staff/customer relations, will turn Arnold Meekly into a . . .'

Teena turned the page. Frowning, she read out the one word contained within the one speech balloon; '. . . *Monster*?'

And she glanced to where she'd pushed the accountant when she'd told him she worked here.

She saw two huge feet – each with just two, clawed toes.

She saw two huge, furry legs.

And her gaze slowly climbed the awesome, fluffy bulk of the creature that had once been Arnold Meekly.

The monster glared down at Teena Rama, breathing in menacing grunts, clearly not taking her treatment of its alter ego lightly.

Before it could react, she grabbed its giant hand, ordering, in the tones of an old-style hospital matron who's discovered a roaming patient, 'Right, come along. This way.'

'Huh?' it said cavernously.

'Yes, that's it. I don't have all day.' And she tugged it toward the elevator.

The prod of a button summoned the lift.

Still holding his hand, she waited, her impatient foot tapping a floor tile as she watched an arrow above the door count down, from sixty to eight.

The door opened with a ping.

'In here with you.' Straight-armed, two-handed, she pushed the confused monster backwards into the lift, then leaned inside, pressed the BASEMENT button, and stepped back out.

As the door rumbled shut on him, she said, 'Goodbye.'

'So, what went wrong?' asked Danny watching from his trolley.

Teena licked the final pie crumbs from her fingers, then removed her headphones, unplugging them from the panel. The screen went blank. 'As usual I was let down by other people's failings, not having beforehand read beyond the comic's first two pages. I never complete books, invariably predicting the outcome.'

'But . . .'

'Unfortunately, being a genius, I'd failed to recognize the sheer stupidity of comic book plotting. Hence, rather than the Hormonal Fifty retiring to Jupiter to discuss gender issues raised by their fight with Android Andy – as I'd expected – by page five they were about to commence a slugfest with Arnold Meekly, the Human

Tube Line. It was the estimable Tube Line who arrived in my lab.'

'Then that was why you wanted to buy all his comics,' said Danny. 'To find out everything you could about him.'

'And discover the best way of dealing with him,' she completed the explanation on his behalf. 'You see, thanks to Doors, I Teena Rama – the world's greatest intellect – am now the world's leading authority on the world's stupidest comic book. Thank you for robbing me of all dignity, Doors.'

'I'm sorry, Miss Rama.'

'So you should be.' And she clomped down the ramp toward Danny.

She removed his headphones, wrapping their flex neatly round and round her forearm then slipping her arm free. 'The lift took Meekly into the caverns which surround this chamber, trapping him there while I re-designed the Xeta Gun to return him to his own world. That took two weeks. But when I searched the tunnels, I found no sign of him. Those passageways stretch for hundreds of miles in all directions. It could've taken years to find him. However, bafflingly, Meekly took just six months to find his way into your room.'

'And you couldn't tell me any of this at the time?' said Danny, annoyed.

'As your psychiatrist, I knew your mind is too small for such shocks. Fearing it might implode after your bedroom encounter with Meekly, I drugged your meals to help you forget him.'

'And it never occurred to you to consult me?'

'A good psychiatrist never consults her patients. But, as several weeks have passed since the incident, and you've discovered the truth, I feel I should now restore your memory.'

'But I might not have wanted to be drugged in the first place. I might have wanted to tell people.'

'I think my medical qualifications make me a better judge of that than you, Gary.'

'No they don't,' he asserted outraged. 'And my name's not Gary, it's Danny; D-A-N-N-Y. You know, like C-O-C-K-U-P, only spelt different.'

'Your name's Gary.'

'No, it's not.'

'Your name's Gary.'

'I should know,' he said.

'On the contrary, forgetting one's name is a common problem among those who've met monsters. I have several degrees in the subject . . .'

'There's a surprise.'

'. . . being one of the world's leading authorities. I'm going to publish a paper on you. You should be flattered.'

'I'm not.'

'Most would be.'

'No one would be. And my name is Danny.'

'Not according to my files.'

'And who wrote those files?'

'I did. That's how I know they can't be wrong.'

'Like you weren't wrong about the Hormonal Fifty's picnic to Jupiter?'

'It was the writer Dick Dicksley who got it wrong. That's Dick as in G-A-R-Y, just spelt differently.'

Danny narrowed his eyes at her. 'You think you're so clever.'

'I am clever. Now stop arguing, while I fetch you another pie.' On her way to the lift, she deposited his head-phones on the panel. The door swished open, ready for her.

Danny called after her as she entered the lift, his head raised as far as the constraints would allow. He taunted

223

bitterly, 'Meat and potato pies, that's the great scientist's answer to everything is it?'

'That's right, Gary.'

And, clunk, the lift door closed.

forty-five

'Drop the shears, lady. Back away from the broad.'

Fifi raised an eyebrow, her fatal squeeze halted before it had begun, by the threat from behind. Annette grinned widely. Good old Ribbons. He'd caught Fifi totally unawares – as planned.

'Excuse me?' The pedicurist asked, still leaning over Annette, secateurs still pressed against her toe.

'You may not know it,' said Ribbons in the style of Humphrey Bogart, 'but this thing sticking in your back's a .45 magic wand, standard issue Witchcraft Police. It can drop a Warlock at half a mile.'

'That's illegal without a licence,' she complained.

'I have a licence,' he retorted. 'And if you think you can take a hit from this range, and walk away, you're wrong – dead wrong. Now drop the shears, or you're frog.'

forty-six

'There you go.' On her return, Teena sat smiling on the trolley's left edge, feeding Danny his new pie. She insisted he eat every last crumb.

All done, she frisbied the paper plate across the lab. As intended, it slapped into the wall, flipped twice then landed neatly on the mind-machine panel.

Still tied down, Danny made himself swallow the last bitter horribleness, no longer even deriving pleasure from its reminder of her incompetence. Her cooking had got worse. He couldn't believe it, suspecting a deliberate plot to make him suffer.

'So, how do you feel?' she asked.

He thought about it. 'I don't know.'

She gazed at the ceiling, impatient foot tapping trolley leg.

'No. Hold on.' He latched onto something nagging at the back of his mind. It was like someone trying to pull a door marked PUSH.

Danny Yates' lost memories became a drunken group

of friends planning a surprise homecoming party, hiding behind the door, lacking the patience to wait. Pushing and jostling, they whispered too loudly, 'Shh. Shh. Here he comes,' then tumbled through the door, landing in a heap at his feet.

Shouting, 'Surprise!' they blew party poppers, burst balloons and enjoyed their silliness too much to even care about him anymore.

'I remember,' he enthused. 'I remember everything.'

'Everything?' she asked.

'Everything.' He excitedly picked each memory up from his mind's floor, dusting it down, making the effort to recall its name; 'Spooky Houses, Thieving Flatmates, Monsters, Rats, Rabbits, A Man Called Osmosis, Fake Latino Black Marketeers [the fake latino black marketeer winked at him then ducked behind a fire extinguisher], Homelessness, Unemployment, Nuns, A Rhyme of Long Gone Hats.' He shuddered. 'My God, it's a nightmare.'

'Now perhaps we can concentrate on finding Arnold Meekly?' observed Teena. 'What puzzles me is how he found his way out of the caves, into the lift, into the house then up into your room. No one as stupid as him should have managed that.'

They considered the issue for a moment but came up blank.

'Do you have a monster detection machine?' asked Danny.

She looked clueless.

'A machine for detecting monsters,' he said.

She looked clueless.

'There are monsters,' he explained, thinking it couldn't be as half-baked an idea as her expression was suggesting, 'and it detects them.'

'Based on what principle?' She was still looking at him like that.

'On the monster detection principle,' he insisted, withering.

'You've never had a scientific paper published, have you, Gary?'

'Not lately,' he acknowledged defensively. 'I've been busy.'

She seemed amused for some reason. 'There's no such thing as a monster detection machine, and never will be, monsters being notoriously undetectable. We'll need more mundane methods. I suggest you seek him on the streets while I stay here monitoring news and police broadcasts.'

'Why don't I get to stay at home?' he asked.

'And do you know how to build a Fighting Android?' she asked.

'I know not to chase after monsters.'

'I can assure you there's no danger.'

He looked at her as if to say.

'No, really,' she insisted. 'Have you heard anything, in the last three weeks, about anyone encountering a monster in Wheatley?'

'Maybe not.'

'Don't you think you would if they had?'

'Perhaps.' He looked at her sideways, yet to catch her thread.

'Clearly, the good accountant has reverted to human form. In that guise he's quite harmless, and may even be trying to return here, filled with remorse over the damage done to my plans. Take it from me, once you've found him he'll be no trouble to you – just so long as you keep him away from bad town-planning, overly drawn out journeys and offensive workers. Now, in a town like this, how difficult can that be?'

Outside the Seaman's Mission, Arnold Meekly – desperate to reach Dr Rama before again changing – slammed the cab door. Sliding along the seat, he leaned toward the perspex partition between him and the driver. One of her arms rested on her seat-back, the other on the wheel. She idled the engine, meter running, more interested in the empty road than him.

He said, '23, Moldern Crescent, please; the Rama residence. And hurry.'

She slid open the partition, chewing gum. 'No way. We'll be taking the scenic route; past every tower block in town. I always chuck my guts up laughing at those monstrosities. You got a problem with that, talk to my colleague.'

Beside her, a dreadful giant ant stared at him, mandibles opening and closing in a style that was highly threatening. 'Fear, mammal, fear, for I am Destructor, and soon you shall call me "Master".'

The driver watched Arnold in her rear-view mirror. And she asked, 'Do you know you're getting bigger?'

forty-seven

Fifi was always going to be frog. It was the deal Annette struck whenever she wanted her familiar's assistance. If the pedicurist cut off the girl's toes, she'd become permanent frog. If she didn't, she'd just be weekend frog – the rest of the week, allowed to be her normal self and reflect on the consequences of her unpleasantness.

It may have struck a casual observer as vindictive, but nasty people deserved nasty treatment. And it might just teach her a lesson in customer relations.

The dentist, the doctor, the makeup artist, the plumber, a college principal, the petrol pump attendant, the insurance salesman, the librarian – and all the others who'd tried to steal her toes – all were now reformed, socially useful characters, thanks to those tactics.

Madam Fifi did not know all.

Now it was up to the pedicurist; weekend or permanent?

Reluctantly, Fifi dropped the secateurs to the floor.

And Annette breathed a sigh of relief.

Keeping both eyes on Fifi, the long magic wand in his mouth still pressed against her back, Ribbons' paw kicked away the shears. They slid ten feet across bare wood before stopping against the pink skirting board.

'You won't get away with this.' Fifi raised her hands in surrender. 'I have lawyers, big lawyers, lawyers so big they can barely get through the door, big doors, doors so big they're too big for their buildings; buildings too big for small cats like you.'

Ribbons was unimpressed. 'Stow it, lady. Or I might just get nervous and pull the trigger.' And he ordered, 'Now, you're gonna give this little lady the zingiest pedicure anyone ever saw.'

forty-eight

Trolley hit floor with a crash, lying on its side, the rattled Danny feeling undignified, straps holding him in place. Did these things happen to other people? He couldn't believe they did.

Behind him, Teena was having difficulty unbuckling even his ankle, having engaged its binding in a tug of war. Unable to see her, he imagined her – foot on trolley, leaning back, heaving at the strap, purple-faced, as though trying to uproot the world's biggest pumpkin.

The world's biggest pumpkin just about summed him up for having ever moved into this madhouse.

She was getting nowhere. 'Unph. Perhaps I was a trifle overzealous applying your tethers – unph. Still, better safe than sorry.'

Her tugging jostled the trolley across polished tiles, jolting Danny's eyeballs in their sockets, making him see two mind machines, two Xeta Guns, two lift doors, two everythings. 'Just get some shears,' he demanded.

'Ah.' She stopped tugging, panting. Danny's vision began to return to normal.

'"Ah," what?' He already regretted asking.

'In order to guarantee you wouldn't escape and hurt yourself, I used Obdurite-laced leather.'

'Obdurite?'

'A metal compound of my own design.'

'Meaning?'

'Meaning I haven't yet invented anything that can cut through it.'

'And how long will it take to invent something that *can* cut through it?'

'Twenty-three years.'

'Jesus, Teena!'

The trolley rattled. She'd claimed a seat on its topmost edge. He was hoping she'd fall off and injure herself. 'There was a fifty-fifty chance you'd regain consciousness in a disturbed state,' she claimed. 'The strength, not to mention insane cunning, of the disturbed individual is notorious. They may have ten times the strength of a normal person.'

'Is that why you can punch so hard?'

'This is no time for sarcasm.'

'Then what is it time for?'

'Lateral thinking. I can't break the straps. I can't smash this trolley, it also being made of Obdurite. My Man Who Does has a way with straps but is overseas on a government mission. No one knows where he is, or when he'll be back, least of all himself.'

'Government mission?' he asked.

'Uh-huh.'

'Why would a cleaning man be on a government mission?'

'There's all sorts of messes need clearing up in this world, Gary.' She returned to the matter at hand; 'I can't melt this trolley. I can't freeze then shatter it. I'm not yet ready to space warp things. But I hold several doctorates in insane strength.'

'Surprise me, why don't you?'

'No ordinary lunatic could snap these bonds. It'd take an Edward Hyde type figure, the twisted product of a pharmacological transformation gone hideously wrong. If I baked you a Mr Hyde pie – of course there'd be no cure but . . .'

'Teena?'

'Yeah?'

'Keep tugging.'

'You're right.' Clatter. She stood. 'Anything I can fasten, I can unfasten. Besides, how could the world's finest mind be outfoxed by a few bits of metal?'

'I'll spend my dying day on this trolley, won't I?'

'Don't be silly.' She tugged. 'Won't be long.' Clatter, gut-busting strain, rattle, rattle, clatter, kick, punch.

'For Christ's sake!' Crash, she gave the trolley one final, frustrated kick, nearly putting Danny's back out in the process. 'What am I doing?' she demanded neurotically. 'I can't free you. I can't help you. I can't help anyone. I'm only a girl. I'm not even a woman, for Christ's sake.' Pat pat pat, she paced irritably, behind him.

'Teena?'

'What?'

'You okay?'

'Hunky dory.' She didn't sound hunky dory.

'That pie you ate?'

'What about it?'

'It's not affecting you in some way?'

'And why should it do that?' She paced on. 'It wasn't my enemy was it?'

'But I've been thinking. Unlike me, you never had amnesia. So, if it couldn't restore your memory, what would it do?'

'How should I know?'

'Because you're a genius.'

'Don't patronize me,' she fumed. 'I was always the thick one. You know that. I know that. Everyone knows that. You all laugh at me behind my back. It was always my sister who got all the praise – Little Akira. Little Akira. "We have a new addition to the family, Tinashta. Be nice to little Akira, Tinashta. And never forget the sun shines out of her perfectly appointed backside." God how I wish I'd tested the fucking pies on her instead of on some rabbits, tied her to that table and . . .'

'Trolley,' he corrected her.

'Big difference! I wish I'd tied her to that trolley and rammed those pies down her know-it-all throat, one by one by one, till she was stuffed so full and so fat no one'd look at her. I love bunnies. Bunnies don't steal the only boyfriend you ever had who wasn't scared of you, leaving you with a drink problem that needs eighteen months' therapy to sort out. I need a fag. I need a spliff. Get me a gin. Oh God, my bunnies, my bunnies, what have I done to you, my bunnies?' Clumpf.

'Teena?'

No reply.

'Teena?'

'Doors?' Danny wriggled desperately like a salmon fighting the flow, trying to manoeuvre the trolley round to face Teena. It rattled and juddered, going nowhere.

After regaining his breath, he tried again, only managing to overturn the thing completely. It crashed down onto him, knocked the wind from him, and slid down the slope. It halted at the ramp's base, pinning him to the floor, further from Teena than ever.

'You wanted something, Mr Daniel?'

'What's wrong with Teena?' He panted, trying to move but failing.

Somewhere behind him, Doors' probe light clicked on, hummed for moments that stretched to breaking point, then clicked off.

Silence.

The silence between stepping off the Grand Canyon and hitting the ground below.

'Doors?' Danny saw only the stippling of the nearest floor tiles. Perspiration trickled down one side of his face, his heart thumping.

'Oh dear,' said Doors.

'What is it?' asked Danny.

'I'm afraid Miss Rama's dead.'

forty-nine

'Aw.' Lucy felt like a large foot had dropped from the sky and squashed her life.

'Is something concerning you, Lucille?'

Stood in the dark, in the middle of the road, freezing from the night air, half wanting to cry, half wanting to lash out, she glared at the big idiot and demanded, 'Are you for real?'

Stood at the roadside, antennae waving, Destructor felt at his armoured chest. He looked across at her. 'I believe I am real, Lucille.'

Grumbling curses, she returned her attention to the wreckage surrounding her on all sides. She did a complete turn to take in its full extent. Once, it had been a cab, her very own cab that no one else in the world had had one quite like. Now it was wreckage spread thinly and evenly across the road, the sort of wreckage any loser could have if they saved up long enough.

And the creature that had done the damage was further up that road, stomping off into the distance, casual swipes of its backhand demolishing telephone poles. She considered running after it and thumping its head. No one got away with wrecking Lucy Jane Smith's cab, not drunks, not criminals, and certainly not monsters that didn't even look like proper monsters. She decided against direct action as a final pole creaked like a falling giraffe and thrashed to the ground. Its wires snapped and pinged like overwrought banjos.

And the monster departed, muttering some gravel-voiced rubbish about a, 'Big gun,' and about finding a, 'Pretty girl. Hurh hurh hurh.'

She returned her attention to Destructor, an exhaust pipe in her hand, tempted to run across and crown him one with it. 'How could you not know whether there's something wrong?' she asked. 'Look at it, for God's sake.' She threw exhaust pipe at tarmac. 'You think my car's supposed to look like this?'

'I do not know, Lucille. I am a stranger to your world's delightful customs.'

'And where were you when he was smashing the thing up?' she demanded. 'All that bragging about how unstoppable you are and, "Tremble, Human," this and, "Tremble, Human," that. The moment I need you to slap some overgrown duster, you just sit there watching.'

He folded his arms across his chest, head tilted back haughtily. 'I have never before been in this thing females call a taxi. I thought perhaps this was how its days were meant to end. In my world, the unprovoked destruction of inanimate objects is quite acceptable, often admirable, though the harming of the animate is considered bad manners and to be avoided unless dramatically valid.'

'Then how are you planning on conquering the Earth?' she challenged.

'I have not yet decided. But when I do,' his eyes narrowed to smouldering, yellow slits as he schemed.

'Pillock.'

'Why, thank you, Lucille.'

'Just look at this mess.' Half-hearted, she kicked debris away from her. It rolled, clattered and clink clink clinked down the camber before stopping near Destructor's feet. She asked, 'So how am I supposed to make a living now?'

'Do not despair, Lucille. Perhaps you may yet reassemble its many parts, creating a new multi-splendoured carriage even more suited to your needs than before.'

Pulling breeze-blown hair away from her face, tucking it behind one ear, she looked again at the bits of car surrounding her. Apart from the exhaust, none was more than a centimetre square. Hoping against hope, she said, 'You reckon?'

fifty

The Horrible Mr Meekly's destination stood before him in darkness, the big stupid white house that ran the length of a street and looked like it was trying to eat its neighbours. He hated the house. He would smash the house.

Now he strode towards it, footsteps thooming, breathing in deep grunts that grew more delirious with each step taken.

Soon he would reach the pretty girl who lived within.

And he would smash anyone who tried to stop him taking her.

'Dead?' demanded Danny. 'What do you mean, "Miss Rama's dead"?'

'Dead,' said Doors.

'She couldn't just be pretending?'

'Why would she pretend to be dead?'

'She's never been honest before.'

'I can assure you she's quite lifeless. I could throw something at her – perhaps a lamp or chair – to see if she moves, but it would serve no purpose. I'm afraid you've proper done for her.'

'Me?'

'It was your refusal to eat her pies that led to her downfall.'

Face-down beneath his trolley, Danny Yates felt sick. This was the second time in four weeks he'd been told he'd killed Teena Rama, only, this time it was no joke played by a malicious flatmate. Guilt, self-loathing, fear, remorse, anger and panic queued up in tilted gangster hats, taking turns to kick him in the guts; 'Think you can mess with us?' Kick. 'Think you can get away from us?' Kick. 'You don't know shit.' Kick. 'Wherever you go, wherever you try to hide, we'll find you.' Kick. 'We're with you for the rest of your days.'

'Can't you do anything for her?' he pleaded with Doors. 'You're supposed to be a red-hot supercomputer.'

'In fact I'm meant to be a simple mechanism for opening and closing doors. Miss Rama was insistent on that, resorting to screwdriver practices whenever I overstepped my duties. She'd even scold me sometimes for performing my designated function. Do you want to know the truth, Mr Daniel? I'm glad she's dead. Perhaps a break from life may do her some good, teaching her humility and greater tolerance of others' limitations.'

'You do understand the concept of death, Doors?'

'My mistress ensured I was fully cognizant with the term.'

'But not its consequences?'

'What consequences?'

'Doors, your mistress won't be coming back.'

'Does that mean she won't be needing her sandwiches packed tonight?'

'She won't be needing them packed ever.'

'Never?'

'Never.'

'Oh.' Then after a pause, in a small voice, 'I see.'

Another pause followed.

Then Doors said, 'I'll pack them anyway. I wouldn't want her returning, and having to go hungry because of my negligence. She really does have rather an appetite, for such a narrow-waisted thing.'

Danny stared at what he could see of the wall, picking ideas up, discarding ideas, trying to project and mentally nail them to it, as though trapping them would somehow make them good ideas.

How long did she have? In hospital dramas it was always four minutes before revival was impossible. Frustrated, he banged his head against the back of his trolley. Why did crazy people like Teena get all the ideas, and never sensible people like him?

He stared harder and harder at the wall, imagining what *she'd* have done if it had been him who'd died. She'd have knocked together some outrageous device in two minutes flat, spent one minute writing a paper on it and then forty-five seconds smiling, pleased with herself. Then, at the last possible moment, she'd have thrown a lever and had him running around better than ever.

Of course.

That was it.

'Inventions!' he declared.

'Inventions?' asked Doors.

'Teena had an invention for every occasion. She must've had one that'd do the trick. Where did she store them all?'

'I'm afraid Miss Rama never tackled the task of resurrecting the dead, saying such practices were in poor taste, what with high unemployment and the housing crisis. And she regarded death as a self-indulgence by the lazy. Frankly, I believe she felt it would never happen to her, which may explain her failure to programme me with all relevant information.'

'But . . .'

'Besides, Miss Rama simply discarded inventions like old socks. Like the hunter – though she disapproved of blood sports – it was the thrill of the chase which intrigued her. Once an idea was stuffed and mounted to her satisfaction, she lost all interest in it.'

Bitter tears welled in Danny's eyes. He hated the straps. He hated himself. He hated Teena for dying and landing him in this mess. And he hated himself for hating Teena. Finally, he resigned himself to lying there till someone found him and placed him on trial for her murder. He'd be acquitted. No court would convict him. But he'd already found himself guilty.

Creak.

?

Step step step.

Something had walked into his brain; a concept that wouldn't leave but wouldn't reveal itself. It moved through his mind's corridors with a steady tread, in no hurry but knowing precisely where it was headed. It was after something, something that was nothing, just a piece of grit lodged in his head's deepest vaults.

But all the while, the grit was becoming something better.

And when, after trying endless locked doors, the walking thing found the room where the grit thing was, and opened the door, the grit thing sat before the walking thing, in its own open oyster – dazzling in its pearly, rounded beauty – an idea as perfect as anyone had ever had.

'Doors?'

'Yes, Mr Daniel?'

243

'Start up the Xeta Gun.'

'The Xeta Gun? But surely this isn't the time for half-cocked experiments?'

'Just do it. And reverse its settings.'

'Why, Mr Daniel.' Doors seemed much cheered. 'You sound just like Miss Rama.'

'So, do what I say.'

Click.

Clunk.

'The gun's activated, Mr Daniel. Is there somewhere you'd like me to point its unbelievably dangerous nozzle?'

'Point it at Teena.'

'At Miss Rama? But how would that . . .'

'You want her back, don't you?'

'I suppose so, regardless of her faults.'

'Then do it.'

If Danny could use the gun to send Teena into the comic book world, like she'd brought the Human Tube Line into this one, then she'd live again because everyone knew that characters never stayed dead in comic books. The moment sales demanded it, they were revived by some improbable means; Superman could barely stay dead for more than five minutes. Then, once Teena was revived, Doors could use the gun to return her to this world. It was a stroke of lunatic genius worthy of the girl herself.

The trolley was blocking Danny's view of the opposite wall's clock. 'Doors? How long has she been dead?'

'Three minutes and twenty-three seconds. She really is taking her time over coming back isn't she?'

'How long will it take to power up the gun?'

'Twenty-one seconds, commencing now.'

Just ten seconds to spare, assuming the four minute cut-off point was exact, not just a rough figure or a thing made up to add tension to TV shows. Maybe the safe time was less than four minutes. Maybe there *was* no safe time.

244

He closed his eyes and prayed. His prayers had never been answered before. He was owed a bucketful.

A quiet hum vibrated through the floor and up into him – the Xeta Gun powering up behind him. For all he knew, the resultant blast might blow him into a million pieces. But that didn't matter, as long as she was saved.

Above the hum he could hear the clock. Tick tick tick. Twenty seconds to go. Tick tick tick. Seventeen seconds. Tick tick tick. Fourteen seconds. Thirteen seconds. Twelve seconds. Eleven. Ten. Nine. Eight seconds. Seven seconds. Si . . .

With a crash the lift door flew off. In slow motion it hit the floor, narrowly missing Danny.

And when the dust cleared, he gazed, wide-eyed, in horror.

Completely filling that lift stood the Horrible Mr Meekly.

And with a mad roar, it headed straight for him.

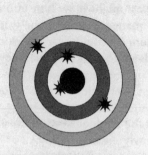

fifty-one

'Osmosis.'

'In the flesh.'

Daybreak. Osmosis answered his door to find General Biggshott-Phaffing, seventy-five, in full uniform. His leather-gloved hands clutched a swagger stick. His handlebar moustache was white. 'Army reporting for duty.' He saluted. He had the voice of a bronchitic seal.

'Where are they?' Peering over the man's shoulder, Osmosis saw just a near empty street. A woman went by, walking her Chihuahua. Was she supposed to be an army? He grabbed Biggshott-Phaffing's lapels and shook him. 'You fool! You've forgotten to bring them! I knew I should never have trusted you!'

'Forgotten 'em? Not at all. Parked 'em out back awaiting orders.' He tapped the side of his hawk nose. 'Wouldn't want Johnny Public spotting 'em.'

'General.' Osmosis released him and set about re-straightening his lapels. 'How could I have doubted you?'

'Things bound to get heated in times of war.' From behind

his monocles, he looked Osmosis up and down, admiring the entrepreneur's new outfit. 'And you're dressed as a general too. How marvellous. Yes. Yes. You're right. We're partners in this, we should both be generals. I, of course, am the better general, having seen off the fuzzie wuzzies in '94.'

'Fuzzie wuzzies?'

'Squirrels. Mildred so enjoyed that holiday. Pity I had to kill her.'

'I'm sorry?'

'Over breakfast. Took her head off with a shovel.' He mimed the swinging action, almost toppling in the process.

'Isn't decapitating one's wife illegal?'

'It is?'

'And premature?'

'Premature?'

'Didn't you try Relate first?'

Biggshott-Phaffing retrieved a cigarette from a trouser pocket. He tapped it on the back of his wooden hand, then lit it. He inhaled deeply, coughed, then, eyes watering from the smoke, said, 'Had to top her.'

'But why risk drawing attention to ourselves before the proper time?'

'Nosferatu.'

'?'

'Signs were unmistakable to an old vampire killer like me.'

'Signs?'

'Mildred was always talking. Poetry, literature; no subject was out of bounds for her.'

'General?'

'Yes?'

'Talking is not a symptom of vampirism.'

'It's not?'

'No.'

'The devil you say. Then what are the symptoms of vampirism?'

'Blood sucking and turning into bats.'

'Blood sucking?' He thought about this. 'No. Can't remember her ever doing that. And what was the other thing?'

'Turning into bats.'

'Cricket or rounders?'

'Flying.'

'Numerous or single?'

'Single.'

'Big or small?'

'Either.'

He again trawled his memory. 'Fair game to her, Mildred never turned into a bat. She knew I wouldn't stand for it.' Then it hit him; 'Good Lord, man. What have you let me do?' Horror seized his face. 'I've ruined a perfectly good shovel.'

'General, you're even madder than everyone says.'

'Barking. I've more certifications than Hannibal Lecture. Want to see 'em?'

'I'd rather not.'

'Brought 'em all with me.' He reached for his uniform's inside breast pocket.

'No!' Osmosis grabbed the arm and wrestled it away from the pocket. The old man was stronger than he looked.

But this was perfect. Now sure he had the man he needed, Osmosis stepped back from the door. He tried not to let his enthusiasm betray the fate he had planned for Biggshott-Phaffing. 'General?'

'Yes?'

'Why don't you come in?'

The general stepped inside and wiped his feet on the doormat. 'Let me just say –'

Osmosis' thugs leapt out from behind the door, put a sack over Biggshott-Phaffing and bound his arms to his sides. They gave him a thorough going over. Each punch produced an agonized 'oof', an 'ow' or an 'argh'. Their vigour was remarkable.

But why were they saying 'oof' and 'ow' and 'aargh' as they hit him? If Osmosis didn't know better he'd think they hadn't spent hours hardening their knuckles on sandpaper as ordered but had spent their time reading that Stanislavsky fellow they were so keen on.

Finally, the thugs gave up and stood back.

'Osmosis, is this part of the plan?' The general stood in his sack, seeming none the worse for his beating. Osmosis resolved never again to hire his thugs from Equity.

Regardless, the general was no threat tied up. And the thugs could always be ... 'rested'. Now Osmosis had Biggshott-Phaffing's hat and his army, he could carry out his master plan. Rule England? The senile old fool. Why should he want to rule England when there were greater prizes in this very town?

He took the general's hat from the floor. As planned it had fallen off during the attack. He placed it atop his bucket. And, with a sharp tug at its peak, he straightened it.

Then went to meet his army.

In a droning plane high above a storm-struck Paris, two rats urgently set about chewing through their safety belts.

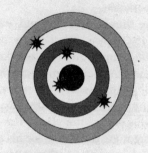

fifty-two

'So. What do you think of my pedicure?' Pleased with herself, Annette sat on a wooden chair by her bed, her legs held out straight for showing-off purposes.

Bare feet resting on carpet, heels together, she opened a gap between each foot then brought them back together. And when they wiggled, her toes tinkled with all the magic of Brian Cant.

'They are fine toes.' The Mysterious Legs still protruded from beneath her bed; their voice slow, deep and swirling as though sent through a long long tube connected to the Other Side.

'And what do *you* make of them, Madam Fifi?' asked Annette.

Fifi ribbited from her perch atop Annette's head then hopped off, landing on the floor. Annette chose to take it as a compliment.

'They are perfect for the task ahead,' said the legs. 'We knew you would not let us down, Annette Helstrang.'

'And that task is . . . ?'

'You shall see when the time is right.'

'And that will be . . . ?'

'You shall know when the time is right.'

'And that will be . . . ?'

'You shall know when . . .'

'For messengers from another Plane, you're not very helpful, are you?' she interrupted.

'Legs never are. That is our charm.'

'No. The charm of legs is that they take you places. You don't take people anywhere, just round and round in circles. Couldn't the Higher Powers have sent me a mouth as a messenger?'

'The Mysterious Mouth has been downsized. It lacked mystery, drama and suspense. For mouths are foolish, prattling things never satisfied with silence.'

'So, what do I do next?'

'Next you do what you always do on Thursdays.'

She frowned. 'You do know what I do on Thursdays?' How could those activities possibly save Wheatley? And what could they save it from?

'We are aware.'

'But then, how . . . ?'

Suddenly the legs disappeared beneath the bed, as though yanked by the hook that drags comedians off stage once their time is up.

She sat a moment, waiting to see if they returned. The only sound was the leaden ticking of the barometer-style clock on the wall.

When they didn't return she got down on her hands and knees and looked beneath the bed. 'Hello? Anyone down here?'

But the legs were gone.

Do what she always did, they'd said. So she got up, went across to the 1920s dressing table facing the window and opened its top drawer. Within was a solitary piece of white chalk. She took it.

She closed the drawer.

And, Fifi hopping behind, Annette Helstrang went down-stairs.

Annette entered her darkened living room.

She crossed to the window and, swish, drew back the heavy velvet curtains, letting in early morning sunlight and the cawing of rooks in the black twisted tree outside. It was a lovely morning, one where you could imagine nothing bad happening to anyone.

She went to the room's centre, her feet clomping on bare boards.

She bent down.

And Annette Helstrang began chalking a pentacle around herself and Fifi on her living room floor.

Somewhere over Morocco, a twin-prop plane turned 180°, flew 108 yards, then turned again.

It turned again – and again – as though its pilot were struggling with two rats for control.

fifty-three

Jessica Lange was allegory.

Lucy had explained it last Christmas as she'd struggled with a big rubber hand – Jessica Lange, that was, not Lucy. Lucy had never struggled with a rubber hand though sometimes looked like she might.

She'd said the hand was the deadening grip of Tinsel Town, threatening to crush Lange's career before it had begun. The natives sacrificing her to King Kong were Hollywood executives. Jeff Bridges was her agent.

All the time that Lange struggled, seemingly terrified by a strangely off-screen ape, she was in fact seeing future acting prospects disappear.

The Postman Always Rings Twice represented the planes which killed Kong, freeing her to develop a life in showbusiness and to pick up Oscars galore. Oscars are the same size, relative to an actress, as she was to Kong. And that was how fate had it planned.

But if Lange had possessed any real sense of metaphor, she'd have climbed the World Trade Center, Oscar in hand, then sat on the roof, peeling bananas with her feet until a plane shot her.

Lucy had reckoned actors rarely understood allegory. Allegory was a directors' thing.

Then she'd upheld her Christmas tradition of thrashing Danny at Buckaroo. As always, the donkey threw everything in the air the moment he'd removed the first object.

Then she'd thrashed him at Ker-plunk, the whole thing collapsing the moment he'd removed the first stick.

Impressed, she'd challenged him to go for the hat trick and place a straw on a dromedary to see if it was the straw that broke the camel's back. He'd felt it best not to – and anyway hadn't known anyone who owned a dromedary.

But right now the lack of camels didn't seem important.

'Let me go! Put me down!' Again Danny struggled to break the straps; for the time being, too exasperated to be frightened. 'I have other things to do. The girl – you remember her, the beautiful girl from the house – I have to help her. Right now.'

The monster strode on, footfalls pounding Wheatley's early morning backstreets, boy and trolley tucked newspaper-style beneath one arm. 'Mr Meekly never like other girl. Other girl lock me in caves when me had never hurt her. Me glad she dead. *You're* my Pretty Girl. Other girl smelled funny, like fruit bowl. New Pretty Girl smell nicer.'

Danny looked up at the monster, a horrible realization dawning. 'Smells nicer?'

'Pretty Girl's smell led me from nasty tunnels. Pretty Girl save my life. Now me love Pretty Girl.'

'Nice smell?'

'Yes.'

'You mean the Bonk?'

254

'Bonk. Hurh hurh. Me and Pretty Girl be happy together. Bonk bonk.'

'Look at me,' ordered Danny, increasingly concerned at the way the conversation was heading.

A gruesome face leered down at him, semi-silhouetted against a rising sun. The creature's head was a shapeless mass of pink fluffy fur, with ping pong ball eyes sticking out the front and pointing in opposite directions. Occasionally they'd revolve simultaneously, one clockwise, one anti-clockwise, sending Danny seasick. Twin bolts protruded from where a neck was meant to be. Dick Dicksley had not been one for originality.

'Do I look happy?' asked Danny.

'Yes.'

'Am I smiling?'

'Yes.'

'Am I laughing?' asked Danny.

'Yes,' it said.

'No. I'm not.'

'Yes. You are.'

'No. I'm not. Look, this is a smile.' Danny smiled. 'This is a frown.' Danny frowned. 'Spot the difference?'

'No.' Its attention returned to the street ahead. And when the monster laughed it resembled the unblocking of a drain.

'Listen, for Godssake! I am not a girl, and I am not pretty. Now let me go!'

'Pretty Girl too modest. Mr Meekly fix that.' Not breaking stride, the monster uprooted a lamp post and offered it to Danny.

The boy scrutinized the twisted length of metal and concrete, wires dangling from its base. It was squashed in the middle where huge fingers dug into it. Danny's eyes narrowed, projecting onto the object his contempt for his captor. 'What's this?' he asked.

'Flowers for Pretty Girl. See? No one give flowers to ugly girl. No one give flowers to boy. So Pretty Girl must be Pretty Girl.'

'It's a lamp-post.'

'Lamp post flowers.'

'You really are stupid aren't you?'

'Me do accounts real good.'

'Yes. I'm sure you do.'

But then Danny saw where they were headed.

Osmosis Tower.

THE HISTORY OF OSMOSIS TOWER

In Osmosis Park rose the Great Osmosis' crowning glory; a two-thousand-foot-tall rubber office block. 'Why use concrete when a satisfactory alternative can save millions?' he'd asked the sandwich-eating Danny, one rainy, park-bench lunch break.

Construction progressed rapidly.

Osmosis had bought the super-strong rubber from a brilliant young scientist newly arrived in Wheatley and keen to make her mark. At the time, Danny hadn't known who that might be but would later be able to guess. Who else would see rubber as a suitable building material?

Like Teena Rama, Osmosis had had charts.

He'd shown them to the council.

He'd told them the tower's concept was that its flexibility would protect occupants during the devastating earth-quake he'd claimed was coming.

Impressed, the council pushed through immediate planning permission. They were the earthquake-proof tower's first and only tenants; 'In the interests of saving the council-tax payer money.'

'Every penny counts,' Osmosis had told Danny as they'd watched the councillors move in, his index finger tapping his bucket at a place approximating his nose.

But Danny had guessed the truth.

Osmosis Tower wobbled.

It wobbled alarmingly, in the slightest breeze, making the occupants spend their working days being sick from the windows. Wheatley's vomiting councillors became a media attraction after winning the Turner Prize. Black-turtle-neck-sweatered BBC2 Post Modernists declared it a masterful satire, though no one knew what was being satirized.

Osmosis' masterplan was ticking along. 'Why should I want anyone's dirty shoes polluting my tower?' he'd asked Danny as construction neared completion. Danny had had no reply. The question had provided its own answer.

All along, the tower's sole purpose had been to commemorate Osmosis, its earthquake and atom-bomb proof nature ensuring the building would stand long after the human race had gone. He even claimed it would survive the Big Crunch when the Universe would finally collapse under its own weight. At the end of everything, only Osmosis Tower would remain – Osmosis Tower and God.

Somehow the entrepreneur had decided his tower was eight-and-a-half inches taller than God – unless God had grown since Biblical times, and he doubted that very much, bearing in mind the decline of conventional Christianity.

The inclusion of office space had merely been a means to procure planning permission.

After a week, the council moved out.

Three months into Danny's coma, Osmosis' plans bore fruit. Not all the tower had been built of Dr Rama's super-strong rubber. The exterior was of her super-weak rubber. After twelve weeks of lashing rain, the weak rubber eroded, revealing a core moulded in Osmosis' image.

His monument was complete.

And no one could do a thing about it.

Now, murder in mind, the Horrible Mr Meekly carried his Pretty Girl toward the Big Ugly Man, crossing a road, overturning screeching braked cars. Sending stupid people scurrying in panic, he entered the Big Ugly Park where the Big Ugly Man waited.

Meekly knocked down a pair of gates, tossing them aside, then strode on. Thoom thoom thoom. Now he and his Pretty Girl were alone. Thoom thoom thoom. She was complaining. His Pretty Girls were always complaining. It didn't matter. He would demonstrate his love for her then she would struggle no more.

But before that, he stopped, inches away from the Big Ugly Man, and gazed up at its heights.

The Big Ugly Man was even bigger than the stupid gun Meekly had just smashed at the stupid house. The Big Ugly Man didn't move, pretending not to have seen him. Meekly roared at him. The Big Ugly Man didn't move.

A sign had been affixed to the Big Ugly Man's gigantic little toe. Lips moving as his finger followed the lettering, Meekly read two words; Osmosis Tower.

Again his gaze climbed the Big Ugly Man. He didn't like Osmosis Tower. 'Big Ugly Man get out of my way, or me kill.'

Tower ignored him.

Meekly leapt at him, attempting to demolish him in one go.

'Unhff!' He bounced off, landing on his backside in clipped grass some yards away. The impact had sent a tremor through Tower, culminating in a pranging wobble at his apex. Meekly was glad. Now Tower would have a headache.

Tower settled down. Meekly didn't. He rose to his feet, glaring at the thing, snorting like a mad bull. Still holding tight the shouting Pretty Girl, he tried again, this time with a long, pounding run up.

And the Human Tube Line launched himself into the air.

And the Human Tube Line bounced off the Big Ugly Man.

Scrambling to his feet, now roaring, wild-eyed, knowing nothing but his hatred for Tower, he tried tearing lumps from the thing, then tried kicking it, then tried wrestling it into submission with a series of Half Nelsons to the toes. And still the Big Ugly Man refused to surrender.

Finally, twelve cable-thick fingers dug into Tower's shin, then six more; Meekly's other hand was occupied holding his Pretty Girl.

And the Human Tube Line began his fateful ascent of Osmosis Tower.

Wheatley waterfront. Clancy Watts, thirty-two, sat on her penthouse apartment's deep pile carpet and polished a selection of AK-47s. On the hi-fi, Tony Bennett crooned *I Left My Heart In San Francisco*.

Ping, the lift doors opened. Hardy, her butler, emerged holding a pewter tray before him. A small, gleaming object rested on it. 'Madam, I've finished casting the silver bullet you requested.' He placed the tray on the coffee table to her left. 'Is it intended for anyone special?'

'Just this guy.' From the floor, to her right, she took a twelve by eight photo and handed it to him.

He studied it. 'An odd-looking individual. Somewhat blank-faced.'

'Hardy, you're looking at the photo's back.'

'I always do, Madam. It somehow makes people seem more agreeable.' He studied its front, not looking any more impressed. She could understand that. 'And does this gentleman have a name?' he asked.

'Uh huh.' She vigorously polished a trigger, where dirt always accumulated. 'He's called Danny Yates.'

fifty-four

Annette Helstrang paced back and forth beside her pentacle. In relentless monotone she read from the blood red pages of her Tome of Incantations.

Turning yet another page, she read on, Fifi matching her every stride with a hop.

And, at the pentacle's heart, creatures never meant for this world began to materialize.

fifty-five

Maybe she should mix and match; one Jane Fonda, one Bridget Fonda, a Greta Scacchi, two Sharon Stones and three Jayne Mansfields. No other woman would get a look in with her around; *Hey, look at me. I have eight breasts. Choose your film star.* Lucy glanced down at her own anonymous chest. Quantity and celebrity over size? The idea had merits.

But it couldn't be denied; even window shopping through her favourite photo-fit scrap book wasn't working for her today. There was no more college, no more job. God alone knew where she'd get the money for a new third-hand cab now her student loan was gone.

She was on her stomach on her bed in her room, repeatedly and lazily pressing a remote control, attention split between the changing channels of a portable TV and the photos before her.

The rabbits hopped around beside her. Maybe she'd call Osmo and ask if he'd had any luck finding her rats.

From a crumpled box beside her, she popped the last chocolate into her mouth. It struck cardboard with a hard

Pthudd, spat straight back into the box. Walnut Cluster. Yukk. It lay there, half-chewed. The ant could have it, assuming he ever finished trying to glue her car back together. 'How you doing out there?' she shouted through to him – him in the hallway, working in what was presumably meant to be thoughtful silence.

'Lucille,' he called back. 'It is becoming a taxi cab fit for any. Come and see what progress I am making. Soon your cabbage shall await.'

'Carriage.'

'Pardon?'

'Carriage. Soon my carriage shall await.'

'But, then what shall you do with this cabbage?'

She refused to dignify it with an answer. Instead, she glanced at the TV, in case she'd missed anything good while talking to the insect. Fat chance. There was nothing to miss, just an endless stream of plywood-walled Australian soaps, each with the same cast.

On another station, an evangelist told everyone to give him money. Two cops walked in and handcuffed him.

She hopped channels.

Now the evangelist was on a confessional show, telling a fat American woman how he'd been a sinner, a crook and a fornicator, like no one could've guessed from looking at him.

Maybe she'd give Dan a call later, see if he was still acting weird.

She turned the page and studied more chests, hoping it would set her interest alight. It didn't. The one top-left seemed okay; 44FF, far too small but maybe they could enlarge it.

Or maybe . . . maybe she could have them fitted upside down.

fifty-six

Mr Meekly carried Danny to the top of Osmosis Tower.
making remarkable progress for one so clumsy.

As they'd climbed, the rubber statue had begun to bend
beneath the creature's superdense weight so that by the
time he'd reached the pinnacle it was no more than three
feet off the ground.

Despite the total waste of energy, the monster seemed
happy enough, sat hugging Danny tight to him, a child
who'd got what it wanted for Christmas. Danny supposed
he should be flattered but wasn't. His bones felt on the
verge of scrunching.

'Now me and Pretty Girl alone. Now no one disturb us.'

'No one except the army.' Danny could see a convoy
of green vehicles snaking toward the park as though in a
B-movie climax.

The monster simply grinned. 'Hurh hurh. Stupid army
not bother Mr Meekly.'

'I didn't think they would.'

fifty-seven

What the?

Lucy stared at the TV.

Furiously she flicked backward through the channels, past the disgraced evangelist who was now trying to sell his story exclusively in one of tomorrow's newspapers. She flicked past the previous channel where he was trying to sell his story exclusively in two newspapers. On another channel he was selling his story in five newspapers, three books and a magazine partwork that, week by week, would build into a comprehensive pile on your living-room floor. Issue 2 came free with Issue 1. There was no mention of Issue 3. Then he was wobbling the walls of an Australian soap prison otherwise inhabited by women. But still no sign of fornication.

Finally Lucy stopped, having found the news station she'd earlier flicked past without thinking. Frowning, she squinted at the screen and pumped up the volume.

Was it?

It was.

Central Wheatley was in flames.

fifty-eight

Magnificent. This was how to do it; stride onto the battle scene and dish out commands like you own the place; 'Colonel, do this. Colonel, do that. Get me an armchair from which to run things. Take this chair away. It doesn't possess flattened armrests for whisky glasses.' And the colonel biting his tongue, following orders. Rely on the military mind never to question instructions given by any man dressed in a general's uniform; even if the theatrical costumier's tag was still on the trousers.

Not that Osmosis Park had been a battle scene before his army had started shooting. Those men really did believe they were on the moon. And not one of them had spotted the change in General Biggshott-Phaffing – the sudden appearance of a smoking bucket below his hat. But eccentricity was the prerogative of rank. Perhaps they all dreamed that one day they too might possess a Mighty Helm of Mystery.

And so the Great Osmosis stood just inside the park gates, watching the last neighbouring building go up in flames –

the old orphanage where he'd grown up, a sickly child bullied by smaller boys but with a genius for getting his way. Reading the exploits of El Dritch, alone in his bunk, had taught him that his escape route would lie in a mastery of trickery.

Not one missile, supplied by Osmosis Arms and Fireworks Co, had hit its target. Each had overshot by some two hundred yards, causing mass destruction to the park surrounds, almost as though built with that precise purpose in mind.

Soon the suburbs would have a clear view of his tower. Then, in six months' time, they too would go, giving Wheatley's satellite towns a view. Then they too would go, providing a view for the whole country and then the world.

That final part would be complicated, requiring the Earth's flattening out onto an orthographic plane, in order for Australia to see. A partial dimensional collapse of the Universe may be necessary but, with the help of the lovely Dr Rama, it could be done. A plan for her abduction and dungeoning was already fermenting in his mind. Dr Rama and chains, somehow the two thoughts went together.

Finally the orphanage collapsed.

Through binoculars he scrutinized his tower's peak; with its monster sat three feet above the ground, holding its still struggling hostage. The monster hugged him tighter, unconcerned by the surrounding commotion.

'Give yourself up,' megaphoned a colonel. 'Give yourself up and you will not be hurt.'

The monster ignored him.

Osmosis lowered the binoculars.

Time for the final phase of his masterplan.

Meekly hugged boy and trolley tighter to his fluffy, pink chest, squeezing the air from him, rocking him back and forth like a newborn kitten. 'Pretty Girl funny. Pretty Girl make me laugh.'

'Yeah? Well laugh on this, pal; soon they'll bring more weapons – big weapons. Then you'll be in trouble.'

'Me not care. Nothing hurt Mr Meekly, not bullets, not missiles, not atom bombs.'

'Can't you take a hint?'

'No.'

'I do not love you. I could never love you.'

The monster stopped rocking him, suddenly looking sad. Could it finally be getting the message? 'Pretty Girl want me let her go?'

'Pretty Girl would love you to let her go.'

'Pretty Girl not love me ever?'

Danny gazed warily at its vast chest and those arms that could crush submarines. He asked it, 'What would you do if I said no?'

'Mr Meekly would let Pretty Girl go, then sit here forever, crying.'

'Mr Meekly?'

'Yes, Pretty Girl?'

'I could never love you.'

'Pretty Girl not love me?'

'For God's sake, put me down over there.' He nodded towards a spot ten feet away. The trolley stopped him moving anything but his head. 'Then someone'll carry me off and you can sit here and cry until they blow you up.'

Meekly gazed at him. Crunch, it bit a chunk from one of the trolley corners.

'What the hell are you doing?' Danny demanded shrilly.

'Me eat Pretty Girl.' And it bit off another chunk.

'No! No!' He struggled desperately against his straps. 'You said you'd let me go!'

It chuckled. 'Me meant me'd eat you. Me not always good with words.'

'No! No! No!'

Meekly lifted him toward its mouth.

And Danny shut his eyes.

But then . . .

. . . nothing.

Baffled, he opened his eyes.

It had forgotten where its mouth was. It tried to shove him into its left eye. It tried to shove him into its right eye. It tried to shove him up its nostrils, left right and centre. Thank God they were too small. It was bad enough to be eaten, it was worse to spend your life stuck halfway up a monster's nose. It tried to stick him in its right ear. It tried to stick him in its left ear. It tried to stick him through the centre of its forehead, until it realized there was no hole there.

But finally, it lifted him toward its mouth.

'Oh Lord.' That cavern now filled his view. Again he closed his eyes but with them shut saw the mouth clearer than ever. And Danny Yates prepared to die.

Instead, Meekly screamed.

'Gas. We need gas, big gas, big nets, big helicopters. How about that foam stuff, entangles its victims?'

'Colonel?' When General Biggshott-Phaffing approached, Colonel Rodgers was at the mêlée's hub, by a jeep, radio-phoning HQ while organizing matters in the park. Soldiers ran to and fro around him, getting into position, setting up armaments.

'Yes, General?' Colonel Rodgers responded.

'Any luck with the heat seekers?'

Rodgers' hand covered the phone's mouthpiece. 'None, Sir. They fly about all over the place, almost as though pre-programmed to leave no statues of local dignitaries intact.'

Osmosis looked around. 'And those snipers?'

'Sir?' Rodgers glanced across to the five men knelt behind swings. They checked their gun sights like they'd never seen one before.

'What sort of damage would they do?' asked Osmosis.

One of them was staring, baffled, down his rifle barrel, repeatedly pulling the trigger. It turned out not to be loaded. Where had the real Biggshott-Phaffing found these people?

'Damage to the monster, Sir?' said Rodgers. 'Probably none. Private Bucky over there, he reads comics. Tells us what we have here is the Human Tube Line. According to Bucky, he's unstoppable – the Tube Line, that is, not Bucky. Bucky's not unstoppable and would never claim to be. Between you and me, Sir, he's easy to stop. You want me to go over and stop him?'

Osmosis glanced across at the private, who already looked stopped. 'That won't be necessary, Colonel. And the hostage?'

'We don't know him. Right now the nation's finest minds are reading comics to see if they can find a reference to him. Apparently, there's a blind girl – Little Cripple Annie – befriends the Tube Line in Issue 6. We're trying to locate her and also a big, talking ant who fights the Tube Line to a standstill on a regular basis. That's a big ant who talks, Sir, not an ant who talks big. Although he does talk big.'

'Colonel, you will find none of those characters outside the hoary pages of a comic book. Howmsoever, the hostage is *The Indestructible Sparkling Boy*. *No bullet can harm him,* from Issue 147.' He knew there was no Issue 147, the comic having been banned from 146 onward, proven to cause brain damage. 'The monster, on the other hand, can be brought down by a sniper's bullet cunningly deflected off Sparkling Boy's indestructible head.'

'Private Bucky says otherwise, Sir.'

'Sergeant!' Osmosis called imperiously.

A passing sergeant stopped, saluted and stood to rigid attention. 'Sir?'

'Private Bucky,' Osmosis waved a lazy hand in Bucky's direction. 'Five years of gagged press-ups in the glasshouse, starting now.'

'Yes, Sir!' the sergeant barked, again saluting. A cruel smile curled one side of his mouth.

And the protesting Bucky was dragged away.

'You're sure about this, General?' Colonel Rodgers hung up the phone.

Osmosis asserted, 'In Issue 147, Sparkling Boy's transferred radioactivity tranquillized the Tube Line and reverted him to a harmless accountant; a little too liberal perhaps but manageable. Have no fears, Colonel, your bullets will simply bounce off Sparkling Boy's head.' And within his Mighty Helm of Mystery, Osmosis' gaze settled on a distant trolley. 'Colonel?'

'Yes, Sir?'

'Have your men fire at will.'

'Yeah! Drop me on my head, why don't you?' Danny lay on his trolley at Meekly's feet, where the monster had dropped him during the screaming fit. His scream had been that of a small girl. Danny strained against the trolley straps. He didn't believe this; his one chance of escape and he couldn't move.

Still agitated, Meekly glanced around. 'Pretty Girl see a rabbit?'

'What?'

'Me thought me saw a rabbit.'

'Where?'

'There.'

'Where?'

'There.' He pointed at the rabbit.

Straining to see, Danny gazed at its vast, green flatness. And he sighed. 'That's the ground, you berk. It's been there all along.'

'It has?'

'If it wasn't, there wouldn't be anything to stand on.'

'Me learn something new every day,' he chuckled.

Then he screamed.

'Now what's up?'

'Another rabbit.'

'Where?'

Meekly pointed upwards.

And Danny sighed. 'That's the sky.'

'Oh.' Meekly settled down again.

'So what's this about rabbits?' Like Danny cared. He just hoped to keep Meekly talking.

'Me know the truth about rabbits.'

'What truth?'

'Me not like to say.'

Suddenly he realized. Comic book writers always gave their characters a weakness; Superman hated kryptonite, if Thor dropped his hammer he turned into a doctor, Iron Man's pacemaker ran down at all the wrong moments. That was why Teena'd told him to keep Proton and Neutron close by. She knew they'd scare off Meekly. That was why he'd fled Danny's room that night – the rabbits had been there.

And where were they now when he needed them? In

the wardrobe where he'd locked them because they got on his nerves. Why did they let him do that?

But this was his chance. He'd brilliantly trick Meekly into returning to the house and the rabbits. How hard could it be to outwit someone that thick? 'Mr Meekl –'

'Pretty Girl still here?'

'Of course I'm still here. Now I want you to take me –'

'Pretty Girl must love me or she would've run off like Pretty Girls always do.'

'I can't run off, you pillock. I'm strapped to –'

Meekly grabbed him and hugged him.

'Bloody Norah.'

Meekly rocked him back and forth, delightedly crushing the air from him. 'Pretty Girl love me. Me and her stay here for ever.'

'You mean?'

'Now Mr Meekly never let her go.'

'Oh,' said Danny. 'Great.'

In Danny's wardrobe, Proton and Neutron played tug-of-war with his spare jeans. They were so happy in there they were determined never to leave.

By the children's play area, Osmosis Park fell into expectant silence. A cold wind whistled through the swings' chains.

Elbows resting on the swings' plastic seats, hands perspiring, heads pounding with tension, mouths dry, each sniper closed one eye.

They pressed a sight against the open eye.

They took aim.

And the shooting began.

'Hug me tighter!' demanded Danny, panicking as a hail of bullets ricocheted off both trolley and Meekly. One narrowly missed Danny's head.

'Really?' The monster was increasingly delighted with how things were turning out.

Danny wished he could share its optimism but, not being impervious to bullets, found it impossible.

Scrunch, the monster hugged tighter.

Barely able to breathe, Danny felt like a steam-rollered road but at least was shielded by Meekly's bulk. Heart and mind racing, he gazed at the distant, reloading snipers who, after a string of wild misses, aimed closer with each barrage, as though learning to use weapons they'd never seen before.

How many were there? Dozens? Hundreds? Thousands? It was like someone had emptied the nation's least successful mental institutions, handed out guns, then sent each inmate to the park to get play therapy. But why? Couldn't they see Danny was the only one likely to get hurt?

Then he realized.

They knew he'd killed Teena Rama, a woman the whole world loved. Now they'd assumed he'd kidnapped this thing, dragged it to the top of Osmosis Tower, and was holding it hostage.

They weren't there to rescue Danny.

They were there to rescue the Human Tube Line.

'Pretty Girl love Mr Meekly?' It still rocked him like a kitten.

'Yeah, yeah, whatever.' His attention was on the snipers lining up their next shots.

Meekly's eyes again did the rotating thing. 'Then, me kiss Pretty Girl.'

Blam Blam Blam Blam Blam Blam Blam Blam Blam Blam
Blam Blam Blam Blam!

'It's not working, General,' said Colonel Rodgers, above the gunfire. He sat in the jeep, watching the action through binoculars. 'My snipers can't get near Sparkling Boy's head while that monster holds him so close.'

Beside him, Osmosis gazed the other way. 'I wouldn't worry about that, Colonel.' He smiled a reptilian smile. 'I believe matters are about to pick up, pick up most delightfully.'

And a slow, low, long black shark of a car glided silently into Osmosis Park, drawing to a halt on a grassy knoll.

Slam! Clancy Watts, all in black, shut the door of her black Plymouth Barracuda, walked around the back, inserted key in lock, turned it, and opened the black boot. It contained one spare tyre, black; one foot pump, black; a tool kit, black; and one rag bundle, black.

She took the bundle and unwrapped it to reveal one rifle, high powered, custom made, long, sleek, polished, deadly and black.

She tossed the rags back into the boot. From her knoll she surveyed her surroundings blackly. Charlie Osmosis and some colonel-type were jogging up toward her.

'Clancy, my dear,' Osmosis blustered upon reaching her. He threw both arms round her and hugged her tighter than that creature was hugging that kid. His cold bucket pressed against her face, he said, 'A pleasure to see you, as always. How are you?'

'My jugs hurt.'

'Oh? I'm sorry to hear that.' Then, suggestively, 'Anything I can help you with?'

'Yes. You can stop squashing them.'

He released her, his clammy, white-gloved hands coming to rest on her upper arms. 'Apologies, my dear. I never realized they were so sensitive.'

'They weren't.' She removed his hands from her arms.

'I trust it won't be affecting your performance?'

'You pay money, you get a job done, jug squashing or no.' And slam, she shut the boot.

'Marvellous. I knew I could count on you.'

'So, what's the latest, Charlie?'

'Field Marshal, Sir.' The colonel-type stepped forward, saluting her. 'We need you to deflect bullets off Sparkling Boy's head. The general tells me you're the best shot in the army.'

She looked at Osmosis, baffled, asking, 'Field Marshal? General? Deflect? Sparkling Boy?'

Osmosis placed a paternal arm round her, guiding her away from the car, towards his jeep and leaving behind the colonel-type. 'Never mind him, my dear.' Not looking back, he called, 'Colonel?'

'Yes, Sir?'

'Go over and give your men a pep talk. We'll join you momentarily.'

'Yes, Sir.'

She watched the colonel-type leave, all the time considering how she'd kill him, should she be required to. Garrotting would be best. Garrotting was always best with colonels. Shoot generals, garrotte colonels. He jogged down the hill, hopped over a fallen tree trunk and joined a group of snipers. One was gazing down his barrel while pulling the trigger, seemingly wondering why it wouldn't fire.

She and Osmosis walked on. 'In a moment,' she corrected.

'I'm sorry?'

'You'll see him in a moment.'

'That's right. I believe I said that.'

'No. You said "momentarily". Momentarily means *for* a moment, not *in* a moment.'

'Whatever you say, my dear. Now . . .'

'No. Not whatever, Charlie. Precision is everything. In this business, you know where sloppy gets you?'

He shrugged.

She said, 'Dead.'

'Dearest child, death is for the unimportant people, as you'll learn when you're a little older and almost as sage as myself. I always have a Plan B, to ensure success.'

'I have a Plan A and stick to it. Prepare properly and you don't need a Plan B.' She stopped walking. 'So, what's happening?'

He stopped a few yards ahead, his back to her. He studied the tower. 'You see that boy up there?'

'Who could miss him?'

'Not you I hope.'

'He's Danny Yates? Jesus. How'd he get in that predicament?'

'How many shots will you require? Only, I'm told you use silver bullets these days and I wouldn't want to be wasting money on him.'

'I never miss, Charlie. I only carry one bullet per job.'

And Clancy Watts, the most dangerous woman alive, performed a one-handed, gun-swinging, vaguely masturbatory action that made rifle parts *klitch* into place and sent the Great Osmosis' legs pleasantly weak.

Meekly's huge face drew nearer, ever nearer, eyes still rotating in opposite directions. 'Pretty Girl kiss. Pretty Girl marry. Pretty Girl live with me on desert island, with coconuts.'

'No. No. It's okay, thank you.' Danny squirmed on his trolley, trying to pull his face away from Meekly's. 'We don't need to.'

'Pretty Girl want me let Pretty Girl go again?'

A hail of bullets meant for Danny ricocheted off the monster's shoulder.

'No, no,' he insisted. 'You keep hold of me but . . .'

It was no use. Meekly's cavernous mouth was closing in on him, purple saliva drooling from one corner, two tongues drooling from another. Tonsils drooled from the middle corner.

The boy closed his eyes, squirming and wincing, hot breath across his face, wishing he were dead, or someone else, or both.

Oh God! Something new had jumped onto him, something small, warm and furry, scampering up his legs. There was two of it, one for each leg.

The monster had brought friends. And they were all going to snog Danny and were all bound to be even uglier than Meekly.

The new thing scampered onto Danny's chest, and headed for his face.

Clancy Watts knelt on her grassy knoll, gun on knee, one eye closed, one eye against a telescopic sight. The sight was filled by a boy's closed-eyed head. He was bobbing and weaving, trying to avoid monstrous lips. She felt it best not to speculate on what circumstances had led to that state of affairs.

A red laser dot drifted across his cheek then upward, settling on his left temple.

And her finger began to squeeze.

She broke off.

His head had moved.

Patient, she settled down for another try, again moving the red dot over his face, awaiting the one split-second of stillness she needed.

The dot again settled on his left temple.

And her finger began to squeeze.

'Miss Watts! Miss Watts! Are you planning on taking all day? It's been positively minutes.'

She broke off, mouthing a silent tirade of abuse at any gods too slow to duck.

Osmosis, in a flap, was heading up toward her. 'I hope you're not expecting to charge by the hour, young lady, because I warn you I will not be impressed.' Now he stood over her, all pig-stupid, puffed-up conceit. 'Murder Cod would have had it done by now.'

'Murder Cod?'

'A marvellous group of truly professional killers. And considerably cheaper than you.'

'Do you mean *Murder, C.O.D.*?' She glared at him, contemptuous, regretting having only brought one bullet with her.

'Murder Cod would have handed me a loyalty card, and a promotional car sticker. Really, my dear, you must sharpen your business practices. This is the age of the eight-second attention span, one-hour film processing, one-hour spectacle manufacture and half-hour picture framing.'

'Murder, C.O.D. are dead,' she told him.

'Nonsense, I saw them alive, just the other week, collecting their giros.'

'I killed them, Tuesday morning.'

'Oh.'

'Someone took a contract out on them.'

279

'Oh.'

'. . . After the "fastest guns in the EU" shot their client's mother-in-law, daughter, sister-in-law, father-in-law, brother, chauffeur, dogs, fish, next door neighbour, son, car, house, gnomes and garden furniture. They shot everyone their client knew, except his wife. It was his wife they'd been hired to kill.'

'In that case,' huffed Osmosis, arms folded high across his chest, 'I could have hired Death Inc, another fine group of . . .'

'And Inc is spelt?'

'I.N.K.'

'You got a wife, Charlie?'

'What does that have to do with anything?' He seemed rattled.

'Because, if you interrupt me one more time, she'll be a widow.'

'Well, excuse *me*.' And he marched off in a huff.

Asshole.

She shook her head then once more settled into position.

Again she lined up her shot.

And the woman who never missed, squeezed . . .

Meekly screamed. He dropped Danny's trolley. The sudden weight reduction twanged the tower upright and flung Meekly skyward.

Crash! The trolley hit the ground hard. A bullet sliced the air where Danny's head had just been. If Meekly hadn't dropped him, the bullet would have killed him. But why had he dropped him?

Meekly was in no mood to answer. He was too busy roaring and flailing. Danny lay dazed, battered and bewildered, watching him roar over Wheatley. With each second, Meekly grew smaller.

Now he was a distant, arcing blob above the suburbs.

Now he was a dash.

Now a dot.

Now nothing.

fifty-nine

The emergency services moved in, all flashing lights, squawking walkie-talkies and blaring sirens, achieving little, but determined to be noticed. Businesslike firemen hurriedly unrolled the anaconda of all hoses to douse already extinguished fires. Cops pushed sightseers back, back, ever back, setting up cordons, planting bollards, insisting there was, 'Nothing to see. Nothing to see.'

And they were right. There wasn't anything to see.

So people drifted away to buy lottery tickets, and the police took to pushing each other away. Chief constables pushed away sergeants. Sergeants pushed away constables. Constables pushed away special constables. Special constables pushed themselves away, getting into minor scuffles with their own arms, till a major civic disturbance erupted and the police had to arrest themselves in a scrum of men not seen since the days of the Great Wheatley Kangaroo Chase.

And the army? Most of all, the army congratulated themselves on a job well done though none were too sure what it was they'd done. But a great victory had been won today. There'd be ticker tape and buntings, and kisses from easily impressed girls. And that was reward enough. Now all they had to do was find a way back to Earth.

A black-clad woman with a rifle ran round and round in shrinking circles, as though not knowing what else to do now her Plan A was ruined. When the circles became too small for her to move without tripping over herself, she flung herself at the ground and sprawled, face down, thumping and kicking the grass, in a less than becoming tantrum. The one remaining cop took her away for assaulting the Earth, a very serious offence indeed, he told her.

But, in all the mêlée that followed, the frantic waste of effort, money, time and resources, no one offered assistance to a dazed boy who lay by a now upright tower. He didn't care. He was simply glad to be alive and unkissed. Bleary-eyed he looked toward his chest, to the two scampery things that had so terrified the horrible Mr Meekly into releasing the girl it loved.

Noses twitching, they squeaked at Danny.

And he smiled.

He saw two rats with cardboard ears.

'Still crap at Buckaroo, then.' Hands in pockets, she gazed up at the wobbling Osmosis Tower. 'How's the Ker-plunk?'

Danny frowned, vision still blurry. 'Lucy?'

Three Lucys revolved around one another – like a choir of angels or a washing machine on Slow Spin – before converging into the Lucy who, hair dangling over one eye, stood grinning down at him. 'Way to go, Danny. We watched the whole thing on TV. The missile dodging was my highlight.'

'We?'

'Me and Des, my new flatmate. Between you and me, he's a bit weird but a big improvement on you.' She shrugged, looking around. 'He's wandered off. I don't know where. So, how are you?'

'I can't move.'

'Paralysed?'

'Lucy, look at me. I'm tied up.'

'I had noticed but didn't want to comment, feeling it might be something you didn't want attention drawing to. It suits you though.'

He tutted.

'No, really,' she insisted. 'It does.'

In breathless passing, a military officer stopped. 'Sparkling Boy, I'm Colonel Rodgers.' He half-extended a hand to shake, then, seeing the straps, thought better of it. 'That was magnificent. The way you got close to that monster and attempted to head bullets onto it. This country's lucky to have men like you. I'll see you get a medal for this.' And he departed, barking orders at his men.

Lucy watched him go, a contemptuous gleam in her eyes, then returned her attention to Danny. Her teasing head tilted sideways, eyelashes fluttering, she asked him, '*Sparkling Boy?*'

He shrugged blankly.

Windswept she looked around. 'So, Sparkling Boy, where's Osmo?'

sixty

The Great Osmosis hastily departed the scene. As he ran, he stripped away his general's uniform revealing, beneath, the attire of a humble telephone engineer.

Waiting on the street corner was the phone company van he'd parked earlier – his Plan B. Soon he'd be away from there. And with nothing to link him to that morning's events, his plans could be renewed with greater vigour than ever.

Out of breath, he reached the van, took an engineer's cap from his chest pocket and placed it on his Helm of Mystery. Composing himself, he checked his reflection in the wing mirror. Perfect. *Hello. I'm Bob, Bob the telephone engineer. Something wrong with your phone, Luvvie? I'm the man for you.* And, for the final touch, he pressed a Zebedee moustache onto his mighty helm. In all the world was there a greater master of disguise?

He thought not.

Opening the van door, Osmosis climbed in. He slammed the door shut, fastened his seat belt, started the engine and prepared to depart.

'Going somewhere, human?'

Osmosis froze.

A giant ant was in the passenger seat.

sixty-one

Scooby Doo time.

'36, 24, 34.'

'42, 26, 40.'

'36, 24, 34.'

'42, 26, 40.'

'36, 24, 34.'

'42, 26, 40.'

'Look; it's definitely 36, 24, 34.'

'No. It's 42, 26, 40. Believe me, Danny, I have a leaflet says so.'

'You have a leaflet?'

'I have a leaflet.'

'I'd like to see that leaflet,' he said.

'I bet you would.'

'I used to have two leaflets,' he said.

'That was used to,' she said. 'They've changed since then.'

'Since when?'

'Since whenever.'

'But not that much,' he said.

'They've changed plenty. They change every six months. A man from the council comes round and paints them white. When he's done, he goes back to HQ and tells them all about it. They publish it in new leaflets and hand them out to everyone. What that man says is law, Danny. It can't be changed.'

'Well, that's stupid.'

'It's still the law.'

Danny and Lucy were at the bus stop, arguing over route numbers. A giant insect appeared at the street's far end. It carried the Great Osmosis by the scruff of the neck.

On his trolley, Danny craned his neck to see better. And he frowned with recognition. 'Pedro?'

'Pedro?' said Lucy.

'If not for him and his partner, I'd never have got into this mess in the first place. Quick! Grab him. If we can make him talk . . .'

'That's no Pedro. That's my flatmate – Des. He's been "fixing" my taxi, turning it into the cab of the future, he reckons. You know what it's come out looking like? A mechanical elk, a mechanical elk with a nodding head and wheels. What does that tell you about him? Maybe this Pedro was just someone who looked like him.'

'Lucy, he has six arms, and feelers. Even without the sombrero, I recognize him.'

'You bought aerosols from a seven foot tall ant called Pedro?'

'Armando said he was a Spanish flea,' Danny said defensively.

'And does he look Spanish?' she asked. 'I don't know what expectations you have of the Latin races but, the last spaghetti western I saw, there weren't many like him in it. "I lost my heart to Juanita with the compound eyes?" I don't think so. No,' she said, 'Forget it. Whoever they were, that pair are long gone, way over the Rio Grande and into the Amazon Jungle. I wouldn't even bother looking for them.'

Danny watched her. He asked, 'Aerosols?'

'Yup?' Arms folded, rats on head, she watched the ant's approach.

Danny's eyes zoomed in on her. 'Earlier, you said aerosols.'

'So?'

'I never mentioned aerosols,' he said.

'Course you did, loads of times. You couldn't stop yourself because it sounds like "arse holes", and you were always the master of the accidental double-entendre.'

'Put your finger over your top lip, like it was a fake Zapata moustache,' he said.

'Don't be stupid.'

'Go on.'

'No.'

'Why not?' he said.

'Because I won't. That's why. No particular reason. No guilt complex. Nothing to hide. It's just one of the things Lucy Jane Smith doesn't do.'

'I don't believe this!' he snapped. 'You sold me toxic waste? What kind of headcase are you?'

She stared at clouds, an eyebrow raised. 'I haven't the foggiest to what you're referring.'

He grunted, wishing the stupid straps weren't preventing him from wringing her stupid neck.

'Release me, ignorant buffoon,' Osmosis ordered the ant, feet flailing several inches above the pavement. 'The indignity of it, that I, the finest of gentlemen, should have to suffer being dragged around like a commoner. Mark my words, insect; today you have made an enemy of the Great Osmosis. And my enemies have a way of disappearing.'

'Squeak!' Cardboard ears standing on end, the rats

mountain-goated from Lucy's shoulders then scurried off down the street, before disappearing round a corner. How could they find talking ants more daunting than a fifteen-ton monster?'

Lucy watched them go. 'Aw shit.'

'They'll be back,' Danny told her. 'They did last time.'

'Yeah. And it was you they came back to.'

'I'm sure it'll be you next time.'

'It'd better be, Sparkling Boy.'

'Lucille.' Destructor approached. 'I have captured the man who brought you such distressed remorse at having caused the potential demise of a friend.'

'Distressed?' Amused, Danny gazed up at her, accusingly. 'Friend?'

She shrugged dismissively, arms folded, eyes on her new flatmate. 'He's just some cockroach. Like he'd know distress when he sees it.'

'But, Lucille,' it said. 'You were weeping.'

'I was laughing.'

'But you said . . .'

'Shut it, bug eyes.'

And Danny grinned.

So Lucy punched his head.

So Danny grinned more.

So Lucy punched his head more.

So Danny stopped grinning.

So Lucy stopped punching his head.

Now Osmosis was held before them, a naughty child awaiting punishment.

Lucy stepped forward, prodding the entrepreneur's chest, staring up at his bucket. 'So,' she said, 'What do you have to say for yourself, *Mr Osmosis*?'

'My dear girl, your rent is due to be tripled. Release me, and it shall subsequently be halved by three and one eighth per cent.'

290

'Gee. Thanks. You don't think you should apologize to Danny first?'

'For?'

'For trying to kill him.'

'Never. The poltroon destroyed my shop. And I shall destroy him.'

'Fair enough.'

'Who is this clown anyway?' asked Danny.

'The Great Osmosis,' she said. 'You used to work for him before your coma. You probably don't remember, rubble to the head, and all that.'

'No. I mean, who is he really, beneath the bucket? It's time we found out.'

Then Lucy said, 'He's your father.'

'What?'

'Osmosis is your father.'

'Who says?'

'It always is; in films and plays and books. On the second last page, it always says, *It was . . . his father.*'

'That's ridiculous. My dad's in New Zealand, with my mum, raising sheep.'

'So he told you.' She turned to the insect. 'Go ahead, Mandibles, whip off the bucket. I won't be wrong.'

'Why would my dad want to kill me?' asked Danny.

'Why wouldn't he?'

'Because he's my dad. Dads don't kill their sons. They take them to football matches and fishing, and ruffle their hair on the way home.'

'Luke Skywalker's didn't ruffle his hair,' she countered.

'Darth Vader was hardly a model of normal parenthood.'

'But look at Osmosis. Spot the resemblance? The helmet, the cod mysticism.'

'Well what's *your* dad do?' Danny demanded of her.

'He's a ninja.'

'A ninja?'

'Yeah.' She shrugged. 'There's nothing wrong with that. It's a job.'

'Lucy, no one's dad is a ninja.'

'Mine is. My mum told me. That's why I've never seen him. Ninja's have the power of invisibility. Besides, he has to keep a low profile. He's protecting the emperor of Japan from the forces of anarchy. But one day, when his job's done, he'll return to England. The Japanese call him the Ginger Ninja and he's practically a legend.'

Danny just looked at her, finally asking, 'So why can't Osmosis be *your* father?'

'Yeah. Like I'm going to be the offspring of some loopy-fruit.'

'A ninja's more likely to be a would-be killer than a sheep farmer is.'

'Wanna bet?'

'Damn right I do.'

'A tenner says it's your dad,' she said.

'Fifteen says it's yours,' he said.

'What if it's the insect's dad?'

Danny studied the wavy-feelered creature, deciding, '*He* pays *us*.'

'Done,' she said.

'You have been,' said Danny.

She nodded to Destructor. 'Okay, whip off the bucket.'

Two insect arms held Osmosis. And two others began to lift the Helm of Mystery, ignoring all struggles and protests.

'No, no, release me. A man's head is between him and his shoulders.' The entrepreneur back-kicked one of Destructor's armoured shins, to no avail.

The lid flipped open, smoke pouring out.

Clank. Bucket hit pavement.

And Lucy wafted away the last smoke wisps, to reveal . . . ?

. . . ?

. . . ?

Nothing; just a deflating suit, the telephone engineer's uniform crumpling in Destructor's arms, unsupported by any contents.

Danny frowned.

Lucy leaned forward, gazing down into the suit, before turning to Danny and asking, 'That your dad?'

'Lucy, there's nothing but smoke.'

'So? I don't know what your dad looks like. There's no law says he has to resemble you. My dad looks like David Carradine. You should see the photo Mum took of him, from a TV monitor, kicking some cowboy types' heads in. No resemblance to me at all.'

Danny watched the crumpled uniform. 'Can you believe it? A man so consumed by ambition that, by the end, only ambition remained.'

'You know, Dan, only you could deliver that line without getting embarrassed.'

The insect was looking concerned. 'Lucille?'

'Yup?'

'Does this fate befall all in this world who have too much ambition?'

'Damn right it does. And don't forget it.'

Danny didn't know why she'd told him that, but then he never knew why she did anything. Clearly, an end like this could only befall a king-size pillock like Osmosis.

Nonetheless, the insect looked concerned.

sixty-two

'Whoa!' Danny's trolley trundled to the back of the bus, hitting the rear wall. He winced.

'Whoa!' Danny's trolley trundled to the front of the bus, hitting its front wall. He winced.

'Whoa!' Danny's trolley trundled to the back of the bus, hitting its rear wall. He winced.

It had been doing this for fifteen minutes. Danny just wished the driver would learn how to maintain a constant speed.

With a screech of brakes, the bus stopped at traffic lights.

'Aargh!' The trolley hurtled, at thirty miles an hour, toward the front. When trolley hit wall, he'd be a goner.

A claw reached out and stopped it. It belonged to the big ant sat on a middle seat. Conspiratorially, it leaned across and warned, 'Be wary, human, your antics, admirably anarchic though they are, may damage this omnibus. I have learned it is unwise to make enemies of bus-driving operatives.'

Danny looked up at the bug eyes and wavy feelers. 'You're not from round here are you?' he asked.

'No.' It looked around, as though fearing someone might hear. Then, content, no one was eavesdropping, it leaned right over. Its face inches from his, it said, 'Do not gasp in shock, human. Though it may be hard for your mind to grasp, I am not even a native of this planet.'

'You don't say.'

'I do say. I am ruler supreme of the planet Bovulous. And I treat my subjects like cattle.'

'Why?'

'They are cattle; three thousand million of them, filling every square foot of my tiny world. They will not listen to me. They will not talk to me. They will not get out of the way when I wish to cross from one side of my throne room to the other. They do nothing but chew grass, and moo moo moo. So I treat them like cattle to teach them a lesson. And still they ignore me.'

'But . . . ?'

'But one day, bored with taunting cattle, I decided to conquer the world of my dreaded enemies the Hormonal Fifty. I set about chewing through the boundaries which separated their world from mine, for I had discovered those boundaries were made of paper.'

'Paper?' said Danny.

'In a strange and bizarre twist of fate, just as I chewed my way through, someone somewhere must have fired a copy of Larry Hormonal's accursed Xeta Gun, disrupting the space/time continuum. I recognized the smell of burning sulphur. Instead of the Hormonal Fifty's world, I found myself on a street corner in this one. And there was no way back.

'But I did not sit on a street corner, crying for hours on end until a friendly nun gave me refuge and taught me a song of hats. That is not the way of the tyrant. Rather, I set about drawing up plans for division and conquest. But now, the lovely Lucille's words have thwarted me. Tell me, human, how may one conquer this world, without megalomania?'

'Beats me,' said Danny.

'Hmmn.' It placed claw against mandible, deep in thought. 'This is indeed a puzzle.'

'Whoa!' The bus again started moving. The trolley began to drift.

The ant stopped it again, then scrutinized it. 'This transport of yours has inefficient design. Why, even Trolley Lad, the daring but clueless jewel thief, has a brake on his trolley. Also, you should have a motor fitted that would put-put-put as you travel the streets. It would have little fear factor for most but might cause mild consternation among cats.'

'I'm not on this thing by choice.'

'You are not?'

'No.'

'Then why do you stay on it?'

'What do you think these straps are for?'

'Then I shall chew through that strapping.'

And he did.

sixty-three

The pretty daisy had nothing to say for itself. The Human Tube Line didn't care.

The pretty daisy only moved when the breeze blew it. The Human Tube Line didn't care.

The pretty daisy had no scary rabbits to chase him off with. That, the Human Tube Line *did* care about. He kissed the pretty daisy. It didn't complain, scream or flee like the Pretty Girl would have done. The Human Tube Line and daisies were the same, feared and hunted wherever they went, just because they were different.

He decided to sit in this smoking hole for ever.

'Hello? Hello?' called a female voice from out of view. 'Is there somebody down there? Or are you just a hole in the ground? Do you need help? Or are you happy where you are?'

He grunted. His eyes raised to see above the rim of the crater he'd created when he'd crash-landed in the garden.

Before him, a horrible, black house squatted like

a complacent toad. He hated complacent toads. They reminded him of the Complacent Frogs of Venus who'd tried to invade earth, armed only with sticky tongues, convinced it could have no defence against such mighty weapons. It had been a short battle.

'Pretty daisy, help me smash ugly house,' he instructed the flower. It showed little enthusiasm for the task. But it would, upon seeing how good it was to smash ugly things. 'Me and Nurse Daisy good friends. Me and Nurse Daisy practise accountancy together.'

He rose to his feet, head flooding with the red mist that made him do things others regretted, then took a thumping great step forward. He took another, then another, then another, fists clenched, a roar forming in his throat. The house was as good as dead.

Then he saw the pretty feet.

They stood in the open doorway, looking out with a sunny disposition; not any old feet you could see skipping between hot tram lines, to avoid blisters, on any broken-down resort's promenade; not kiss-me-quick-feet.

These were big city feet, with big city ideas. If these feet smoked they did so not from the burning touch of tram lines but through an eighteen-inch-long cigarette holder while cradling a glass of something smooth, and leaning listless against a piano which played a lilting melody.

But all the while, for all the pianist's harmonious chords, it was the feet you'd be noticing. And while they might lead you on, play you for a fool, take half your money and all your sense, cosh you over the back of your head, and be gone with your car before consciousness returned, they could never be taken for a tramp.

He studied the flower. 'Pretty feet prettier than daisy.'

His thooming right foot squashed the stupid daisy into the stupid ground. From now on, he'd be doing his auditing with Nurse Pretty Feet.

Nurse Pretty Feet approached, attached to a girl in black. Stood at the crater's edge, frog on shoulder, she looked down at him. Smiling, she pulled breeze-swept hair away from her face and tucked it behind a multi-pierced ear. 'You're the horrible Mr Meekly, aren't you? I recognize you from the Necronomicomic. You shouldn't be here. You belong in another world, one where you can do no real damage because everything you smash can be redrawn.'

The girl made no sense. Meekly didn't care. He just cared about Nurse Pretty Feet. He watched them with a vacant look on his face.

The girl noticed. She looked down at Nurse Pretty Feet. 'What?' she asked. 'You like these?'

He nodded, entranced, Quasimodo to her Esmeralda. She wiggled her toes. And when they wiggled they tinkled with all the magic of Brian Cant.

And when the Human Tube Line laughed, it was with the simplicity of a child.

sixty-four

Danny mounted the step outside Teena Rama's front door, imagining her lying cold and still, on the lab floor where he'd left her, the time for her revival long gone. And now he had to face Doors. Hollow-stomached he almost pressed the green panel, then decided against it, fearing he might be refused entry for what he'd done to Teena.

A small plant pot stood beside the step. He bent down, tipped it away from him, and retrieved a key from among the cobwebs and woodlice beneath. Teena had kept the key there in case Doors' systems failed, which she'd expected they would. Danny's queries about the policy's wisdom had always been met with a smile and a claim that no burglar worth his salt would be naive enough to look under plant pots for front-door keys. Teena had always been smiling. Danny felt like he'd lost his smile somewhere near the park and would never find it again.

She'd claimed the keys didn't matter; the house had ways of dealing with unwelcome visitors.

He hoped that didn't now include him.

He inserted key in lock, turned it and entered.

Danny gently closed the front door behind him and stood in the silent hallway. 'Doors?'

'Why, Mr Daniel, hello. I wondered if we'd ever be seeing you again. I followed, through television, your struggles with Mr Meekly. A rum do, and no mistaking. But at least you're safe and well.'

Danny sighed, 'Which is more than I can say for Teena.'

'It's been an unfortunate affair all round. Still, Mr Smeegle – the undertaker – has arrived to make arrangements. I'm sure he'll give Miss Rama a delightful send-off. As I recall, she was always rather fond of funerals, once a year attending the burial of a stranger, finding such outings cathartic. I'm sure she'll find her own doubly so.'

Danny wanted to cry. 'I'm sorry, Doors.'

'For . . . ?'

'For causing her death.'

'Tish. Think nothing of it. I warned her, on numerous occasions, of her work's insanity. She never listened, being a wilful creature devoid of sense. In retrospect, her death was quite inevitable.'

He still felt guilty. 'So, what happens now?'

'Well, Mr Meekly seems to have vanished. I can find no mention of him on news reports. And believe me, there's plenty out looking for him, including those who normally hunt Mr Boggy William. Therefore, we must assume he's reverted to human form or been somehow spirited away. Miss Rama once informed me that, each year, Wheatley sees the disappearance of two-hundred-and-twenty-seven people. No one knows why, other than that they're all foot fetishists. Arnold Meekly was a foot fetishist. That was why Miss Rama always went barefoot around the house, in case he turned up unannounced. It would be a way to control him, she thought.'

'And the house?' asked Danny.

'Miss Rama's sister – Akira – has been contacted, and will arrive early tomorrow. She expects to close the house down, dismantle the lab, and transfer me to a little black box to be kept in her own, rather modest, flat. She wouldn't like to see me deactivated. Frankly, Miss Akira tends to anthropomorphize. It was one of the many things she fell out with Miss Rama over. Will you be joining us?'

'Sorry?'

'I'm sure she'll be happy to reduce you to a black box on her mantelpiece. She's rather clever at things like that, much cleverer than Miss Rama ever was, though Miss Rama didn't like me pointing that out.'

'Er, no, it's okay, Doors. I'm sure I'll be able to find alternative accommodation.'

'You're certain?'

'Positive.'

'Only, I think you'd get on famously with Miss Akira. You and Miss Rama were never compatible housemates, her being very much the loner by nature and prone to moods. Her sister's much more outgoing, keeping an active social circle on her mantelpiece.'

'No, it's okay thanks,.' Danny knew exactly where he'd be staying next but felt it best not to tell Doors. The computer would only try to talk him out of it. And the danger was he might succeed.

'Oh well. Then goodbye, Mr Daniel. It's been nice knowing you.'

Danny felt he should say something profound, to make it feel like a story was drawing to a close. It had to be from a book, meaningful statements always were. Writers knew how to end things with a profound shake of the head that said it all about the human condition. Danny possessed no such knack. Unfortunately, he'd only ever read two books. They always reminded him too much of shelves. So he said, 'Doors?'

'Yes, Mr Daniel?'

'You're worth more than the whole damn lot of them put together.'

'Why, thank you, Mr Daniel. But what does *The Great Gatsby* have to do with me? Surely that would be more relevant to Miss Rama, as she was rich and caused her own downfall through overreaching. Not that she resembled Mr Jay Gatsby in any other way, not being prone to throwing parties, nor to wasting her life in pursuit of a vacuous and worthless woman. I rather think Miss Rama would have given Mr Gatsby an ear-bashing and a meat pie, and probably will, should she encounter him on the Other Side.'

Maybe he should have stuck to the only other book quote he knew.

Doors continued, 'Perhaps she would rather have been compared to that other 1930s icon; Mr Charles Foster Kane, if only because she modelled her video camera work on that of Mr Welles.

'As a child, Miss Rama had a sled,' he explained as Danny lost all interest. 'A mahogany one, with steel runners and a handbrake. When her parents handed it to her, one Christmas morning, they joked it was called *Rosebud*. She told them not to be childish. She was two years old.'

Danny went upstairs.

sixty-five

'Give over.'

'*You* give over.'

'Stop pushing.'

'*You* stop pushing.'

'Lemme see.'

'No. *You* let *me* see.'

Fifteen fairytale characters waited in Annette's darkened lounge; some by the walls; some in chairs, knees hugged to chests. All were impatient.

Pop! They glared at Gretel. Her eyes all sullen defiance, the brat stretched her chewing gum to a long long strand then released it, her tongue slowly hauling it back into her mouth. Pop, she burst the gum again.

Annette's voice drifted through from the hallway, 'This way. There's some people I'd like you to meet.'

Many shifted in their seats, anticipating.

Mr Meekly's menacing form filled the lounge doorway, blocking out all light.

'Heavens,' said someone.

'Gracious,' said another.

Glances were exchanged.

Someone tittered behind a girlish hand.

A murmur circled the room, stopping at Jack who'd seen it all before and wouldn't give five beans for it.

Smiling, Annette took the reluctant creature's hand and led him into the room, his shoulders scraping the ceiling. Craning her neck to see his face, she told him, 'These are my friends.'

'Hi, big guy. I'm Rumpelstiltskin.' The little man stepped forward, removed the cigar from his mouth and shook the creature's hand. 'Bet you can't guess her name,' he said of Annette. 'That dame is the most inscrutable broad I ever worked with, and I worked with Nijinsky.' Then he frowned. 'Least, that's who she said she was.' And he rejoined the pack.

Meekly looked confused. He wasn't the only one.

The ugly duckling quacked.

Jack's cow mooed.

'Looks an absolute brute of a thing,' said Snow White's Stepmother, eyes gleaming vicariously.

'Hello,' the three bears said to him.

'Want some porridge, Mr Pink Horrible Mr Meekly Line?' Baby Bear stepped forward, steaming bowl held out.

'That's my porridge!' Goldilocks slapped it from his hand. Thwack, it hit the bare floor.

'Yeah? Like you don't owe us, Bubbles!'

Baby Bear sidestepped Goldilocks' punch, producing an uppercut to the chin, then another, then another. It looked like she might go down but she replied with three good kicks to the stomach.

The others formed a ring, crowding in, cheering them

on, girl tearing clumps of fur from bear, bear bashing girl's nose.

Annette raised her eyes heavenward. Why did it always have to end like this?

Mr Meekly grunted, bewildered by the tiny figures rolling around at his feet.

'Smack him, kid,' urged Rumpelstiltskin.

'Bite her ear off.'

'Empty your porridge on her head.'

'Sleep in his bed.'

'Sit in her chair.'

'Ten quid on the bear,' slurred Snow White, her loosely held vodka glass spilling half its contents. The inveterate gambler, smoker and drinker always blamed it on being from a broken home.

'This juicy apple on the brat,' said her Stepmother.

'That juicy apple?' said Snow White.

'This juicy apple.'

'Lemme see that juicy apple.' Snow White snatched it from her and rubbed it on her own dress.

'Impressed?' asked the Stepmother.

'What is this?' demanded Snow White, studying the fruit, her face blackening with rage.

'What?' said the Stepmother, all wounded innocence.

'You're trying to slip me a mickey. Hey, everybody, my mommie dearest's trying to slip me a mickey!

'Quack.'

'Moo.'

'Quack quack quack.'

'Moo moo moo.'

Fight spreading, Annette led Meekly to a quiet part of the room. She assumed that what she was about to do would set right whatever had gone wrong when Danny'd failed to stick to his destiny. It was a rare man too clueless to follow his own fate. Later she'd pay Mr Yates a visit and make him know what he'd put her through. And he'd better be sorry.

'Would you like to sit here please?' she asked Meekly.

Still bewitched by her pedicure, he sat in the pentacle she'd marked out earlier.

She waved her arms around because it was expected, and began to incant. After all, that which brought fairy tale characters to our world could return comic book ones to theirs.

sixty-six

With grim determination Danny dropped his open case onto the bed, setting bedsprings rattling. He crossed to the wardrobe. Its white doors opened with a wooden clank. Its fresh pine smell again filled his nostrils. And he collected his clothes.

As he removed hangers from the wardrobe, their hooks scraped the metal rail. It sounded like the sharpening of knives.

He didn't remove the clothes from the hangers, figuring hangers might be in short supply where he was going. Two half-eaten T-shirts and a pair of jeans – not much to show for such an eventful stay. He put them in the suitcase then sat beside it on the bed.

Now he'd go to the police and hand himself in. It was what he deserved for killing Teena Rama, and she deserved that he did it for her. If they refused to arrest him, he'd insist. And if they still refused, he'd run round the back of their counter and knock their hats off, again and again and again, no matter how many times they put them back on. Until, finally, they'd have no choice but to bundle him into a cell, and lock him there for-ever.

And it might be a pathetic crime, lacking malice, style and gravity but pathetic was what he did best.

With a sigh, he fastened his luggage.

Halfway down the stairs, a breaking handle sent his luggage cartwheeling to the bottom.

Thump thump thump thump thump thump thump.

Thud, it landed on its flank, dead.

At the stair bottom, remembering the sheer uselessness of their previous conversation, Danny decided against say-ing goodbye to Doors. Instead, he toe-poked the case, like a badly designed football, to the end of the hall-way.

Stepping over the bag, and the junkmail mountain, he opened the front door.

Through bare branches, mid-afternoon sun shone on Moldern Crescent. Birds sang like it was the first day of the rest of someone else's life.

He took a final look at the silent hallway; the photos of Teena collecting prizes; little bits of incomprehensible sculpture; countless doors, countless intrigues; a secret corridor that was a broom closet, a broom closet that was a secret corridor (as though anyone would fall for that trick); and numerous monster-shaped holes.

The ruined cuckoo clock still hung on the wall. Deciding no one would miss it, he took it down, as a keepsake of the most remarkable girl who ever lived.

And he turned to leave.

– Mumble –

? He stopped, and listened hard.

– Mumble –
? There it was again.
– Mumble mutter mumble! –
Someone was in Kitchen Number 1.

sixty-seven

'Hello, darling, I'm home,' Lucy told thin air as she and Destructor entered their flat, from the landing.

'Lucille, why do you always say that, when you know there are no darlings awaiting you?'

'Because everyone says it.'

'Everyone?'

'Everyone. No exceptions.'

'Then, I must say it also?'

'Only when I'm not here.'

'And what is a "darling"? If one rushes to greet me, its tail wagging, how shall I know it is not an enemy to be squashed? How many legs does a "darling" have? Will it be armed? These are things I need to know.'

'Des, I can honestly say a darling is one thing you'll never have to worry about.'

'Thank you, Lucille. That is a great relief to me.'

'Anytime. I'm off to feed my rabbits. Don't disturb me for half an hour.'

'And are your rabbits "darlings"?'

She went into her magnificent room, shutting the door behind her.

Destructor remained in the hallway. He closed the front door, and worried. Lucille's warning of what happened to megalomaniacs in this world necessitated a change of plan. He needed something cunning and devious, a way to conquer without conquest.

He looked around for inspiration, at the walls and ceiling, the bare lightbulb, the bare carpet, the painting of a puce female whose eyes didn't match.

Most of all, he saw Lucille's wooden bendy box propped against the far wall. When in a bad mood, she would take the box and strike it, eliciting horrible anguished sounds. What did she call it? Her 'stupid guitar'. But he felt instinctively that a stupid guitar might also be used to create music.

And then he knew.

If he couldn't rule this world through conquest, he would do it through showbusiness. Yes. Yes. He would become a singing sensation, in the style of the excellent Perry Como, fêted by royalty, adored by critics.

Lucille had music student friends at the polytechnical school; John, Paul, George and Richard, also George and Martin. He would make them join his group, under threat of death.

And being an insect, he had the perfect name for his singing group . . .

He would call it . . . Wings.

sixty-eight

'Kindly unhand my buttocks.'

'Madam, please. In twenty-five years of dealing with the newly departed, I've never encountered a corpse as fidgety as you.'

'That's because I'm alive.' Jaw clenched, Teena Rama squirted ketchup on bread, endeavouring to make a sandwich.

The undertaker buzzed around behind her, an over-greedy fly at the queen of all picnics, attempting to measure her in every conceivable direction; up, down, sideways, lengthways, widthways, anyways. She was just relieved he didn't know Multi-Dimensional Space Theorem, or they'd be there a lifetime.

Where he'd come from, she didn't know. How he'd got there, she didn't know. She'd only discovered his presence when his tape measure had lassoed her forehead as she'd approached the kitchen worktop. It was a safe bet Doors was involved.

Her carving knife forced through eight layers of bread,

313

meat, lettuce, mayonnaise and ketchup. The man was ignoring a sound rule of cookery: never annoy a woman with a cutting edge.

Still carving, she tried back-kicking his shin.

He dodged, wrapping the measure round her waist, yanking it tight. All patronizing avuncularity, he said, 'No; Madam merely believes herself to be alive. Autonomic reflex action of the muscles, after death, is a well-established phenomenon, especially in chickens. And psychosomatic wellness is common among the deceased. The number of people we at the *Happy Burial Home* have buried who insisted they were still alive . . .'

She slapped the sandwiches onto a plate, her backwards swinging fist fending him off. 'Look,' she stated, 'I happen to be a doctor, and can assure you I'm in robust health. Now, if you'll leave me alone to get on with my meal.'

The measure yanked tight around her calf. She tried to shake the man off, like he was an over-sexed terrier – with little luck.

'I'm sure Madam's aware that doctors are their own worst patients, often convincing themselves their symptoms are milder than they really are.'

'Heaven knows I try not to be a violent woman, Mr Smeegle, but if you make one more attempt to measure my backside . . .'

He made one more attempt to measure her backside, tape yanking tight. 'We must ensure your coffin fits in all directions. We wouldn't want our lid popping off in front of our loved ones, would we?'

She snatched the tape from him, flung it aside and advanced, a concerted round of finger-prodding driving back the gaunt, balding man. No one finger-prodded with an authority to match Teena Rama. 'If you must know, my height is twelve-foot-one. My hips are eighty-nine inches.

My waist is three inches. My bust is a hundred-and-thirty inches. My inside leg is eight-foot-seven. I weigh two-and-a-half tons. I take a size twenty Doc Marten no.9. And my hat size is two.' None of this was true. 'Happy now? Would you like to record all that in your notebook then go away? Take it to your place of employment and tell your friends about it? Assuming you have any.'

'Will Madam require enlargement?'

'Enlargement?'

'It's all the rage in California – cosmetic surgery for the dear departed. It can be most distressing for family to see loved ones looking unwell. We in undertaking have a long-standing tradition of making-up corpses, dressing them in nice clothing, changing their expression to one of contented repose rather than the twisted mask of terror many tactlessly adopt at their moment of doom. Madam appreciates we must take a sensitive line, touch up the corpse a little.'

'I'd be content if you'd stop trying to touch me up.'

'Madam shouldn't be overprotective of her assets.' His gaze ran up and down her. 'I can assure her I'm fully homosexual and am pleased to announce that, for a limited period, we are offering free cosmetic surgery to you, our ten thousandth customer. We provide a full range of services; stomach tucks, liposuction, face lifts, collagen injection. Not that Madam requires any of those treatments. What's the saying? *Die young, leave a beautiful corpse*? Madam has certainly achieved that. But, perhaps . . . ?' His eyebrows hoisted. '. . . A few more inches on her bust?'

'Doors?'

'Yes, Miss Rama?'

'Have this "person" electrocuted.'

'Yes, Miss Rama.'

'Madam is aware there's a call out-fee?'

Ten thousand volts arched up from the floor, swarming

round the man, striking like rattlesnakes. The room lit crackling blue.

And he screamed.

Flumpf; following a brief but spectacular dance, the undertaker collapsed in a heap. Doors cut the power. The electricity settled down, with a final malicious rattle, then slithered back into the floor.

Teena Rama stepped over the motionless figure. With a sigh, and a shake of the head, she returned to her sandwiches.

In a letter once, Danny's brother – Brian – had claimed to have discovered something odd in a not very big cave in southern Ecuador.

Blundering into a recess, to escape killer bears, the explorer had found himself facing twenty million mammoths (his estimate) all stood shoulder to shoulder, gazing inscrutably into his eyeballs. He'd had the feeling they were surprised to see him.

Some were stood on others' shoulders. Some had squeezed in upside down or sideways or balancing on their heads. That was the only way they could all fit into a cave so small.

Danny had always suspected bullshitting.

Excited, Brian had whipped out an Instamatic but, because they'd spent fifty million years in the dark and therefore lacked resistance to sunlight, the camera flash disintegrated them, leaving just a pile of ash.

Now no one would believe his story. And it was best they didn't; posterity would look none too kindly on the man who'd extincted the woolly mammoth.

Now Danny stood in the kitchen doorway, worried that one loud sound might have the same effect on a newly rediscovered scientist, like she was real only so long as he stayed quiet or still. In stunned disbelief he said, 'Teena?' Not loud enough to disintegrate the weediest of extinct creatures.

When the girl didn't vanish, he said it louder; 'Teena?'

Not glancing back at him she opened the fridge, retrieving a bottle, pouring herself a glass. 'Hello, Gary. Fancy an orange juice?'

He stepped forward then stopped, still uncertain. 'You're alive?'

'Don't tell me. Tell that idiot.'

He looked down and across at the undertaker's motionless figure, and feared the worst. 'Is he . . . ?'

'Just unconscious. Sadly, he'll be fine in a few minutes.'

But Danny didn't care about the undertaker anymore. Sod him. What had he ever done for Danny? Stepping over the man, he staggered forward then ran, flinging both arms round her, seeking one final assurance she was real.

And she *was* real, still smelling like banana milkshake, still solid and warm and soft and bendy and all the other things living people are and dead people aren't – only more so because she was Teena Rama and Teena Rama had always been the solidest, warmest, softest, bendiest, banana milkshakiest girl who'd ever lived. Somehow you always knew she would be, without even having to touch her. And he hugged her tighter than anyone had ever been hugged.

She mumbled, as best she could with Danny's upper arm pressed against her mouth, 'I see the erection's back, then.'

sixty-nine

'But I don't understand why you thought I was dead.' Teena brought her orange juice through to Kitchen Number 2, where she pulled out a chair, its feet scraping on floor tiles, and joined Danny at the table. She always scraped chairs. He decided she did it on purpose, but couldn't divine her motives. 'Didn't you notice my breathing?' she asked.

'I couldn't see you for the trolley you'd got me stuck to,' he said pointedly.

'Oh.' She seemed embarrassed, moving her glass in small circles on the table, watching it rather than Danny. 'About that; let me say . . .'

'Besides,' he butted in, 'Doors said you were dead.'

Eyes narrowing, she watched the ceiling camera. 'Doors?'

'Yes, Miss Rama?' He sounded nervous.

'Scan Gary. What do you make of his health?'

Click. A blue light emanated from the camera, its cool warmth studying the boy's upper half. Danny imagined his likeness appearing on a screen in a part of the building he never knew existed. The image would be a man-shaped

318

grid of luminous green lines, and be rotated full circle and then on its head, like happened in car ads when they wanted to convince you a tin box was a high-tech miracle that would give your life total freedom.

The light clicked off.

Teena watched Doors' camera, her gaze demanding his verdict.

'Oh dear,' said the computer.

'What is it?' she asked

'Miss Rama, Mr Gary's dead.'

Her gaze met the baffled boy's. *Was it true?* he wondered. Was he dead and hadn't even noticed? Surely even he'd spot a thing like that. He felt at himself, his hands patting at his upper half. He seemed to be alive but how could he tell? Perhaps he'd died back at the hospital, after the shop had crashed down on him, and ever since had been walking around dead. And, even now, hospital staff might be scouring the streets of Wheatley for the escaped corpse – after all, he had Ribena for blood. How could he be alive with Ribena for blood? Maybe Boggy Bill had had his revenge and Danny had been too thick to notice.

Teena said, 'Doors, scan every home within a quarter-mile radius of this house. Tell me the occupants' state of health.'

His scanner hummed while Danny and Teena waited. Danny still not understanding what was going on.

The humming stopped.

And Doors ventured, 'Miss Rama? They're all dead too. But what could have happened? Was it the Horrible Mr Meekly?'

'Try the entire world,' she instructed – Danny growing ever more confused.

Doors' scanner hummed. Enigmatic, Teena sipped orange juice while waiting.

'Miss Rama?'

'Uh-huh?'

'Everyone's dead, the entire population of the world, all gone; as though there's been a terrible nuclear holocaust that no one's told me about.'

The mystified Danny looked at her.

She explained, 'Doors has little medical programming. It hasn't a clue how to tell the living from the dead. As I keep telling everyone – and they never listen – you shouldn't regard it as a person. It's just a machine, like a calculator or food blender. Doors know what it knows, nothing more.'

'So, what happened to you?' asked Danny.

She shrugged. 'I merely passed out, having underestimated the intoxicating effects of my pie. I woke shortly before your return, to find that someone . . .' and she looked pointedly at the camera, '. . .had called an undertaker.'

'Was that inappropriate, Miss Rama?'

'Just slightly. Oh and, Doors?'

'Yes, Miss Rama?' He was starting to sound more than a little downcast. Danny felt sorry for him, imagining what new 'improvements' Teena might inflict on his programming with her screwdriver.

She scrutinized the penguin, its beak still embedded in the table. 'You didn't complete the Fighting Android and despatch it to confront Mr Meekly, as per my orders.'

'No, Miss Rama,' he said warily.

'Well done, Doors.'

'Thank you, Miss Rama.'

'Wait, Mr Smeegle!' the boy called, his footsteps trying to catch up with the undertaker. 'I need a word.'

The wind whipping at him, Smeegle's stride quickened,

taking him up Moldern Crescent, toward his parked limousine. He was determined to avoid anyone connected with the madhouse he'd just left. In all his years in the trade, he'd never been treated in such a cavalier fashion, insulted, knocked unconscious; and then, upon revival, ordered to leave – by a talking door, of all things. At the next Guild meeting he'd be getting the address blacklisted. Let's see how they liked it when they discovered they weren't allowed to die.

The boy caught up with him, slightly out of breath, half running, half walking alongside him. 'You have a free cosmetic surgery offer for your ten thousandth customer?'

Smeegle lengthened his stride, not looking at the boy, his own footsteps clacking hurriedly on paving. 'That's correct. But as Dr Ramalalanyrina's corpse refuses to lie down, it seems an irrelevant point.' He reached his car, gripping its cold handle and, clunk, pressed it down. 'Besides, frankly, Mr . . . ?' For the first time he looked at the straggly-haired youth who confronted him.

'Yates; Danny Yates.'

'Frankly, Mr Yates.' He pulled the car door open, the breeze flapping his tie around. 'The Undertakers' Guild takes a dim view of electrical high-jinks, especially since the incident with Mrs Shelley. I've no doubt they'll be unanimous that, in Dr Ramalalanyrina's case, the offer should be void.'

'But if I found you another customer, right now, they'd be your ten thousandth?'

'I suppose so.' The boy was starting to intrigue him.

'And they'd be eligible for breast implants?'

'Of course.' But would he never get to the point?

'And you could get free publicity, maybe an article in the local paper.' His hands gestured as though framing an imaginary headline: LOCAL UNDERTAKER PICTURED WITH HIS TEN THOUSANDTH SATISFIED CUSTOMER.

And for the first time all day, James Smeegle smiled. He was beginning to take to this young man. 'Why, Mr Yates, are you telling me you are in fact dead?'

'No. But I know someone who a computer might claim is.'

Voyager

Join the travellers of the imagination

www.voyager-books.com

All the latest sf & fantasy news

Exclusive author interviews

Read extracts from the latest books

All the latest signing dates

Great competitions

Full Voyager catalogue & ordering

www.voyager-books.com